The
Dark

The Dark

Carrie Brown

St. Martin's Press
New York

M
Bro

Library of Congress Cataloging-in-Publication Data

Brown, Carrie.
    The dark / Carrie Brown.
       p.   cm.
    ISBN 0-312-11769-8
    I. Title.
    PS3552.R6852D37 1995
    813'.54—dc20   94-45767
                                               CIP

First Edition: April 1995

10 9 8 7 6 5 4 3 2 1

for RD

Thanks

Frank Atwood, Rita Balkey, Malcolm Brown, Bill Bult-
mann, Phyllis Bultmann, Susan Cary, Teresa Chris, Jim
Davis, Nanette Davis, Hope Dellon, Chauncey Eaves, Pa-
tricia Gardner Evans, Steve Hager, Ben Hall, Lynne Hall,
Stuart Hall, Charlotte Hamlet, Bob Huff, Laura Kalpakian,
Edna Kiel, Thelma King, Tasha Mackler, Gary McKinney,
Carol McRandle, North Campus Pharmacy, Jenny Notz,
Willo Davis Roberts, Chuck Robinson, Dee Robinson,
Knute Skinner, Herb Taylor, Arnold Williams.

1

STOP, LINDY THOUGHT, BUT SHE DIDN'T YELL. THE RULE OF half a lifetime kept her from resisting before she was sure.

She watched a wildly waving patch crash through the elderberries buffering her home clearing. The disturbance was coming her way, helped along by human grunts. What was all the thrashing *for?* she wondered. There was a perfectly good trail only a dozen feet from the noise.

It's a stranger, she decided, because none of her regulars would destroy her peace by clattering at this hour. They all knew she launched every day by sitting on her south deck, watching the sun rise. Getting to see the sky lose its copper in silence was one of her reasons for buying the old Sunstrike commune.

Three miles beyond the city limits of Bellingham, Washington, by eagle, and eight miles by road, Lindy's one hundred and eighty acres of woods was the best of all worlds, to her. She lived alone in the lodgelike main house, but the original Sunstrike commune had scattered homemade cabins out of sight in the dense timber, and wanderers still used them.

She had objected in the beginning, but bewildered communards kept appearing anyway. After four years of struggle, she accepted the tradition as just part of her bargain. Still, her tolerance didn't stretch as far as letting someone break down bushes the birds enjoyed.

Lindy opened her mouth to yell, but she stopped when a man staggered free of the shelterbelt. He paused at the edge of the meadow which served as a lawn, and she saw he was a

1

teenager. His overworked sweatshirt had its sleeves ripped off at the shoulder, his jeans were hacked off above the knees, and his slouch socks draggled above black hightops. The party clothes didn't make sense. At dawn? It had to be last night's party.

Abruptly he stretched out his hands and strode forward, slinging his feet crazily.

Was he babysitting? she wondered more cordially, as he continued acting elaborately, re-creating some ancient kid's game. She didn't know what game it would be, from the look of it, and there weren't any young families on the property at the moment, so far as she knew. Still, she smiled, waiting for shrieks from whomever was being entertained.

Nobody laughed.

Crossing the meadow path, he plunged into the pond.

The pond had been trouble from the start. It was dug by a man who planted dwarf reeds along the banks and filled the water with lilies and cress. He added small mouth bass which he warned should not be fed because the pool was balanced. Lindy hadn't commented because he obviously believed he was on the old Sunstrike. He had finally noticed that the commune had moved on, and so he drifted away, too, not waiting to see his theory tested. Lindy could imagine what he would have said about a splashing teenager in his balanced pond.

She didn't like it, herself, because diving in couldn't be part of any game she knew. Outside water never got comfortably warm this far north, and especially not in September, when nights were cool.

Her trespasser lifted his face clear of the lily pads and simply sat in cold water up to his chin. Even on the Sunstrike, that reaction was alarmingly wrong.

Lindy set her coffee mug down and headed for the pond. Her trespasser turned when he heard footsteps on the bark path, but he didn't explain, and so she waited until she was close enough to speak in a conversational voice.

2

"I'm Lindy," she said in the casual way she had learned to use with Sunstrikers. "What's up?"

His large eyes were squinted to anonymous slits. She didn't recognize his nose as thin as a blade, his dark hair too short to fall into his face, tangled with water weed.

"Hi, I'm Tim," he answered. "Uh, this seems to be some kind of—" He paused to think. "Is this a wetland?"

Lindy didn't tell him he was in no condition to deliver a statement on local politics dealing with green issues, because his reaction wasn't a surprise. Strangers looking for the Sunstrike often rejected her purchase by teaching her about who owned the earth.

"It's more a pond, actually," she said.

He bent his head as if to study the water.

"It's pretty cold in there, isn't it?" Lindy asked. "I could help, I guess, or did you want to do it yourself?"

"Get out, you mean?" he said.

She didn't react to the defensiveness. "If you want to," she said.

He turned his head slowly, to survey the extent of the pond, but his eyes were squinted so nearly shut Lindy didn't see how they could be much use.

"Did you lose your glasses in the brush?" she asked as if any sensible person might have done the same. "Shall I go look?"

"I don't wear glasses," he said even more defensively.

He's too nearly blind to be helped, Lindy thought, regretting her earlier annoyance. He must have hitched to get here, but *surely* no one would have just dropped a handicapped teenager on the highway. It was all very well to respect his independence, but he shouldn't have had to find his way alone through woods so thick they confused even fully-sighted, fully-adult wanderers.

"This bottom's clay," Tim said before Lindy could think of anything to offer. "Too slick for anything."

"Just a second. I'll find something to help."

Leaving footprints in the dewy meadow grass, Lindy

crossed to the burn pit beyond the rhubarb patch and selected a pole from the forest slash she had picked up after the last windstorm. When she came back to the pond, Tim paid no attention. He seemed absorbed in shivering.

"Here's this stick," she said. "Grab the end, don't you think? If I get into the water with you, we'll both slip."

"Right."

She leveraged the pole against her hip and swung the far end toward him. He waited expectantly, not noticing the pole. It seemed like proof that he couldn't see much of anything. Lindy coped with distress by reviewing the rules concerning handicaps. Masking her feelings was essential, she was pretty sure. She forced pity out of her mind.

"Are you righthanded?" she asked.

"Yes."

She eased the far end slowly toward his left shoulder. He didn't react until the tip touched him. Her heart ached over the evidence. He's used to it, though, she reminded herself, it's casual to him. And so she said, "oops, too far, sorry," as if it were casual to her, as well.

"That's okay," he said, grabbing the pole and using it for help in standing up. "Are you set?"

"Let's go."

She tightened her grip, intending to walk backwards as he scrambled out of the pond. Instead, he dragged her forward. When she instinctively let go in order to save herself, he managed to stay on his feet.

"You're a lot heavier than you look." Lindy inspected the bone-thin arms which didn't suggest how strong he was. "I'm going to sit down and just try to stay put. I don't weigh enough to balance you, but it might work, if I get braced. Can you use this pole to hand-over-hand?"

"Sure."

Whoever he was, he belonged to an active family who hadn't babied him, Lindy saw. Good for them, she thought, not sure she could have done as well in their shoes. She sat down in the dew-soaked grass, bent her

4

knees, and dug her heels into the drought-hardened ground.

"Ready," she said as she clenched her hands around the pole and lay back to brace her whole body against her heels.

Tim tried to pull himself out of the pond, but the bottom was too slippery, as he had said. After landing face down in the water a couple of times, he decided on a different approach, leaning backward as if rappelling. That worked.

When he made it out of the water, he flopped on the grass, puffing his cheeks to blow. It was such a normal reaction, Lindy smiled. He didn't notice. Discouraged by the reminder that she would have to find a replacement for eye contact to show friendliness, she glanced at her hands, the palms scraped and bleeding from bark cuts.

"Are you living here on the Sunstrike?" she asked.

"No, and that's what I wanted to ask about," Tim said. "I'm fifteen, so I can't drive legally. My brother's old enough, but he can't see."

Lindy's heart plummeted. *Two* handicapped kids?

"Where's your brother?" she asked.

When Tim squared his shoulders to emphasize his chest, she realized her voice had been too emotional.

"At that birder cabin, down on the river," he said. "He's not scared. He knows all these rules."

"What kind of rules?" Lindy asked, worried that Tim probably *was* scared, since he wanted her to know his brother wasn't.

Tim pondered lengthily. "Karl's rules cover everything," he said at last. "He didn't want me to ask for help, because he says he can drive if I sit beside him and tell him when to turn, and stuff. But I'm not sure."

"No, you're probably right, that doesn't sound too good," Lindy said, glad he couldn't see her face as she visualized them careening down the highway. "How did you get out here? Hitch?"

"Hitching's dangerous. You really shouldn't do it," Tim advised her.

"That's true," Lindy said, aching at his readiness to teach her safety rules when he was in such need himself.

"Karl drove us," Tim added. "He could see, yesterday."

"Why can't he now?" Lindy knew alarm made her voice too loud, but she couldn't seem to help it.

"I'm not sure. Karl says it's nothing, just temporary."

Lindy didn't see how it could possibly be "nothing." "Should we go get your brother?" she asked, trying to keep her voice calm so he wouldn't feel managed.

"No, he wants to wait down there till he feels good enough to leave. We parked over on the other side and used a boat to cross the river."

"I suppose that is the best route," Lindy said as she thought about the perilous trail on the Sunstrike's high-bank side of the river. She wished her feelings would get out of her way so she could decide what to do. Over the years, people looking for the Sunstrike had exposed her to all the recreational vegetable smells, but she was beginning to catch a puzzling aroma which seemed entirely different. Sharper. More chemical. It was vaguely familiar, in spite of being mixed up with the stench of the pond water Tim had wallowed in. What was it—like opening a cartridge for her ink jet printer? Or, like that grain-based substitute for gas? She recoiled from the thought, because Tim's situation suddenly began making sense in a way she couldn't bear.

"Your brother isn't the only one, is he? You can't see as well as usual, today, either, can you?" Lindy asked, hoping to be contradicted.

"It's just this headache. It makes you feel like, even if you *could* see, you wouldn't want to."

"That must have been some party," she said, hoping he would take it as a sign that anything could be discussed.

"Oh, it was just this *stuff!*"

"Stuff?"

He shrugged. "Karl was in it anyway, he *wanted* to be. But the only reason I was along— See? my grandad says I have to keep an eye on my brother. Karl's nineteen, but

Grandad says common sense doesn't relate to age which Karl's the proof of."

"That makes sense," Lindy agreed. "Even without knowing your brother."

Tim nodded. "I hardly drank, but Karl had to be the man."

"I don't know much about hangovers," Lindy said. "I've never had one."

"That's good," Tim said. "But forget I said anything, because I'm pretty sure it's against the law."

"Probably." Lindy tried not to hear the outraged lectures on fair play, on brotherhood, on chemical recreation which jabbered in her mind. "Shall I drive you somewhere?"

"Well, see? I don't want to be rude or anything, but my mother'd *die* if you drove me. She totally freaks about older women, because of who one of the guys—" he stopped tactfully. "I don't mean you're *old*, but—" he squinted with his entire face, as if determined to inspect her. "Are you?"

"I'm thirty-two."

He pressed his lips together in a meditative gesture. Finally he said, "my mother might let it go if you were ninety, or along in there, but I wouldn't want to count on it."

Lindy sighed as she stood up. "Let's go back to the house while we figure this out, and I'll get you a blanket. I'm cold, just from sitting in this dew, and I can't stand to watch you shiver."

When he stood up, she could see more clearly that his goose-bumped, blue, bare arms and legs were covered with long, blood-beaded scratches from his thrashing through the brush. He started briskly toward the river bank. It took Lindy a moment to realize he thought he was following her suggestion. She wondered what it was about the Sunstrike that attracted people who took emergencies in stride, who coped as if they didn't even notice an emergency. She wanted to cry.

"The house is over here behind us," she said instead.

Tim stopped.

"Put your hand on my shoulder, don't you think?" she asked.

Tim came back, waving his arm in a reaping motion. She stepped into his hand, accepting the cuff on the temple as nothing anyone could help. He slid his hand down the side of her head to rest it on her shoulder like a flexible block of ice.

"One of my buddies says a man lives here on the commune," he said, as Lindy led the way toward the house.

"A couple of men live around here, and it isn't really a commune," Lindy said. "It used to be."

"My mom thinks it still is."

"No, the commune sold out and moved on. Now, it's just my home."

"But people live in the cabins," Tim said.

"Sometimes," she admitted. "In some of them."

"One of them's a writer."

Lindy hesitated, as she always did when someone wanted to talk about her residents. Most of them had even more secrets than everyone else, regardless of the fact that people in conventional neighborhoods believed life on a commune did away with privacy. She tried not to argue about communes, since she had to keep insisting she didn't live on one.

"He writes science fiction," Tim said, as if to jog her memory.

"Nick?" she asked uneasily. "Were you going to visit Nick?"

"No. But writers don't work, so he could drive me home, one of the guys thought. My mom will freak, but not as totally if a man brings me. Is that clueless? I keep telling our counselor at school they need to run sex education classes for parents, but my grandad says to leave it."

In spite of their situation, Lindy smiled. "You sound like you have a nice family."

Tim looked taken aback.

Finally he shrugged. "Anyway, if I can just get home, my grandad will know what to do about the others."

"It wasn't just you and your brother down there?"

"No, but the others are friends, so Grandad knows them."

"Four steps up, here," Lindy said, pausing before she started up to the deck. "Are the others— Are their eyes not working very well today?"

"They're blind right now. Maybe one of them not quite. It's hard for him to tell, with his headache. I know you're having to help me, I see that, but I'm pretty good, compared."

Oh, please, Lindy thought, surely not. She looked at his face, contorted to help his eyes.

"Karl says to wait it out. He knows all about hangovers. He wants to wait in the cabin so we don't have to listen to any adult until we're feeling better. He's calling me just about everything because I want to ask my grandad if Karl got these rules right."

Lindy couldn't stand it. "Tim?" she asked. "Should you tell me about this?"

"No! People say you give advice. They say people come out here just *for* advice."

"I suppose they do."

"It's too late for it."

"But isn't that when people usually give advice? After it's too late?"

He snorted, and the laugh made him trip on the top step. He grabbed her instead of the railing. They both almost went down.

"I shouldn't drag you into this," he said as they clung together to find their footing, "which is how it would look if you knew."

His protectiveness made Lindy want to keep her arms around him, but she suspected he wouldn't want heartbroken sympathy, any more than advice.

"There's a chair to your right," she said. It was hard to sound cheerful, but she cleared her throat and tried to seem at least practical. "I'll bring you a towel and a blanket. I don't have any men's clothes, but you can strip out of your wet things and wrap up in the blanket. There's no one around to look, except me, and I'll have my back turned, calling Nick."

"Thanks."

As pragmatically as if it were a normal morning, Tim began groping in the direction of the chair.

2

IT TOOK NICK ONLY MOMENTS TO REACH LINDY'S HOUSE.
Tall, rangy, comfortable in fatigue sweater and jeans, he
stepped out of his ancient reddish Volvo with a cheerful
grin. In his mid forties, he projected an aura of having seen
it already, no matter what it was. He needed barely a glance
at the situation in order to decide on a wry man-to-man approach which left Tim his dignity. Lindy watched gratefully
as he shepherded her blanket-shrouded guest to his Volvo
and settled him into the passenger seat as if no situation had
ever been more routine.

After the station wagon disappeared among the trees,
Lindy stopped worrying. Whatever Tim had gotten into
was surely illegal, as he said himself, but she had long ago
decided that kind of thinking didn't belong on the Sunstrike. Listening to former communards had taught her
how many ways there were to break the law without feeling
guilty or responsible. If Tim went home to trouble he
couldn't handle, she knew Nick would help him. That was
one of the good things about how she lived—any of her regular residents willingly got involved whenever someone
asked.

After lunch, a package service returned the blanket Tim
had borrowed. It was freshly laundered. She was grateful
for the proof that he had gone home to someone who cared
about him. Nick didn't check back with her, which seemed
like further evidence that getting Tim home had been
straightforward.

Still, she wasn't surprised, the next afternoon, when a

dark green sheriff's car lurched up the buttercup over-grown two-track which led to her clearing. Apparently Tim or one of his friends must have told their story. County teenagers had a habit of gathering secretly at different places where they could be unsupervised, and if word of the party got out later, the sheriff questioned the owner of whatever building had been used, making sure the underage drinking hadn't been by adult consent. No property owner ever admitted knowing what had happened, but the ritual had to be gone through anyway.

She had been sitting on her east deck, reading, and so she propped her book facedown on her lap as she watched the official car park in a graveled area at the end of the flag-stoned walk. Two men got out. One of them was a stranger, and not the sort she was accustomed to seeing, anymore. About six feet, styled haircut, suede jacket, blue shirt the right tone to make his eyes vivid, dress jeans, lizard boots. He gazed at the tops of the hundred-year-old cedars like a tourist, but his face was cop-blank.

The shorter, homier man was one of her former students.

"Hi, Brent," Lindy said.

The stranger smiled. "He said you wouldn't recognize him."

"It's been eight years," Brent said, looking suddenly young.

Lindy didn't explain that teachers were likely to remember their very first class. She smiled instead. "You were in Philosophy 102, isn't that right? Logic. When I saw in the newspaper that you'd joined the sheriff's department, I wondered if a C in logic helped or hurt."

All three of them laughed. The men trooped loudly up the wood steps to the deck.

"I brought Detective Sergeant Richison along," Brent said, adjusting the collar of his baggy field jacket as if he had just noticed the discrepancy in how they dressed. "Richi-son's with the Bellingham police, new there. We're borrowing him."

12

"Because of having to question your former teacher?" Lindy asked. "I won't make it hard."

"No, that's not it," Brent said, but he looked uneasy.

"It's more like being fresh from California makes me supposedly an expert on communes," Richison said.

He wouldn't have had to say where he was from, Lindy thought. He spoke with his throat relaxed, in a way Northwesterners didn't do. The streaks in his coffee-colored hair were natural. His tan was bitten deeply into his flesh in a way parlors couldn't achieve. It was appealing, but anyone who loved the Northwest had to lament Californiazation.

Lindy gestured toward chairs made of the plastic-sprayed metal webbing which was practical in a wet climate. "Communes?" she repeated as the men sat down. "I don't know how much help I'll be. People from the old Sunstrike drift through sometimes and tell stories in exchange for a meal, but I never know how much to believe."

"Not the old Sunstrike," Brent said.

Lindy smiled at him.

"*Your* commune, Dr. Adair," Richison said.

Lindy leveled him a chilly gaze, since his comment was exactly the reaction her elaborate explanation had been meant to forbid. "Out of those four words, I'm going to have to object to three of them, Sergeant Richison."

Richison nodded. "Okay, you earned your title, doctor, but you prefer everyone to call you Lindy, I heard about that. So that leaves us the commune."

She studied his aggressive face. He had more jaw than he needed, but his surprisingly sweet smile balanced that, when he chose to use it.

"Is this how cops are in California?" she asked.

"I expect that's a hostile remark based on watching the news. I'm from San Diego, which has a cleaner reputation, besides which I *left* California. Even in San Diego, your perpetrators take pride in what they call tripped-out behavior because of living in a tripped-out universe, and so some of your cops finally trip out, too, from the constant exposure, which I don't really want for myself. I was hoping around

Bellingham I'd find logical people making rational choices to break the law for dignified reasons which I could figure out and respect."

It sounded like a recitation, but it was amusing anyway, and so Lindy smiled. "Welcome to the great Northwest."

"Thanks." He gazed at her house, a nonarchitected board-and-batten structure stained woodlot brown, the glass half of its walls brightened by plants crowding forward as if trying to break out. "Now about your living arrangements," he said.

"I'm sure Brent's told you all about it."

He turned to her, his eyes intent. "It won't bore me to hear your version."

That sounded as if it had developed out of the kind of line a younger man might use. What was he, mid thirties? she wondered as she studied the faint beginning of sun wrinkles at the corners of his eyes. He probably didn't need a line anymore, so it was no doubt just an interview technique. She decided to cooperate.

"I bought this property because I like space," she said. "I couldn't have afforded it, normally, but the price was way down because people worried there was a curse on it."

"This curse—how does it work?" Richison asked with California-style acceptance.

"I'm not sure. The real estate agent talked about it because of those full disclosure laws on real estate sales, where you have to list everything bad."

"And your agent said what."

Lindy hesitated, because she couldn't remember how much of what she knew came from the real estate agent, and she didn't want to admit the curse had fascinated her. "Centuries ago," she said slowly, "in England, they could put a curse on property they donated to churches. It was called a 'malediction.' Anybody who tried to cancel the deal was going to suffer."

"So, you're a church group, here? It's why you were safe to buy out a cursed commune?"

"No," Lindy said.

14

"You teach religion," he reminded her in a flat tone.

"I used to."

"And now you run a church, with this malediction to protect you."

Lindy glanced at Brent, who was looking embarrassed. No doubt it would shock any Northwestern cop to work with a fellow professional who expressed an interest in the function of curses, she thought. The tension between the two men was intriguing enough to help her deal amiably with Richison's insistence.

"No, I don't have a church," she said again, "and as far as any malediction, it would have been intended to work the other way. We don't seem to have that kind of a law, though—I looked it up in the Washington State Code. I thought the property would be all right because the people who wanted the malediction were told it didn't qualify as a lien or an easement, or anything you've heard of like that."

"These people who wanted the curse—what was their basis?"

"One member of the commune owned the land," Brent summarized, when Lindy hesitated. "He decided to move out and sell the property, so the rest of them tried to block him."

Richison turned a completely expressionless look on Brent. It was all Lindy could do to keep from laughing. He really must be freshly arrived, she thought, if he didn't understand that, in Bellingham, cops were just your neighbor.

"What *does* go with the property, setting the curse aside?" Richison asked, turning back to Lindy.

"This is the main house." Lindy nodded toward the building they sat beside. "There are fourteen other dwellings scattered around. Some of them you reach only by trail. They're charming, so I didn't want to tear them down. At first, I planned to leave them vacant, but people from the old Sunstrike sometimes use them while they try to think what to do, now that the commune's gone."

"Everyone living here is from the old commune?" Richison summed up.

15

"No. A couple of students followed me out here. It's close enough for them to commute, and giving away housing seems better than scholarships. They word-of-mouth, so there are usually a few around, even though it's been awhile since I stopped teaching."

"How long?" Richison asked.

"Four years."

Brent inspected the deck, which a confused slug had left a slick trail across, but Sergeant Richison met her gaze steadily. He had the blazing blue eyes most people needed contacts to achieve. He didn't have to tell her gossip had explained more than she had.

She sighed. "I also have links with Bellingham's women's groups, so sometimes there'll be someone hiding out from a batterer. Most of them try to give something back—maybe stock a cabin with canned goods, if they've got any money, or borrow tools and split a few cords of wood, if they're broke." She gestured toward the open toolshed at the north end of the deck.

"So. How many of your residents are on the run?"

Lindy regretted his ability to select out the police element of everything she said. But she had been a university professor for four years, and so she met his gaze without any trace of discomposure.

"I won't talk about that," she said.

Brent intervened. "Dr. Adair? It would help everybody if you talked up front."

That seemed like an odd reaction, Lindy decided as she inspected his embarrassed face. Some of Richison's questions were very far afield from a teenage party investigation, which wasn't surprising, given his newcomer's need for background information. But what could Brent's motive be? she wondered. Maybe they weren't here about Tim's party, because they seemed to be asking only about the Sunstrike. It was hard to imagine why.

"I'm perfectly willing to talk about most things, Brent, surely you know that," she said, waiting for him to meet her gaze, "but if you're going after any of my residents, I'm sorry. You're on private property without an invitation, and I don't see any warrants in your hands. Even the roads are private."

"We're not sure who we're looking for, is the truth," Brent said.

Lindy gazed at him. "Would you care to amplify?"

"You used to say that in class."

They grinned at each other.

Richison's interrupting sigh was irritable. "Our questions concern this illegal still out here."

Lindy looked surprised. "I thought all stills are illegal, aren't they?"

"Yes, professor, they are," Richison said heavily. "Let me rephrase that."

"Sorry."

They sat silent. Both men stared at her, but Lindy waited as if she didn't notice. She was glad of the pause because it gave her a chance to think about what he had said. A still. Had the boys *made* their alcohol? The possibility seemed worse than for them to simply drink something they shouldn't have, as she had imagined them doing.

"Bellingham police have received a complaint that whiskey is being made here without a license," Richison said at last. "We decided to team-work instead of debating jurisdiction."

Lindy nodded. "I've heard the sheriff's department is shorthanded, so that's generous of you."

Richison's square jaw became more prominent. "I don't need emotional support, Dr. Adair, I need answers."

"About a still?" She shrugged. "I don't know of any still."

"Do you know a cabin on the river by your pumphouse?"

"Yes."

"Tell me about it."

Lindy planned her answer carefully since she wasn't sure what Tim and his friends might have said. How much trouble were they in? she wondered. If they had set up a still down there in the river cabin, that was breaking the law much more seriously than if they had just drunk whatever kind of alcohol they could get hold of already made. But this conversation seemed to imply they must have confessed, so why were the police asking more questions? Shouldn't they just be dismantling the still, if there was one? She wished she knew more about the laws governing such things.

"That area down there is classified as primary wetlands," she said, deciding the safest reaction would be to talk about local history, as Sunstrikers did in answer to questions they considered overly direct. She wasn't glad to be adopting their methods, and yet she began to see the use of them.

"You usually can't build on primary wetlands, but the new cabin was exempted because the pumphouse was already in place, and because the public schools did the asking. The schools bring ecology classes out on field trips because we've got so much natural variety here. Last year, they asked to build a shelter so they could spend more time watching the birds come through." She turned to Brent. "The river's a migration flyway, you know. Geese. Eagles. Woodpeckers. Some little things like bumble bees, but noisier—I don't recognize them all."

Brent nodded.

"I said building was fine, provided they got permits for everything. By the time it was legal, they were required to build a real cabin butted up against the pumphouse, and put it on pilings above the hundred-year floodline, with an elevated septic system and a catwalk trail in to protect the environment. It's a nice place. They invited me down for a housewarming."

Richison nodded. "Have you been back since the housewarming?"

Lindy shook her head.

"It's a still."

Lindy shrugged. "Not that I'm aware of."

"Who else uses it besides the high schools?"

"No one so far as I know."

"But would you know, Dr. Adair?" Brent asked.

His urgent tone alerted Lindy. How much, in fact, *did* she know about what went on in her cabins? Not enough, apparently. But that was right, because she didn't want to know. She hadn't been a residence hall advisor, after all. She had been just a professor, and she wasn't even that, anymore.

"You're right. I guess I *don't* know," she said at last.

"What about people from the community on the other side of the river, beyond the cabins?" Richison persisted.

"Nugent's Corners?" Lindy stared in the direction of the informal cluster of stores, services, churches, and homes which couldn't be seen from her deck. "I don't know," she admitted. "Anyone can go to the cabin, but I don't know that anyone does. Look—" She hesitated. "If there's a still down there, then I guess the law was broken. But aren't you coming down pretty heavy on just some rowdy kids?"

"I'm interested in your definition of 'rowdy.' " Richison was grim. "There were five youngsters down there night before last, drinking moonshine. One of them is stone blind at the moment, prognosis uncertain. One of them can detect light. One of them can make out shapes well enough to get around. One can see in splotches."

Lindy couldn't seem to catch her breath strongly enough to make her voice come out. "Blind?" she tried to echo. "I thought they had hangovers. I thought one of the boys knew the rules about whatever they were into."

"He thought so, too," Richison said.

"We need to find out why he was so wrong, Dr. Adair," Brent explained. "Was he just pretending to know? Or did he honestly misunderstand? Or did someone deliberately mislead him?"

"No! They just messed up. They probably aren't cooks. They aren't used to following recipes."

"There's some evidence they were set up," Brent said.

"It can't be true," Lindy said.

Her unwilling gaze came to rest on the balanced pond where Tim had landed. After a moment, she added, "I can never understand why people hurt each other. But if that actually is what happened, then I have to notice that you said four of the boys are having trouble seeing. If the fifth boy wasn't hurt, maybe he's where you could start, with your questions. Maybe he arranged trouble because of some quarrel and didn't realize how serious something like this could be. I mean, I wouldn't have known, if you weren't sitting here telling me."

"The fifth kid was murdered, according to his family," Richison said.

"*Murdered?*"

"When Tim didn't come back soon enough to suit him, this other kid, Vance, decided to follow him out. He wasn't as athletic as Tim, so he fell off the catwalk," Richison said. "He could swim, but as far as the other kids know from listening, he couldn't figure out which way anything was, once he hit the water. They were hoping he made it ashore anyway, because they stopped hearing him scream for help after the current dragged him down river. Did you hear him?"

Lindy shook her head as if her joints had frozen. "Maybe if I'd been standing on the bank, I might have heard," she murmured, "but the cabin's a long way off, and even if I'd heard, I'd have thought it was just a party."

"This sort of thing goes on routinely?" Sergeant Richison asked.

"No. We all like quiet. It's why we're out here. I just meant, if I'd heard shouting, that's what I'd have thought, from when I used to live in town."

"You were aware what they use the cabin for?"

"I thought they watched birds," she said.

The men were silent for a little while.

"Don't take it as your responsibility, Dr. Adair," Brent said eventually. "I guess nobody heard this kid. Or at least nobody phoned it in to us."

She looked at him sadly. "There's no one else out here to hear him."

Sergeant Richison sighed. "Yeah there is. He drifted

20

downstream past several communities. He didn't beach until the flood debris under the Everson bridge, which is miles from you. Of course, Everson wasn't going to hear him. He was dead before he got that far."

"Oh God."

"His family believes the kids were attacked deliberately, with a careful plan, not just on impulse," Richison added. "We'd take their statement seriously in any case, but especially so since other evidence backs them up. As Deputy Fuller just told you."

His tone told her that Brent shouldn't have admitted anything to her, in Richison's opinion. She wasn't willing to watch their power struggle, and so she looked into the depths of the drought-darkened sky and tried to imagine a grief which would need to lash out, place blame. Finally she rubbed her eyes.

"Brent?" she said in almost a classroom tone. "I can't help feeling you should have said you're investigating a death. You must have known I'd assume this was just follow-up on an underage party."

"Would it have made a difference in your answers?" Richison asked.

"No." She turned to Brent. "But it matters to my feelings."

"I didn't want to say, because I didn't want you to try to protect someone," Brent said uncomfortably.

"What did Tim tell you when he came for help?" Richison asked.

"I don't remember the words, and unless I could quote exactly, I won't quote." She paused. "I guess I'm not going to discuss it anymore. Too much of what you ask doesn't make sense to me."

"There's physical evidence connecting the still to the Sunstrike, Dr. Adair," Brent said, refusing to see Richison's frown. "I know there's a good explanation, but we need to hear it. It's why we're here."

"Evidence," she said, not even trying to hide the utter emptiness which seemed to have replaced her mind. "I

21

don't know how there could be. What evidence?"

"We can't tell you," Brent said. "We need that kind of detail to be unknown, for the process of our investigation," he added. "Our first step is here, getting it established that you're entirely out of it."

"But if I don't know what we're discussing, how can I answer?"

"Just tell the truth," Richison said.

"Everything I've said has been the truth," she said, "and what good has it done?"

"Look, Dr. Adair, we have to figure out where the still came from—the equipment, supplies, information, everything about it," Brent said in a voice which showed he knew every word was objected to by his temporary partner. "This kid who died, he can't be classed as a controlled substances homicide if the boys themselves figured the whole thing out, because if you're part of the crime you die committing, your death isn't classed as manslaughter, much less as murder. So you see, these really are important questions."

"Controlled substances homicide?" Lindy repeated faintly. She seemed to separate from her body and leave her physical self on its own, far below. Nightmares were part of modern life—she accepted that—but she had already done her lifetime's share, four years ago. Hadn't she? She had thought so.

"I didn't know there was such a thing," she murmured.

"Yeah there is," Richison said. "One of your state laws."

The deck was silent while Lindy studied the meadow where nothing but a faint breeze moved. Yesterday, she had discovered a tiny clump of blue-eyed grass among the daisies. The fragile blossoms had delighted her. As if they were safety, she tried to see them now so she could focus her thoughts.

"All I've done is own that wetlands," she said in a voice which didn't seem to be hers. "The cabin is thanks to Bellingham high school's science teacher, who helped the kids design the environmental compliance program, and the history teacher, who signed as the supervising adult when they filed for permits, and the woodshop teacher, who watched them do the actual building. Why aren't you hassling them? They at least deal with the kids, which I don't."

"Maybe. But Tim knew where to come for help," Richison reminded her.

3

DAN RICHISON TRIED TO ESTIMATE HOW MUCH DEPUTY FUL-
ler's attitude was costing them. Small-city procedures
weren't like what he was used to, and he accepted that.
Even so, it couldn't be routine for Fuller to spill their entire
case and leave them with no way to create a surprise.
Maybe Fuller was just reacting to his former prof, or possibly he even knew what he was doing, because these Northwesterners were hard to judge. They never told their whole
story in thirty seconds, the way he could expect in California. They seemed good natured if someone else was into
full disclosure, but they apparently never felt compelled to
explain themselves just because he happened to be standing
there looking at them.

Their being so casual about cops made investigating
harder than it should be. Lindy, for example. At least some
of the kids' equipment came from her commune, so she
should have been pouring out nonstop explanations. Instead, she was looking at him like she was on the secret side
of a one-way mirror. He couldn't believe she didn't know
furnishing supplies for manufacture was as bad as deliver-
ing the abusable substances themselves, when kids were involved. She didn't have to stand down there in the cabin
and tell them what to do next in order to be up to her neck.
The boys were refusing to talk, but they didn't have to in a
situation this obvious.

On the drive out from Bellingham, Fuller swore there
had to be a different explanation for the equipment carry-

ing the Sunstrike logo, but Lindy's attitude contradicted that. She wasn't wearing makeup, and her skin was extremely fair, almost translucent, so he would have been able to see the least hint of a flush. But here she sat, apparently serene. An innocent person ought to be rattled.

"I have to wonder why you're so calm about this, professor," he said, hoping the use of a title she rejected would be irritating enough to get her going without rousing Fuller to her defense.

"I'm not calm." She cleared her throat. "It's just that I've faced official threats before."

"No priors, Richison," Fuller said hastily. "She probably means when she left the university."

"I'd like to hear your view of that," Dan said, hoping to block Fuller from leaping in with an explanation. He had been glad to work with someone who could provide local knowledge, but that was before he found out Fuller had graduated from the local university. Campus types were problems, in his experience, because they expected to discuss the law instead of obeying it, but the situation got worse when Lindy turned out to be one of Fuller's own profs. A sheriff's deputy should have been helping to create a feel of investigative confrontation. Instead, Fuller kept rescuing his teacher.

Lindy seemed to take that attitude for granted. If he hadn't known how much she had to worry over, he would have believed she frowned only because the sunlight bothered her.

"My relationship with the university can't possibly be related to this," she said eventually.

"I won't know until I hear it."

She looked at him for a while, in a way which told him although he just had a cop's habit of keeping his feelings out of his eyes, she really was crouched down inside herself somewhere safe, totally out of view.

"I suppose everybody loses even the pretense of privacy when something like this happens," she said.

"Yeah you do."

"It doesn't matter, Dr. Adair, everybody knows your story," Fuller said.

Lindy glanced at him as she brushed her fingers through very short temple hair. The gesture was useless, although it would have worked with hair long enough to tuck behind her ears. As attractive as she was—especially with that blue-black hair—she probably wore it long, before she turned professional, Dan decided. If the gesture was a retreat to the past, it might be a sign of stress. The thought was encouraging.

"Our state laws say our curriculum has to treat women equally," she said. "Our nondiscrimination laws aren't just about women as workers. What we teach has to be fair, too."

"Okay. I crammed your criminal law so I could join the force here, but this sounds like I should learn the civil code too, because Washington does seem to be different."

He intended to sound friendly, to keep her talking by suggesting he appreciated any kind of information, but she stared at his face as if she'd read his mind and recognized that improvement was called for.

"The philosophy department worried about having only male faculty," she went on after a few moments, "so they hired me. My academic training is in comparative religion, so I do know about some women's faiths. When they offered me a contract, they mentioned that's what they were looking for."

"Right," he said.

"I designed some women's courses," she went on. "Some of my students liked philosophy and religion. They wanted to major in it. But when they got into the other classes, where they were supposed to take it for granted that all belief focuses on men—" She stopped abruptly. "I mean—" She hesitated. "My students started asking questions in other classes, and that made the traditional faculty uncomfortable."

When she paused again, apparently absorbed in rear-

26

ranging her book, he realized what she must have been like in class. She didn't appear to have canned answers. She would have described this situation a thousand times, given the legal maneuvering he had been told about as background on her, and yet she acted like she was gathering it up all new.

"They told me it was bad enough to have my point of view added to faculty meetings," she went on in a sad tone, "but they said it was totally disruptive to have my students in their discussion classes. That was success, in a way, because it was what they hired me for. But you can see their side," she added, offering eye contact that felt insulting, since it assumed all men—including him—had to be coddled. "They wanted to get back to what they considered normal," she told him, "so they fired me."

"Is that legal?"

His question seemed to shift him to a different category in her mind, because she looked at him more analytically, which he preferred. Apparently she did, too, because she went on without any pausing. "No, it isn't, so I filed a grievance case, mostly for the sake of my students who wanted to study philosophy. Everybody outside the department admitted my suit was justified, but the trouble is, it's hard for a university to change. Faculty committees make most of the decisions, which means bad individuals can hide behind a group vote. When I saw that *nothing* was going to help my students, I settled out of court. I'm not supposed to speak against the university—I hope it doesn't sound as if I have been."

"Everybody else does that for you," Fuller said.

She caught his gaze with a smile that was personal without being intimate at all. Dan was glad to see it. Apparently being a teacher was one of the things that governed her, which might mean being alone would get him a better reaction. A private talk could definitely be arranged.

"Okay, so evasions and silence are what you give the university," he prompted. "What did they give you?"

"Two years pay as a cash settlement, plus lifetime faculty

27

privileges at the library, plus contributions to my retirement program as if I were still employed." She shrugged. "If I live to sixty-five, I'll be rich."

He made a show of glancing around the clearing. "You don't look poor, right now."

She breathed deeply—for stress control? He watched her chest rise and wished he had caught her in more interesting clothes. Sweatshirts seemed to be universal around here, and it was a shame, he thought.

"I used the whole cash settlement as a down payment," she said. "It means I *am* poor, because there's a huge mortgage, and I don't have a guaranteed income."

"So show me how that ties into our situation here."

She looked puzzled. "It doesn't. You asked, so I explained. As a courtesy. There's no connection."

"If you were still teaching, you wouldn't have bought out the Sunstrike, would you?" Fuller prompted.

"Oh." She nodded. "No, you're right, Brent—I couldn't have. I wouldn't have had a down payment."

"So. Getting yourself fired put you into ownership of this still," Dan said.

"Provided I do own it, which I'm not sure of. Maybe I just own the land under it. I'll have to ask my lawyer, I guess, if you feel like it's important."

"I have trouble believing you think it isn't," Dan said.

She didn't react in any way he could see, but she must have done something, because Fuller leaped in, asking, "Can you think of any other connection, Dr. Adair? I know we haven't given you much to go on."

It was a novel approach, Dan thought as he watched them look at each other—hand a suspect a loaded gun, ask them to hold out their own foot and shoot it themselves. Whatever he thought about it, though, Fuller's method seemed to be working, because Lindy began clutching her book.

"I don't usually think in terms like this, but there might be something you could call a connection, because making the grievance claim was worse than struggling with the men who were being disgraceful. So, I promised myself I would never, never, never again involve myself with any kind of law."

Dan studied her white-knuckled grip on her book—some sort of philosophy tome. "Well, we're sitting here," he told her, "so you apparently don't live up to your promises."

She closed her eyes. Tears seeped into her eyelashes.

"Oh, come on, Dr. Adair, don't take it like that," Brent urged.

"I'm not sure how to handle this," Dan interrupted. "What I'm used to in California everyone keeps current on the cop shows and the law procedurals and the infomercials, and they choose their attitude from something out of that. But if you're coming from somewhere, Dr. Adair, I don't spot it."

"I'm just myself, Sergeant," Lindy said unsteadily. "That's usually hard enough, without borrowing from the media." She released her book and brushed the backs of her hands beneath her eyes. "Besides, I couldn't act like someone else, even if I wanted to, because we don't get TV out here. It's this river valley. Stewart Mountain blocks off all the cities."

"Cable?" Fuller asked as if he had dropped by for nothing more crucial than neighboring.

Lindy shook her head. "Cable doesn't come out this far. And if we wanted to put up a satellite dish, we'd have to clear out *acres* of trees."

"We?" Dan repeated, grateful for a discrepancy which might force her to deal with the real topic. "You mean the commune?"

"I. I should have said 'I.'" She clenched her jaw. The gesture seemed oddly more emotional than her tears. "If *I* wanted to put up a dish, *I'd* have to hire foresters to do the clearing. It's an art—logging trees as old as these. But it'll never happen, if I can block it. If *I* can block it," she corrected.

That seemed to be her version of a tantrum, and Dan

abruptly realized what he was facing. She assumed he and Fuller were playing good-cop-bad-cop. Since she definitely saw her former student as good, she automatically labeled him as the bad cop. But forget that, he thought as anger replaced his frustration. When cop roles were being chosen in San Diego, he always played good-cop, and that wasn't going to change.

"Look, Lindy, let's start over, get this settled," he said, as if they had been working together from the beginning and their only problem had been that she was slow to notice. "Everything we've got is circumstantial. You always need to be careful with that kind of evidence, because it may not prove what cops think it does."

He paused for acknowledgement. When she caught his gaze before nodding, he felt like they were making progress. He was more used to reading emotions in dark eyes, but even with her foggy blue, he seemed to catch a glimpse of understanding.

"Okay, but even granting that," he went on, "you're involved because this situation includes juveniles and it occurred on your land, you allowing it in the sense you apparently allow anything."

Lindy sniffed. "I suppose it looks that way to you."

"Yeah it does. So. What we need is for you to change my thinking. How about cooperating? Like Deputy Fuller says, it ought to be to your advantage."

"I *am* cooperating," she said.

"Maybe, but here's my problem. If people are going to cry, I prefer they do it in situations where I'm not professionally required to withhold sympathy," he told her. "And Deputy Fuller, here, he doesn't want to see it from his prof."

Lindy cleared her throat. "I wasn't crying at either one of you. I was crying about Affirmative Action."

Her answer was so unexpected Dan couldn't block a laugh, and so he was relieved when Fuller joined him. Could she really think her first obligation was to reassure them, regardless of the mess she was in? Granted, this wasn't much of an interrogation, with Fuller undercutting him every other sentence, but even so, she must realize she had attracted police interest—never a good thing to do. She evidently had her own rules, though, because she sat up straighter and blotted her eyes on her sleeve as if their reaction had relaxed her.

"I don't really *allow* things in the cabins," she said. "I just don't supervise. Do you see that as a difference?"

He nodded. "Maybe."

"And especially with the birder cabin— I'm not really aware of it, because you don't see it from here."

"You don't see *any* of the cabins from here," Dan said, with a quick glance around to verify.

She rubbed her forehead. The gesture looked spontaneous, so possibly this approach was working, he decided.

"That's true," she said. "If I had to look at the cabins, I'd tear them down. I came out here for privacy."

"You're a recluse because of the uproar with the college?"

"No."

She studied his eyes. He sat still for it, but he had to wonder what she imagined she was seeing.

"A teacher gets stared at, even if nothing has happened," she said. "It wore me down. So, I decided to get clear away."

"Okay, I can probably understand, because cops have the same problem."

She nodded so promptly it felt friendly, and he found himself half ready to line up with Fuller and hope for an explanation which could put her in the clear. Everyone who talked about her assumed these people she called "residents" had rules which were different from the old Sunstrike. But what if that wasn't true? If people from the glory days were still around, one of them could be the source for these kids, and she genuinely might know nothing of it.

"How many of your communards know distilling procedures?" he asked.

She closed her eyes briefly. When she opened them again, he saw that the thaw was over.

"I don't discuss my residents," she said.

"If you could make an exception this once, Dr. Adair?" Fuller said. "It would save us from interviewing anybody who *doesn't* know about moonshine. We might have to talk to everyone eventually, but at least for now, we could spare people who don't seem to be involved, if we know which ones they are."

"All right, Brent." She rubbed her eyes. "What expertise would that be? Technology? Health sciences? There's no one here along those lines," she said when no one answered.

"What do they use to get high?" Dan asked.

Lindy looked in the direction of the road. "I guess I did see someone walking in from the highway with a six-pack last weekend, but mostly they're into herbal tea. Chamomile at the moment, but it can change."

For a person who didn't run a commune, she seemed to know a lot about her so-called residents, but Dan decided to save that thought for later. At least for now, *avoiding* confrontation seemed to be what worked.

"If you had known what the kids were doing," he asked, "would you have stopped them?"

"I don't know."

"Estimate."

While she thought it over, she gazed up at the hundreds of small dark birds who twittered excitedly as they swarmed the tops of the tallest evergreen trees, picking seeds, apparently. "I've never challenged any of the residents," she said at last. "I'd hate to start, because where would I draw the line?"

"Easy. Draw the line at self-destruction," Dan said.

"And exactly where is that?" she asked. "Should I include drifters moving on to nowhere? Runaway wives giving up and going back to their abusers? Burnouts paying any price rather than face useless detox again? Your values might benefit from a little sympathetic visualization, Sergeant."

"Yeah, well, sign me up for a workshop," he said, deliberately sounding rude so she wouldn't notice that she had given herself away. Negative attitudes toward anyone she protected brought her out into the open. She admitted she had sued the university for the sake of her students, and he had watched her turn high-handed over the idea of cutting her trees, and now she was losing her temper in defense of her residents. Since the pattern was clear, it seemed like enough to learn in a preliminary session. There was no point in hoping for any damaging admissions, with Fuller sitting here helping her instead of the case, so leaving now should be a good tactic. She would imagine the questions were over, so she'd have no reason to work out a better story. In a day or two, he could come back on his own and use her protective instincts to get her goat, and then he should have a chance to listen.

4

"WE'RE GOING DOWN TO LOOK AT YOUR CABIN," RICHISON
said as he stood up.

"Fine."

"There's access from this side?"

She nodded.

"Show us?"

He probably knew the way, and Brent surely did, Lindy
thought, so why was he asking? Did he hope she would un-
veil an alternate pathway which would be safe and easy,
making Tim's route less heroic? Not that it mattered what
he wanted, she decided, because cooperating would move
them off her deck, and that was what she cared about.

Leaving her book on her chair, she led the way down the
steps and along the meadow path. At the edge of the clearing, she entered the woods trail Tim hadn't been able to
find. Beyond the shelterbelt, the trail crossed a glade which
had been opened years ago by the fall of a giant maple. Un-
dergrowth had been prevented by falling cedar needles, but
tiny mushrooms like new pennies scattered the duff.

It was one of Lindy's favorite spots. She hated having
strangers in it with her. Brent paid no attention, but Richison gazed around as if visiting a park.

The trail wandered through a belt of cedars framing the
far side of the clearing before reaching the riverbank, a two-
hundred-foot clay cliff. The abrupt drop gave a panoramic
view of the miles-wide meander basin which was green with
young alder on every high spot. The river itself was a blue-
green wash, loafing between gray gravel bars and riprapped

curves. Beyond, forest-shrouded ridges led into the Cascade Range, where Mt. Baker blocked the head of the valley and supplied the glacier-melt which turned the river chalky, in summer.

"You *own* this?" Richison asked.

"No one really owns land like this," Lindy said apologetically, "but I pay the taxes on it."

"No wonder this one family wants to beggar you," he said.

She wished her body would remember how to breathe. "I'm not sure what you mean," she murmured.

"The dead boy's family is preparing a civil suit," Brent said. "I told them they'd do better to wait for the criminal investigation to be complete, so they can sue the right person, but I guess they're going ahead."

"I don't understand," she said.

"Your state has this specific crime Fuller mentioned, controlled substances homicide," Richison said. "What that amounts to is, you're going to pay the cost of rehab and any other damages, when you deliver a controlled substance to a minor."

Lindy caught her breath. "It offends me for you to just assume I'm responsible."

"Yeah, well—"

She knew his pause was meant to draw some reaction from her, but she couldn't bear to look at him.

"I have to wait for proof, you're right," he admitted when she didn't answer. "But the family needs to go ahead. Delay doesn't matter in the wrongful death claim for the dead boy, but one of the blind kids is his brother, and he's got to deal with that. His family hopes legal justice may help him see the whole guilt isn't his."

"When the papers are ready, they want to deal with the lawyer who represented you against the university, so they don't have to pay someone to come out here to serve you," Brent added. "Is he still your lawyer?"

Lindy simply nodded, because she couldn't manage a voice. Could he *really* be thinking only of how much bother the suit might be to the people who were hoping to destroy her? Or was he just treating it as routine? Maybe it actually was routine, to him, she admitted even though she couldn't stand the thought.

Overwhelmed by their intrusion into a life she had strained every nerve to make peaceful, she walked on rapidly, hoping to get away from them before she dismantled into mindless rage.

"Here's the trail." She looked at their feet. "It's meant for spiked boots, but you can probably manage. The clay's fairly dry because of this drought."

The trail pitched down at an irregular angle across the face of the cliff, using eight hundred feet of riverside to reach the gravel bar two hundred feet below, where a pair of Tarzanish shacks showed through a fringe of young alder. The newer structure was the more elaborate, having a deck cantilevered over the river to provide a birder's view. The access trail took advantage of an occasional small bench and widened to accommodate a rare, struggling vine maple, but mostly it was just an eight-inch-wide pathway chopped in the blue clay.

"The Sunstrike built this so they could get to their pumphouse," she said. "Everybody who comes through from the old days talks about it as if they had built the pyramids. They count up how many people fell in the river, how many broken legs, broken arms, cracked ribs, concussions."

"People actually use it?" Richison asked.

Lindy hesitated. "Once in a while, I guess," she said.

"Is it the only way to get down there from this side?"

Lindy nodded.

"Did Tim come up this trail?" Brent asked.

"Apparently. I didn't ask."

"You might save yourself grief if you did a little more asking," Richison said irritably.

Lindy didn't answer. She set her jaw and willed herself to wait as if she had the patience for it.

She was relieved when they finally started down the narrow trail. The woods were parched, but the bank was a northeast exposure sheltered from the sun, and the clay absorbed the river mist which rose most early mornings, so it was never completely dry. The two men crept as precariously as if each step would pitch them into the water far below. Eventually, as they got lower, they gained enough confidence to walk more normally. When distance turned them into toys, Lindy left them.

Heading back through the dry woods, she tried to believe their visit was no more bizarre than anything else attracted by the Sunstrike. That didn't work, because no Sunstriker had ever made her in the least uneasy. Sunstrikers were invasive, using the washing machine or the stove and paying for borrowed supplies by talking, but they were never judgmental, whereas this overly tanned cop seemed to run the world, in his opinion.

I can't lose this place, she thought, trying to face her most terrifying fear. But if they win a civil suit, I own nothing else to give them.

Unable to look at trees she might have betrayed through inadvertence, she fought for hope, determined to imagine that the forest would remain intact and peaceful despite this family's anger. But by the time she reached her house, her spirit had taken the opposite journey. All she could see was Tim, floundering bravely in the pond, marching off toward the cliff in his struggle to help his tragic friends.

Was she really responsible for them? she wondered. And whether or not she was responsible, was she to blame? It was a question for experts, she realized. She went inside to look for her insurance company's phone number.

When she called, her agent's reaction made her realize how totally confusing her situation was. She could report an event on her property, but she didn't know whether it was an accident, and she didn't know the last names of the kids involved. Admitting her feelings of helplessness, she offered Deputy Sheriff Brent Fuller as the best source of information.

Going back outside, she sat on her deck and struggled to

understand what was happening. As a first step, she thought about stills until she was sure she knew nothing about them. Next, she closed her eyes and thought about blindness. With only her other senses, would life seem worth it? She could hear chipmunks chatter. Tree limbs creaked in the light breeze she felt on her face. Wing feathers rubbed audibly as large birds wheeled above the clearing. She opened her eyes in panic and focused on the sky. She couldn't bear to never see it again.

How can these kids be my fault? she wondered. I couldn't have controlled them in the first place, even if I'd known, and I can't control them now.

The thought was true, but it didn't comfort her. She had begun life like everyone else, trusting to luck and counting on justice, but her conflict with the university had taught her otherwise. Not willing to feel like a victim, she had decided everything that happened was values-neutral. When things progressed from bad to awful, you could give up and call yourself defeated. Or, you could struggle on until you gained something out of every horror. Either way, the end was yours to choose.

That worked, in theory. The trouble was, this time she couldn't see how it might apply. She went inside, hoping for distraction.

She loved her home, which had been built by enthusiastic amateurs. The inside walls were rough-sawn cedar boards. The ceilings were bridge planking. The main floor was chopped in half by a vast brick fireplace. In the kitchen half, the walls were cupboards, except for built-in machinery, and except for windows under which bookshelves were topped by plants.

Protecting this property is the most basic point, she thought as she ground redskins in her food processor. I'll build from that, she decided as she split a home-baked soda roll. Until this suit is settled, the woods come first, she thought as she spread the roll with the impromptu peanut butter and added sprouts growing in a counter jar. I feel sorry about Tim and the other boys, *terribly* sorry, but that's a separate matter, she assured herself as she poured a glass of buttermilk.

She took her snack outside. Relieved that the sheriff's car had disappeared, she moved a chair to the west deck and tried to think of nothing beyond the way late afternoon air turned gold as the sun descended. Keeping her mind blank was a struggle. She was glad when it was finally time to dress.

She had a regular obligation Tuesday and Thursday evenings at a downtown women's bookstore. The situation had begun when she was still a teacher. Her class in Philosophy 485—Women's Fellowships as Charismatic Faiths— hadn't wanted to lose touch at the end of the term. They had continued as a study group, asking her to sit in as a moderator. She had refused, using her failing marriage as a polite, woman's reason.

She knew it was wrong to blame the university for her divorce, because her problems at home had begun long before work troubles were added. As soon as the first companionship glow withered, her husband had become perfectly frank about seeing her as a resource—an income and a link to the university. She was career driven for her own sake, and so she didn't get her feelings too badly hurt. After all, she had thought, even if her husband entered the marriage for advantage—couldn't love accompany advantage? She was sure it often did.

She hadn't quite reconciled herself to this more realistic view by the time she had to bring home the news that she would lose her job at the end of the year. Her announcement produced a clarifying moment. Without a salary, fringes, a university office, what good was she? her husband had asked. She wasn't sure, she had admitted, because being fired was a bewildering jolt. She had hoped he would comfort her, help her use this shock as a checkpoint, a basis for reexamining her personal goals and their joint future. But by the time he finished loudly restating his own personal goals in light of her job loss, it turned out he didn't foresee a joint future. When he packed up and moved out,

39

she turned to the women's group which constituted her remaining hope for continuity.

The group's reliable companionship had seen her through divorce, she remembered gratefully, and so they would surely support her through this new nightmare, as well. She let her mind rest in that belief as she climbed the stairs to the spare room she used as a dressing room so her bedroom would be uncluttered. She changed into well-worn jeans and walkers, and rummaged through the closet in search of a flower-print shirt to balance the tough image, which was almost a uniform for the group. Grabbing a wool sweater off the built-in shelves which replaced chests of drawers, she picked up the Spanish-leather bookbag she carried instead of a purse and headed back downstairs.

Outside, she stepped into the scuffed gray Subaru which combined fuel economy with the four-wheel-drive she found useful on the Sunstrike's handmade roads—uneven two-tracks which meandered aimlessly enough to prove that no tree had fallen to make room for wheels. She idled her car through the belt of giant black cottonwoods where spur routes plunged into the evergreens. A flag pole marked each cabin's drive or trail, and a personal ensign flew when the place was in use. Only two of the flagpoles were bare, Lindy noticed.

Muscling into the Mount Baker Highway's steady traffic was like stepping onto a conveyer belt since the two lane road had too many curves and hills to allow passing. The pace was set by the county's old settlers, who had plenty of time. Driving so sedately was one of the adjustments Lindy had made in order to live on the Sunstrike. As the dignified stream of cars rounded Stewart Mountain's shoulder and headed into blinding level sunlight which didn't hide the city sprawl, she sighed.

Bellingham had begun as several small communities ringing a mostly enclosed shallow bay. The early Anglo settlements had depended on lumber, mining, and shipping, while the Lummi settlement focused on fishing. Eventually, the separate communities grew together, but they refused to lose their individual identities even after they officially disappeared into a group name taken from the bay.

The current city flourished as an international port, a shopping town for Canadians, a host for a popular university, and a last resting place for the laidback university fringe. Mountain ridges to the east and south confined the pollution, bouncing it west over salt water, and north across dairying sea-level flatlands which reached beyond the international border to Vancouver, the major city on Canada's sunshine coast.

Suburbs crept up the city side of the hills, gaining stunning views of the bay, the islands in the salt water channel, the untouched Canadian mountains. Inside the suburbs, a chain of malls clasped the basically two-story city—except for a handful of downtown commercial buildings, Bellingham depended on geography for views.

Used to clean, river-valley air, Lindy began to cough as she entered the city. She drove down the long slope toward the bay, centering her thoughts on her group, which met at the Old Mall. The city's first, it had lost its Canadian customers as other malls leapfrogged northward. Hoping to survive by appealing to local use, the Old Mall's directors had launched a total rebuilding which would identify it as the closest easy-access shopping area for the university. They established a park-and-ride for students and negotiated for stores congenial to Bellingham's singles and gave rent reductions to university groups meeting unofficially. Lindy was grateful. Bruised by the job loss which had thrown her bad marriage into crisis, she suspected she wouldn't have felt able to join a group which met on campus.

She waited for a pair of runners to pass, their fluorescent sweatbands flashing in the shadows which had begun to fill the lower part of town. She entered the mall and picked her way among the road graders, backhoes and skyhooks which crammed the parking lot. Leaving her car under one of the few lot lights which would still turn on as darkness fell, she skirted sawhorses guarding a section of freshly poured concrete and entered the women's bookstore, *Ours*.

"Oh, Lindy," the blonde clerk said, breathy so she wouldn't sound critical. "They were beginning to wonder if they should call or what."

Lindy smiled ruefully. "Sorry. It's been a little bit hustly today."

"Which is why they worried. You could miss, no problem, even though you never do, but after what was in the newspaper? Absolutely not."

"Sorry," Lindy said again, her pulse frantic. She had forgotten about the newspaper, but she managed not to say so as she threaded her way through the jammed store, which was dusty with remodeling. At the back, the meeting room was set off by a smoked-glass wall. It was the only part of the store where redecorating was complete, its floor covered by pioneer-look rag rugs and its walls lovingly crazy-quilted by posters of famous female faces. Competing with the life-size mugshots, the Tuesday group of living women seemed outnumbered as they stared toward Lindy through the dark glass, their eyes agog and huge.

5

LINDY WORKED HER WAY INTO THE CLOSE-PACKED GROUP. Some of the members were students, and some were professionals, but all had dressed for the occasion in jeans and sweatshirts. The clothing blended them together, as if being women erased the more conventional divisions of age and income. Normally there would have been the hum of many conversations, but this time there was utter silence. Avid staring replaced the usual friendly smiles.

The moderator, a lean redhead with bitter eyes, cleared her throat. "We set our announced topic aside when one of us is in crisis," she said in a public voice.

Her listeners nodded.

"So, Lindy?" she said.

Lindy looked around, soberly meeting everyone's gaze. "The worst part of all this is not knowing," she said quietly. "What *did* happen? I'm not sure. What *will* happen? I haven't even seen the newspaper, in case it says."

Rattling papers were thrust toward her from everywhere. Their faces told her they were sharing the shock, and so she accepted everything they held out. When she had built a stack of newspapers on her lap, she smoothed the top copy and stared down at it. Local policy ruled out identifying juveniles, either as offenders or as victims, and so there were no names or faces. Instead, there was an artistic shot of the birder cabin. Normally it would have looked charming, but melodrama took precedence because of the crime scene tape. Lindy clenched her hands around the edges of the stack. She was grateful for her unlisted phone, which

must have protected her from interview requests. If this re-
porter had tried to catch her face-to-face, he would have
asked for directions to her house as soon as he found the
entrance to the Sunstrike, and the residents closest to the
highway would have sent him away—she knew she could
count on them for that.

"What does the article say?" she asked.

"They told the history of the cabin," one of the group
said while the others waited their turn.

"There's stuff about that old commune."

"It's mostly about substance abuse."

"Among kids."

"They must not know what happened, it sounds like."

"No. They know." The contradiction brought everyone
to a halt since the speaker was Yvonne, a small blonde with
a discouraged mouth. As the friend of the wife of a sheriff's
deputy, her insider status made the jammed room tense.

"*What* do they know?" the moderator finally asked.

"I'm sworn to secrecy."

"This group is sworn to secrecy," someone reminded
her.

"Okay, well, a call came in on the tip line," Yvonne said.
"According to someone anonymous, what happened in the
cabin was planned, and Lindy knows about the whole
thing."

The gasps were whispers.

Lindy shook her head doggedly. "I don't know anything."

"Maybe you know stuff you don't know you know," the
moderator said.

"You hear that's true sometimes," someone affirmed.

Lindy didn't exactly stop listening, but she wasn't really
able to hear. She bowed her head and tried to be fair. If
someone thought she knew tragic details, she ought to consider it. But if she knew something, what would it be? What
would it even be *about*? Teenagers? She had never been a
parent and didn't expect to be. Drinking? She had been
drunk only once, mildly, eight years ago, to celebrate get-

ting the teaching job she had hoped would be her life. Birding? She loved birds, but more as neighbors—not as someone to use binoculars on. Moonshine? She wasn't even sure that was what people called it, outside of the Westerns she had read as a child.

When the talk around her thinned, she roused to hear the moderator say, "Well, actually, our topic here does blend in with our planned program. Five boys, one dead, four blind—it's almost a case study, isn't it?" After the briefest of pauses, she added, "so let's move on to our announced question. Question: How does a woman raise a son without hating him in a society which tells him he's the Image of God?"

No, Lindy thought, no—the real question is larger: How do you raise children at all, in a way that leaves them their independence and also protects them? But she kept silent. She knew her reaction was focused by what she had just been through with Tim. It wouldn't be fair for her to drag the rest of them down from their safe, theoretical approach.

At the end of the two-hour session, they were still debating the terms of the question. Their attitudes divided them into rough groups based on whether they had children, and if they did, whether they had nothing but sons, or nothing but daughters, or a mix. Lindy wasn't able to offer anything. In her condition, that might be just as well, she suspected, but she was sorry, anyway, because not talking left her mind free to follow its own path—five boys, one dead, four blind. She couldn't seem to get beyond that.

When the meeting broke up, each of the participants murmured support or touched her gently before drifting outside. She nodded and thanked her way toward her car, clutching her stack of newspapers as if it was a shield. She struggled under a rush of exhaustion as she saw that a newcomer was loitering to catch her alone.

"Can I buy you a cup of coffee?" the waiting woman asked as Lindy approached. "We could go over to that fish place."

45

Lindy didn't want to. She wanted to go home.

"If it's complicated, I'm not sure how much help I'll be, but coffee sounds good," she said.

They picked their way along the destroyed walkways, hopping across rubble-filled gaps.

"I'll get it," the woman said as they entered *The Fishery*. She went to the self-serve counter confidently, although she had seemed diffident, outside.

Everything else about her didn't match, either, Lindy decided as she chose an orange plastic booth well away from a group of teenagers romping noisily over cokes and chips. All of them wore argumentative tees, and they seemed to be playing some sort of space game involving Star Trek roles. The kids who had used her cabin to blind themselves— would they ever be welcome again in such a group?

Not able to bear the question, she turned to study her hostess. The oversize denim jacket looked wrong on a person her apparent age, but her worn jeans fitted in with the women's group. Her blue shirt seemed to be recycled from a man's, but her rough-out laced boots were new and very expensive. As Lindy decided she couldn't evaluate the look, the woman set mugs on the table and slid into the booth.

After their ceremonial first sip, she held out a snapshot. "My son claims you know him," she said.

Lindy looked at the picture of a teenager offering an unconvincing grin. His light hair was long, curving upward at the ends. His face was baby-smooth, but his ancient eyes suggested he should have had a beard. He looked elongated, like a potato sprouted in the bag in a cool-room.

Lindy smiled. "Stash. Yes, I see him in the woods sometimes. He's yours? You must be proud of him."

"I'm Faith, I don't know if he mentioned it."

"Hi, Faith," Lindy said, wondering if the name was real. Faith's conglomeration of clothing made sense if it stood for the generation which had chosen names symbolically.

"No, Stash doesn't talk much," she said. "Just, oh, can you make sugar out of vine maple sap? that sort of thing.

We have a lot of vine maples out at my place," she added.

"He's one of the blind ones they were talking about."

"Oh, Faith! I'm *sick* about it. Stash!"

"He's not completely blind. The doctor says he'll be so no one but him notices, once he adjusts. Stash says it's like a fishnet inside his eyes, and if he could get windex in there, no more problem."

Lindy rubbed her own eyes as if it might clear his. "What happened, do you know?"

"Sort of." Faith sipped her coffee before she began a harrowing story. One of the boys was nineteen. In most states, he could have been drinking legally, according to the laws in force when he was born, and so he took personal offense at the recent changes which let him vote but not drink. He was out of high school but unemployed, and so he was looking for a low-cost way to occupy his time. His younger brother wanted to raise marijuana, but the older boy insisted that was illegal, whereas drinking wasn't—only their ages were illegal. They started talking about how hard it was to buy liquor without an ID and moved on to discussing moonshine as a joke—or at least, Stash thought so. Looking back, none of them could remember exactly when the idea turned serious.

Lindy sighed. "If the boys organized everything themselves, the bad part couldn't have been deliberate, like they were saying there in the group."

"I'll tell Stash what they said, but he wasn't part of the group to start with, so he may not exactly know." Faith frowned, activating facial lines etched by a non-Northwestern sun. "He doesn't usually get involved," she added, "but I think— Well, he grew up on a commune, so they probably thought he'd know about do-it-yourself."

"You were on the old Sunstrike?" Lindy asked.

"No, a place in NorCal. It was finally over for me, for a bunch of reasons. Leaving's hard, but I threw my trust on a change of scene, which had saved me before. Bellingham seemed right because I knew I couldn't leave the coast. Once you've come west, once, you—" She looked into the space above Lindy's head. "And I'd heard of the Sun-strike," she said, canceling her reverie. "I wasn't going onto a commune, but it was easier if one was handy, if that doesn't sound too stupid."

"No," Lindy said, "changing your life's hard."

"When we first got here, I went to the women's rescue house, out there in the Lettered Streets, you know?"

Lindy nodded.

"Before I could move on, their manager left. It worked out lucky because I have a college degree. I can't remember it, but it looks good on a resumé," Faith said, pausing for a god!-life! smile. "So they hired me, and I've been there, well, I forget how many years."

"That's a great getting-it-together story," Lindy said.

It also explained the contradiction of stooped shoulders, neglected hair, and confident manners.

"Except about Stash," Faith agreed, apparently not no-ticing Lindy's inventory. "It was okay while he was a kid, but he's a man now." She inspected the tabletop. "Some of the women who come to us are really just kids, but even into their twenties, they forget how young Stash is, because he acts older." She fidgeted her coffee mug. "If there's a way to convince a kid he ought to resist, when women start coming on to him, I haven't figured out what it would be."

Lindy sighed. "I remember the first time a stranger drove past me in a mall parking lot and yelled something. It took me years, really, to realize that isn't flattering."

Faith caught her gaze knowingly. "The shelter tries to protect women from their impulses. So I had to tell Stash to leave."

"For his own sake, too," Lindy said.

Faith nodded. "But I feel bad. If he hadn't had to find someplace to stay, he might not have agreed to get involved with this stuff—the other kids covered up for him living in that cabin if he promised to watch their still."

"I like him, Faith," Lindy said. "I'm glad there's a rea-son."

Faith sipped her coffee. "But the cops sealed the cabin."

"I suppose they did."

"So, now, he truly has no place to be. His dad's in jail again, and I can't afford separate rent for Stash. I wondered, though. I'll scrape something together somehow, if you'd let him live in one of the other cabins out there on the Sunstrike?"

"Sure. Of course. Except there isn't any rent. And it isn't the Sunstrike anymore."

"I'm not asking for charity."

Lindy shrugged. "And I'm not willing to be a landlord."

Faith drew the long breath of a successful marathoner. "He's in shelter care at the moment. But even with the doctor saying he can take care of himself, the cops still say he can't live on his own. Kids in trouble lose their rights, even if they haven't broken any laws."

"I guess the cops think of moonshine as breaking the law," Lindy said.

Faith looked surprised. After a moment, she went on as if Lindy's comment was incomprehensible and therefore tact required her to set it aside. "What I thought was, I could come out and make a home for Stash, and you wouldn't have to know whether I actually live there with him or not."

"Sure. Do that. I don't watch the cabins, so I truly won't know. Most of them are in use right now, so you'll be stuck with one of the ecological ones that don't have power, but you're welcome to whatever there is."

"Stash can string power, install outlets up to code, the whole thing. I mean, he knows how, if you don't mind having the cabin changed," Faith said.

Lindy smiled. "Wonderful, then. You're satisfied about rent, and I'm satisfied about no rent."

Faith laughed as if she had forgotten how. They left *The Fishery* together, and Faith walked Lindy back to her car. Lindy assumed there was something more—something even harder to say—but Faith simply knocked on her roof to send her off. It was a shock to realize Faith had walked with her to protect her. In quiet Bellingham, it was hard to remember the women Faith dealt with did need protection.

WHEN A NEW stranger walked briskly out of the woods next morning, Lindy remembered the commune's supposed curse and wondered if she was bringing herself bad luck by sitting on her east deck to read. This woman's rose business suit wasn't intended for bushwhacking and her open-toe pumps weren't meant for forest duff, but she didn't seem concerned. She inspected the clearing with large, dark eyes and bent her head inquisitively toward the pond as she passed.

"Deb Wayne, from All Perils Insurance," she called out as she spotted Lindy. "You're Professor Lindy Adair? Owner of all this including that down there?" She made a clicking noise for lament. "Looks disastrous, all right."

"You've been down?" Lindy asked.

Deb rolled her dramatic eyes. *After* an hour of arm wrestling with the cops. Feel possessive of their precious crime scene. They've never seen a still, the way they act."

Lindy smiled and pointed to a chair. Deb sat down and rummaged a notepad out of her briefcase.

"Did you walk up that trail, dressed like that?"

Deb looked at herself. "Yes. You enforce a dress code?"

Lindy laughed. "No. It's fine."

Deb nodded. "You've been assigned to me. I know your call wasn't about loss to yourself, but we look at that, along with liability questions. Now, what we've got here, All Perils doesn't cover criminal enterprise, so the still, we don't cover it. But subsequent damage, we look at the situation. Slip-and-fall, yes, so falling off the catwalk and drowning, we cover that regardless. Blindness, a gray area from any fool knowing you can't drink moonshine, but three of the kids are juveniles. Kids can be held to behavior other kids their age can manage, and their parents are supposed to supervise. On the other hand, you provide them with

50

that cabin, a perfect place to escape control. But two of the kids being eighteen or over should help us negotiate you down as to proportional blame. You argue it's not your personal criminal enterprise, so, loss of use from the crime scene restrictions, also *for* you."

Lindy didn't try to follow it, from an insurance point of view. "Where did they get the still?" she asked.

"Good question." Deb slapped her pen against the notebook. "You talked to Timothy Patrick, right?"

Lindy nodded.

"Okay, Timothy's grandfather is The MacOwen, in the old country, as he says, where they made their own whiskey as a regular thing. They pronounce it more Magown, according to him, but he's Max Owen here, being born in the United States, in moonshine country, as he puts it, and so he knows all about white whiskey, as he calls it, but these kids didn't get it from him, so he swears. His proof—" She held up fingers. "For one, if they'd gotten it from him, they wouldn't have gone blind because he'd have taught them precautions. For two, he disapproves of drunken kids—get old enough to do it legally is his rule. For three, moonshine delivers an apocalypse instead of a hangover, as he describes it, so real moonshiners go down to the local liquor store when they're thirsty."

Lindy smiled.

"Yes, I liked him, too," Deb said.

"Why does moonshine make you blind?" Lindy asked. "You hear that, but I thought it was like what they tell little kids to keep them from fiddling with themselves."

Deb laughed. "I know zip, but Owen just got through telling me all this stuff to where I could go into the business. You might ask him."

"Where *did* they get the information, if not from him?"

Deb frowned. "The survivors willing to talk all put it on the kid who drowned, Vance Crayson."

"That's convenient, since he can't contradict."

"I told them so, but they swear anyway."

"Where did Vance learn?"

Deb shook her head. "He didn't. Not even chemistry at the high school."

"If blaming him is supposed to cover up for one of the other boys, which one really was responsible, can you tell?"

Deb produced deep dimples to show thought. "We're in difficulty there. Al's the oldest of the group. A strong personality, so probably the ringleader. Nineteen, so technically of-age, but letting him live at home gives his parents protective rights. Plus his doctor says he's stressing, which excuses him from everything, in the law's view. Your cop, Richison, says when he asked so much as the kid's name, both parents and their lawyer answered to drown Al out, if he had tried to talk, which he refused to do."

"Richison?" Lindy said. "I thought I gave Brent Fuller as the police contact."

"You did, but Richison does most of the talking."

Lindy sighed.

"I'll keep after Al," Deb assured her, "because it would be *extremely* convenient if we could show that the of-age kids were the ones who set the whole thing up. That way, you're just the property owner. Plenty bad enough."

"I guess I don't see why I'm at fault at all," Lindy said.

"Being an insured is a serious responsibility," Deb answered in a textbook way. "You think you just pay a premium and say what coverages. But that's not it. You're required to be prudent, which letting half the world crash here is not. You're to supervise what's yours, which housing teenagers in cabins no one can see is not. You're to warn of known and potential dangers, which—"

"I get it," Lindy interrupted.

After a moment she tried again. "I took out one of those Personal Umbrella Policies for more insurance because this is a little unusual out here."

Deb nodded firmly. "The downside of your PUP— that's our term for it—is, paying for added coverage advertises you know you're living an at-risk life. The same with putting up a sign: BEWARE OF DOG. It doesn't put any responsibility on your trespasser, it just proves you know you've got a vicious dog. Now. Suppose this underage kid, Vance, was at fault, which we have to consider unless the detectives come up with something else. Everyone is supposed to help minors stay *out* of trouble, so that means everyone who helped him get *into* difficulties is in a jam. We can lay out some of the blame on the school, for building their cabin, but quite frankly, you're a deeper pocket than they are, if you've ever tried to sue a school district which is not the same as your collision with the university."

Lindy sighed. "I always feel pure dread when anyone tells me something frankly."

Deb laughed.

Lindy hadn't meant it as a joke, and so she approached her worry more directly. "Why would you think I'm a deep pocket?"

Deb lifted one hand to indicate the woods.

"No," Lindy insisted, "the former owner got a forestry basis for the tax assessment. We aren't considered—what do they call that?"

"Highest and best use," Deb answered. "Right, you aren't at the moment, which probably confuses you about your value. From the claimant's point of view, all they have to do is declare an intent to remove the forestry classification. It costs them a few years of back taxes at full assessment, instead of the reduced rate you paid, plus interest on the difference, and then there they are, at full value, which is what? Twenty, twenty-five thousand per acre? On a hundred and eighty acres—you do the math."

"I paid about two thousand an acre."

"Land values rise so fast around here, I can't be sure I've kept up."

Lindy bowed her head. "I don't mean I don't believe you. All I mean is, I can't stand it."

"No, people in your situation usually can't." Deb stood up energetically. "Is this your story—you didn't know what these kids were up to?"

Lindy nodded as she stood up.

"Don't give up yet. But realistically, I'd see my lawyer, in your shoes. We represent you only to the extent of your coverage, so you'll need help with the rest of it. Our lawyer and your lawyer had just as well work together from the first."

"I have a million dollars of coverage, with that Umbrella policy."

Deb nodded. "Whereas you're talking five kids."

Lindy found it hard to breathe. "Two pairs of them are brothers, so isn't that three families?"

"Each child had a life, before this, so, no, it's five." Deb slid her notebook into her briefcase as she started down the steps. When she reached the path, she turned to walk backwards so she could talk without slowing herself down.

"What do you figure?" she asked pragmatically. "A million bucks a kid, average? We should be able to hold it down to that."

6

LINDY STARED AT THE WOODS WHERE DEB WAYNE HAD DIS-
appeared. After a blank moment, she went inside to stare at
her phone in the booklined entryhall. She knew her lawyer's number—it had memorized itself inside of her during
the bad days with the university—but she didn't like being
the sort of person who could dial her lawyer by heart.

She dialed and asked for Harry. She hated it that the receptionist recognized her voice.

Harry was talking to someone else as he picked up the
phone. "I was going to call you in a little while, Lindy.
We've been notified to expect papers on a civil case. I
agreed to accept service for you, is that what you want?"
When Lindy agreed, he went on, "I figure it's time for a
planning session. You're penciled in for eleven, does that
sound all right?"

It didn't sound all right at all, but Lindy managed not to
say so. She trailed upstairs to change into cords so she
could go to the campus afterwards. Scooping up an armload of books, she headed for her Subaru.

Harry's office was on the far side of downtown,
crouched on the shallow bank just before the land dropped
away to sea level. The building was a pleasant brown-brick
structure, with wide halls and copious windows looking
out over the working docks surrounded by fish markets
and come-as-you-are taverns on pilings which allowed the
bay tide to surge beneath. Even so, Lindy dreaded it. She
had been there too many times, during the end of her university career.

She paused for a trio of runners with swinging pony tails before she entered the parking lot. She walked down the empty hall, reliving anguish. Harry's receptionist smiled and waved her on without interrupting a phone conversation. Lindy stepped behind the screen which gave the partners privacy.

Harry's office was the head of the row. Books lined the side walls, but two of the walls were glass. One gave him a view of South Hill, and the other faced the hall to protect him from any suspicion of misusing his privacy with clients.

He grinned and took his feet out of his bottom drawer when Lindy tapped on his open door. "Well, Lindy," he said in a humorous tone.

"I'm afraid so." She sank into a black leather chair.

Harry chuckled and lifted his arms to lock his wrists on top his luxuriant gray hair, kicking his chair back to get comfortable. As always, he was in his shirtsleeves. Lindy noticed that he still preferred small checks on white, but his tie showed he kept up with the current power color, even though his pants were banker gray.

"I thought I'd get started, so I called this new detective, Richison," Harry said. "He seemed cooperative."

"Supposedly someone called the tip line," Lindy said. "Did he say anything about that?"

Harry stared at the ceiling. "He probably hinted. Tip lines attract people who have a lot of free-floating anger they want to express to someone who won't talk back, he told me."

Would that attitude help? Lindy wondered. She hung her head to think about it. The sheriff's department evidently took the call more seriously, or at least her group thought so.

"Richison told me they have evidence that what happened wasn't an accident," she said. "Did he say what their evidence is?"

"No."

Lindy rubbed her cheek. "I was hoping it was just this tip line, but if he thinks that doesn't matter, then what *does* matter must be something else."

"Yeah, sounds like it."

Lindy pressed her knuckles against her mouth. She knew it made her hard to understand, but she needed the comfort. "If someone really did mean for all this to happen, shouldn't they be investigating everyone who had an attitude about the boys?"

Harry scowled. "Don't meddle in this investigation, Lindy. Stay clear away. Cops generally know what they're doing, even if they don't act like it."

"You just say that because you're part of the justice system," she insisted.

"I say it because I don't want to visit you in jail or in the hospital."

"Thanks."

"I mean it! Suppose you start asking questions all over. Given your mental training, suppose your questions are too good, too close to the point. Somebody might decide they need to get you stopped."

She frowned. "Surely not."

He shook his head, not really patiently. "This new detective's looking into it. Leave it to him. He says your problem is going to be the complaining family. They're divided, which keeps them going. The father just wants criminal charges, but the mother doesn't care anything about jail. She just wants money, which is where your civil suit comes in."

"So they're compromising on both?"

Harry laughed. The sound transported Lindy back to her university ordeal. When his clients were in real trouble, Harry laughed as often as he could find the least excuse. At first, it seemed like hardheartedness, but eventually it came to seem supportive, almost like encouragement. Lindy recognized it as a bad sign that he was laughing now.

"My insurance includes extended liability coverage,"

she said, "but the adjustor thinks a million won't cover it."

Harry snapped his chair forward and reached for a legal pad. "What's her name?"

"Deb Wayne." Lindy explained as she watched him write. "I don't have much actual money, you know. I thought I could tie everything up in that property because I live low-profile, but I didn't plan for something like this."

"Nobody does," Harry agreed in a voice intended to sound comforting. "You're looking at the worst possible?"

Lindy nodded.

"For civil, if they demand a jury trial and bring in this parade of blind kids—" He didn't need to finish the sentence.

Lindy fidgeted. "The insurance agent seems to think the property is worth a lot."

"Yeah, it is," Harry said. "I remember you didn't pay a lot, but with this housing shortage here in the county, values are going out of sight."

Lindy stared at Harry's doodles, which looked like dollar signs. "What about that malediction? Could that help?"

"You mean, they might be afraid to demand the land, because of what's happened?"

She nodded.

"Don't start believing in curses." He held her gaze, frowning. His face was basically cheerful, and so she knew it was an effort for him to look dire. "What happened here is too bad, but it's absolutely routine. You don't need anything supernatural to explain it."

Lindy couldn't bear to visualize the tragedies his clients must have presented him, in order for him to call this situation routine. "I wasn't thinking about my own beliefs," she said at last. "It was more that I wondered what other people might feel."

"Stick to the law."

And what would the law do? she protested silently. Trying to face the worst in order to look for ways around it, she imagined losing the case, losing her property. Would the new owners let her walk on the trails she had built so laboriously, using only hand tools in order to keep the work low impact? No, if the land went for a court judgment, they would want as much money as they could get. They would sell to a developer who didn't believe in curses. There wouldn't be any trails, because they would apply for a rezoning. The county's housing shortage was most severe at the lower end of the price range, so they would plan for that market, packing multiples into the highest possible density, building row after row of yardless two-story apartments along bare, narrow streets.

"We'll string it out," Harry said in his kindest voice. "Quite often people come to their senses."

It was his way of admitting he was a top-notch arbitrator. Lindy tried to believe it would apply this time, too.

"Sergeant Richison said their evidence is circumstantial," she said. "Could that help?"

He ran his lower lip over his upper lip in order to consider. "You're thinking empty chair defendant?"

"I don't know what that is."

"You say it seems like someone was involved, but it wasn't you. You're not obliged to say who it was."

"Does that work?"

"Sometimes."

"It would be better to come up with some definite possibilities, wouldn't it?"

"No, that gets you into slander. Leave accusations to the cops—they can get away with it."

"But it seems like citizens are having to get involved, these days," Lindy insisted. "You see it everywhere. Kidnapings. Deaths the cops make a mess of and then claim they were shorthanded."

"Forget the news. You're dealing with law here, not journalism. I know you like to talk theory, but concentrate on facts until we get this settled."

Trying to accept advice, Lindy stood up. "I'll write a check out front, to get you started," she said.

Harry walked her to the door. Lindy paused at the edge of the screen.

"I suppose there's no point in my telling you how much this scares me," she said.

"No. No point at all in that."

Feeling as if she had traveled back in time, Lindy wrote out a retainer, barely able to concentrate while the secretary chatted about how nice it was to see her again. Lindy left the building in a cloud of depression so thick it dimmed her view of the street. Maybe Harry was right, maybe what she faced was just a matter of simple facts, but she always saw everything in terms of larger patterns. She knew she wouldn't be able to make sense out of the facts until she had a structure to fit them into, but how was she to find a structure she could bear to look at?

Returning to her car, she crossed town toward the university which ringed the west face of Sehome Hill, Bellingham's highest point. She didn't like returning to campus, although hindsight helped her see that losing her job had been like divorce. At first, she had hated the whole hill, but gradually she remembered her battle had involved only five people out of a faculty of hundreds. She had tried to imagine what those five were like inside, to behave as they had. Finally she saw they didn't have an inside—that was exactly their problem. The recognition helped.

Still, she was tense as she drove through the Visitor Center for her day-parking permit and left her car in the lot nearest the central campus. Since fall term hadn't started yet, she was alone as she climbed the long rise of steps masking the rib of bedrock on which the library perched. Dumping her returns in the slot, she checked the card catalog and went upstairs.

The library owned a number of books which discussed the structural distinctions among alcohols. A few books mentioned recreational use and explained that some alcohols were more dangerous than others. None of them said why.

Lindy was too absorbed to notice footsteps approaching.

"How come you're in science?" the humanities librarian asked.

60

"Hi, Nan," Lindy said to the comfortably round woman who filled the end of the aisle, her bright rugby top and dark stirrup pants looking like a campus uniform. "I was trying to find out about moonshine."

"Are you sure you're in the right area?" Nan said.

Lindy smiled. "Well, I'm not finding much, if that's a sign of anything."

"What about lunch?" Nan asked with a glance at her watch.

"Sounds good."

They strolled outside together. Crossing the street to the union building, they went downstairs to one of the smaller dining rooms. Since Lindy didn't trust the food service's opinion of additives, she chose a carton of yogurt and a tea bag. Nan was more accepting, landing chowder, chips, bean salad, beef sandwich, and carrot cake onto her tray with no apparent pause for thought.

Four tables were pushed together in the center of the main room so a noisy all-male faculty group could linger over their meal in order to debate campus politics. Nan led the way toward the windows.

"Has it been long enough that you don't worry about meeting any of your so-called colleagues?" she asked as she unloaded her tray.

Lindy sat down while she thought about it. "I met my former chair down at the fish market once. We discussed the ling cod. The skin was going a little orange, and he wanted to know if I could tell how fresh it was."

"And could you?"

"I said it was fresh, but I think it wasn't."

They both laughed.

"I guess, after that, everything's easy," Lindy added.

Nan laughed again, reminding Lindy of the part of campus life she missed. It was a community. A teaching contract was the only thing you needed in order to join. The downside was that the moment you left, you disappeared.

Her situation was different, because most chairs and deans had been on careful behavior ever since Lindy's case proved they couldn't get away with absolutely everything. A lot of the women on campus were grateful, and so she could still count on a welcome.

"I've been reading the newspaper," Nan said as she reached her dessert.

Lindy set down her spoon. "It's why I was looking up homemade alcohol. I was hoping there might be something about it that would make me not to blame for those kids."

"Like what?"

"I'm not sure. All I've found out so far is what to call it. Anything from 'panther's breath' to 'who kicked me.'"

Nan laughed. "Really?" Her smile faded. "You aren't to blame, surely?"

Lindy shook her head. "I *swear* I'm not, but I seem to be the only person who feels that way."

Nan studied her face while she sipped her tea. "This isn't going to make you shut down on letting our students crash out there, is it?" she asked. "I mean, I'm sure they do things they're not supposed to, but I can't see why that's your problem. Are you going to be stuck for child support if a baby's conceived accidentally—that sort of thing?"

Lindy rested her chin on her fist, wearily seeing she might be well advised simply to disappear entirely and forever.

"I hadn't even thought of that," she said faintly.

"Sorry I suggested it. The thing is, I send our work-study kids out there when they can't find anything cheap enough any closer, and I don't know what they'd do if you shut down. School's starting pretty soon, you know, and I've already sent somebody to you."

Lindy studied her friend's round face, its line-free openness proclaiming what a safely bookish world she lived in. She tried for bravery, but her affectionate smile was nostalgic at best.

"Maybe you shouldn't Nan, you know? They're still welcome at the moment, but I really may lose that property. There are laws I'd never heard of about it. I feel like, if the legislature's going to pass laws that make us guilty, even when we're innocent, doesn't it seem like they ought to warn us?"

"What kind of law?"

"Controlled substances homicide. It's a law about kids."

Nan drew a sharp breath and clattered her fork onto her empty plate. Lindy watched the noise abstractedly.

"And they're applying it to *you?*"

"They want to, I guess."

"How *can* they? Everybody knows protecting students is what got you into trouble here at school."

Lindy shrugged.

" 'Who-kicked-me,' " Nan quoted, "is that what you're saying?"

Lindy smiled wistfully.

Nan reached across the table toward her hand. "I'll talk to the documents librarian, see what he can find about defenses."

7

A HIGH FOG WAS WHITENING THE RIVER VALLEY BY THE TIME Lindy got home. She walked into the silent woods, searching inside herself for confidence. When she found only dismay and fear, she turned her thoughts outside. Fog was always beautiful in the breathlessly still woods, and she concentrated on that. Water droplets beaded each separate, individual needle on the cedars, but the tops of the Douglas firs had already disappeared as the blanket of white sank dramatically down the trunks.

"I can't lose you," she whispered to the trees. Greed wasn't driving her. She was sure of that, because underneath her personal yearning was a more primal fear. Without the protection of her ownership, the forest was gone forever. The construction machinery she had seen at the Old Mall would arrive as if by evil magic, and the soul-renewing woods would fall before roaring blades.

She clamped her eyes shut to erase the image. The darkness inside reminded her of the blind teenagers. She opened her eyes in horror. Whatever was going to happen, maybe she couldn't stop it, but she didn't have to stand and wait. Harry might be right—maybe it truly was safer to leave investigation to cops—but she had never been passive, and she had never put safety at the top of her values list.

Feeling sure, she set off through the woods without using a trail, clambering through the limbs of fallen trees and skirting moss-lined sumps which had managed to remain boggy despite the drought. When she reached a two-track, she followed it around the head of a blunt gully to reach a cabin on the other side.

The cabin had begun as a standard Sunstrike design, a shed roof sloping against a chimney wall. But in this case, a second shed had been built against the first, with a gap left between the rooflines to accommodate the clerestory windows which were so much more practical than skylights in a dripping climate. An in-ground greenhouse extended from the original kitchen. A long woodshed, designed like a corncrib, had been added beyond the living room on the other side. A plume of white smoke curled out of a brownish lava chimney above untreated cedar shakes.

Lindy rapped on the open door which gave directly into the kitchen. "Nick?" she called.

"Yo!"

She stepped into the galley-style room which matched Nick's choice of the Coast Guard's ensign as his trailhead flag. Latched cupboards of seagoing mahogany topped a prefab unit of kitchen built-ins. Opposite was a counter serving as both pass through and eating space. A galley-style wood stove straddled the dividing line between the kitchen and living room. Firewood cut to stove lengths stacked the outside wall up to the level of the casement windows which stood open despite the fog.

She came in past the stove, to find Nick sprawled back in an oversized executive chair, his boot-socked feet crossed on the enormous desk he sat by, a computer keyboard balanced on his midsection. Despite his comfortable pose, his muscular build showed through his checkered western shirt and tight jeans.

"Top me up and help yourself?" he said, holding out his coffee mug.

Lindy smiled and reached around the corner of the pass-through for the coffee pot without having to look. Nick was one of her earliest residents. Originally from Arizona, he had met Lindy at Vikingcon—the annual science fiction gathering sponsored by the university. Lindy had attended because one of her students wanted her to lead a discussion about off-world belief structures in science fiction. Nick, as Rascal Dunn, had been signing his current novel, *Faultline on Frenzy*. After their separate performances, they met on a panel where they discovered how easily their minds sharpened off each other.

It would have been the beginning of a friendship, if Nick had been local. The geographical problem had straightened out when he raved about the area, insisting he had never seen trees before. One of the listening students mentioned Lindy's Sunstrike as the area's best collection of trees. By the time Vikingcon was over, Nick had decided to send for his belongings.

He had moved in cautiously, not quite sure Lindy was as casual about her excess cabins as she sounded. But as the months passed and other people accumulated, he decided to take her at her word. He began renovating his cabin, for exercise, he always claimed. He rewired the cabin for kitchen and computer equipment, but everything else was ocean-going, as he liked to explain. It amused him to insist he wanted to be battened down, in case he someday slid into the river.

Lindy supposed it might be partly true, since he had chosen a cabin on the lip of a steep gully which dumped dramatically into the valley floor. He had wanted the view, he said—on clear days, he looked without obstruction across the twenty-two miles between the Sunstrike and Mount Baker. But Lindy suspected his real motive was privacy. Visitors were even less likely to discover his house than they were to find hers.

"Can I interrupt you?" she asked, picking a mug out of the drain rack and filling it for herself.

"Sure." He blanked his computer screen and set his keyboard aside in order to balance his coffee mug on his middle, where the keyboard had been.

Lindy described her situation. "I wondered if Tim said anything when you drove him home the other day," she ended.

He lifted one arm to show evenhandedness. "His folks

are divorced, so he gets this divided world effect. He talks to his mom, one set of things drives her berserk. He talks to his dad, a whole other set of taboos. Since they don't talk to each other about values, at least not in front of him, he never has a chance to see how what they say meshes, if it does. His mom is no more evil than all the other mothers, he claims, but she's wired about older women because one of the kids took up with this older woman and the mothers who know about it are all sure their little darling is bound to be next."

Lindy nodded. "He said something about not being allowed to let me drive him."

Nick laughed.

"I know it." Lindy smiled faintly. "He's not my type, anyway, however old he might get."

Nick laughed again, filling the small room. "What sets his dad off is how to be a man in this modern world," he added in an amused, quoting voice. "He thought I might have some hints on that, since I write about the future."

"Were you any use to him?"

"I hope so. His dad says to protect women but not to let them know you're doing it, and I said forget it, they're bound to know, and they'll clobber you for it. Even now, much less his generation."

"Well, that ought to leave him nice and confused," Lindy said.

"Teenagers are always confused, it's what they're for."

Lindy laughed. Nick had a point-blank way with people, as if standing within voice range meant they had accepted his plan to question them invasively. And usually they did seem to accept it, partly in reaction to his obvious interest, and partly because of their curiosity about writers. Surely Tim would have reacted like everyone else, she hoped.

"Did he say where they got the idea for this moonshine?" she asked at last.

"He's always known about it, he said. His grandfather tells family stories, and apparently the grandfather's father was a commercial moonshiner. Tim just thought it was fun,

67

he never realized there was anything dangerous."

Lindy sighed. "I wonder if he told that to the cops."

Nick shook his head. "Apparently not, if he talked to the same one I did."

"They questioned you?"

"Yeah. A sheriff's deputy. For driving Tim home," he said. "He wanted to know what Tim told me, so I described the trouble he's having in sophomore writing. They're supposed to do persuasive essays, which he can't get the knack of, and he wondered if I knew how."

Lindy smiled. "Did he really?"

"Close enough." Nick studied her face a moment. "Someone questioned you?"

Lindy described the police visit.

"You need a lawyer," he told her.

Lindy described her lawyer's view.

"Good God, Lindy, you can't lose this place." Nick looked around his tidy cabin. "If I didn't have free rent, homegrown vegetables, free firewood for heat, I'd have to get a *job*."

When Lindy laughed, he grinned.

She carried her mug to the galley. "What are you working on?" she asked, to end their conversation on a pleasant note.

Nick groaned. "I've got to invent this alien life form. I tried out a description on Tim and he said no way, so I'm back to go."

Lindy washed her mug and set it in the drain rack. "This alien, what does it need to do?"

Nick explained, using off-world gestures. Lindy leaned on the counter to watch.

"Sounds rough, all right," she said as he fell silent.

She paused at the door to wave her thanks. Nick grinned and reached for his computer keyboard.

Lindy set off down the two-track feeling somewhat cheered. If Tim's grandfather was the source of the information, that might explain why the survivors were blaming the dead boy, Vance. Tim liked his grandfather. Maybe they all did. They might be protecting him by placing blame on someone who wouldn't have to care, ever again. If they were, then maybe it was a way out, for her. Surely it would help if she could show that another adult was involved directly.

The first step was to meet this grandfather.

Pondering this not quite hopefully, she reached her clearing to find a gunmetal Cherokee parked next to her car. Sergeant Richison stood beside it, his head tipped back as if he enjoyed the fog which had descended low enough to bathe his face. He was dressed more informally this time, a pearl windshirt over a navy turtleneck topping his dress jeans and signature boots. Lindy wondered if he was trying to look Northwestern.

"Hi," she said.

He straightened. "Got a minute?"

"Sure," Lindy said, smiling at the neighborly greeting, even though she would have given a great deal to banish him forever from her clearing.

8

DAN HAD WONDERED IF LINDY WOULD INSIST ON SITTING outside in the fog, as resistant as she seemed behind her casual greeting. It was a relief when she gestured him into the house, because he wasn't sure he would ever adjust to Northwest temperatures. She led the way to a room which looked more like the lounge in a hunting lodge than a private living room. Bookshelves lined one wall. An entertainment bench holding a TV, VCR, and CD player filled a corner, beside a built-in couch. Easy chairs formed a half circle in front of the huge fireplace. Since the room itself was entirely wood, except for the brick fireplace, the dark blue couch and chair cushions served as a sufficient color accent.

"I'll build a fire while we talk, okay?" she said as she opened the fire screen. "Once the fogs start, it's damp enough to feel chilly even when it isn't."

Dan watched her transfer logs from the built-in woodbox to the grate. She kept in shape, he decided. Not that he could see her muscles, under all that clothing, but she turned and crouched and twisted and lifted as if it took no effort. She had been so still, sitting through that first interview, and she seemed so accepting, he had thought she must be passive. He'd have to revise that judgment.

She grabbed a box of matches off the mantel and lit the paper underneath her kindling before brushing the wood dust off her hands.

"I thought we might talk easier if you weren't outnumbered," he said as they sat down.

70

"It's all right."

"I've interviewed just about everybody." He tried to sound confidential. "Most of them aren't talking."

"The families, you mean?"

"Yeah, plus the kids, their doctors, and the high school."

Lindy glanced at him. "That didn't take long," she said.

He shrugged. "It should have taken longer, but most of them just shut down. I didn't know if it was because I'm not from around here, but your student, the sheriff, didn't seem to get anymore out of them than I did."

"Northwesterners can be silent when they decide to," Lindy agreed. "It isn't being shy, or being hostile, it's just—"

"Comes from spending so much time with trees, no doubt."

Lindy smiled.

"Are you going to the services for the kid who drowned?" he asked, even though he suspected rapid changes of subject wouldn't rattle her as they did most people.

"No. I'd feel unwelcome, I guess, with no one knowing whose fault anything is, but wanting someone to blame. And I don't know them." An edge of impatience in her voice made him feel she thought his topic shifted around because his mind was disorderly, not because he was controlling the conversation.

"They belong to one of those charismatic churches, at least the mother does," he said. "Did you get an announcement?"

Lindy nodded.

"Fuller tells me you have a lot of different churches here."

He had hoped it would be a leading remark, but Lindy just nodded again, not looking at him.

"This particular one—Fuller thinks the minister sometimes takes people to task from the pulpit. I've never seen that, myself, but I thought you might know how to handle it."

71

Lindy folded her arms across her solar plexus. The self-protective gesture answered his question—absolutely she had seen such performances. Nevertheless, he waited for the words, which were slow in coming.

"It shouldn't be a problem for you," she said, instead of talking about herself. "It sounds like you were thinking of attending."

"Yeah."

"Well, at most, he might exhort you to do your best, something along those lines."

"Maybe I'm already trying to."

She glanced at him only from the corners of her eyes, not turning her head to face him, but her smile was sympathetic, so maybe they were making progress, he decided.

"I need to know a couple of things, Lindy."

Her smile disappeared.

"We have witnesses that the original Sunstrike ran a still. I'd like to hear what you know about it."

"Nothing." She breathed deeply. "I didn't know this place existed, until it was for sale. The commune was gone, by then."

"You admit communards drift through."

She nodded. "Yes, they do, but only as individuals."

"Suppose some of the old-timers are rebuilding the Sunstrike, and maybe not mentioning it."

Lindy got up to stir the fire. He studied her back as she crouched on the hearth, looking defenseless even with a lethal-size poker in her hand.

"I feel combative when you turn everything I say into something bad," she said without turning around. "Could you stop planning traps and just *talk*? I'm willing to tell you whatever I know, provided I'm not getting someone into trouble."

"Okay."

She turned to look at him, her eyes narrowing as if his acceptance seemed aggressive to her. The reaction was puzzling.

"Here's what I need to know. Are you carrying on the Sunstrike?"

"No."

"The kids got help from the Sunstrike," he said in a tone meant to sound aggressive.

"They couldn't have. You must be misinterpreting."

He let her stare into his eyes until she had her fill of it.

"What makes you think so?" she asked eventually.

"Our investigation established the connection."

Returning to her easy chair, she stared into the fire as if she were thinking. He decided to wait it out.

"Something must be wrong with your investigation," she said after a long silence.

"I'm willing to entertain that, but it would make sense for you to run a commune. You told me you aren't a recluse, which says you probably miss campus networks."

"I do. But campuses aren't communal."

"Buying a former commune and going right on holding open house might seem like a substitute," he told her.

"I guess that's true." Lindy watched flames lick around the pale bark of an alder log in order to move beyond twigs and kindling. "It wasn't a plan, and I didn't really put it together that way. I like land. I like to be useful. The two things just added up."

"What about the rest of what you lost? Teachers get to invent the rules and also enforce them. Accidental people moving in on their own don't make up for that."

"You're right about teachers being managing—they're as bad as cops. But I don't have any vocation to tell people how to live. Once I was out of it, I could see the university had done me a favor."

"Maybe. But Fuller says you're a preacher, which is worse than cops and teachers both put together."

She rubbed her forehead. "No, I don't preach."

"Fuller says you go on these two- and three-month trips, preaching every night."

"My income is doing workshops, which is not the same as preaching," she said.

The irritated tone was encouraging, but Dan wished she would look at him, because eye contact was important to her, he noticed. Apparently that wasn't going to happen, though, and so he tried a different tack.

"I was going to do this the easy way—factual public records," he said. "Here's my thinking: If your residents pay individual utility bills, you're probably just a neighborhood, like you keep saying. So what do I find? None of you buy water, you just have an 'appropriate public waters' permit for that pumphouse by the still."

Lindy shrugged. "The water system was here when I bought the place. I got the permit because I like to be legal. Not that I always agree with the law."

"You also don't buy public power," he told her.

"The Sunstrike built a windfarm where the property sprawls up the side of Stewart Mountain." She pointed vaguely southwest. "That provides far more than I use, so why shouldn't the cabins use it, too?"

"I'm from California, remember?" he said. "I know about windfarms because California owns most of them. It's as quiet as a coffin out there today. You can't possibly be running off a windfarm."

"Ours isn't terribly effective," she admitted. "It was built for the fun of it, I imagine."

"So what do you do when there's no wind? I hear your fridge running."

They both looked at the fridge, visible through the wide arch which connected the halves of the downstairs.

"It's going to sound wrong," Lindy said.

The comment suggested she really was cooperating, her version. "Tell me anyway," he said.

"Well, one of the people who came through here a while ago was an inventor, but he was too peculiar to attract venture capital. You know, a bird's nest beard, blackheads instead of skin, can't half talk because of all the phlegm. But you can get used to that, and so I bought what he said he needed and he set us up for hydro power. I don't ask to understand it, when Sunstrikers do that kind of thing, but

74

this man said his structure is just this tube with insides like a jet engine. We got a permit to hang a gang of them in the river. They don't break loose and float off, the way a water wheel does during floods, and they don't stall at low water, which is another waterwheel drawback. It's a wonderful invention, but he didn't stay long enough for me to persuade him to get development funds and make a commercial product of it."

"He just turned up one day?"

She nodded.

"You didn't know him?"

She shook her head.

"Are you really that casual about who lives here?"

Lindy frowned. "I've already said that, how many times?"

"Right. But you keep contradicting yourself by sounding like a commune."

She gritted her jaw, which he was beginning to spot as a violent gesture from her. "I sound like myself, Sergeant."

"Okay, but here's my problem. Everything I see tells me this is a commune. Tell me *one thing* that says it isn't."

"Communes have ceremonies," she said in an absolute voice. "We don't."

He was startled enough to laugh. She didn't look at him, but apparently his reaction helped, because she fidgeted with her watch, even though fidgeting wasn't a habit. "Why does it matter?" she asked.

He was torn. If she truly was uninvolved, then the question was legitimate. She might even be helpful, if she knew what was under discussion. On the other hand, they had so little physical evidence to work with, he hated to give away what they had.

"Part of the kids' still was a copper kettle from the Sunstrike," he told her. "Ownership is dug into the copper quite artistically—copper's soft, you know."

She turned her head to look at him fully, her eyes defenseless. "A kettle?"

He nodded. He glanced at her chest. She wasn't breathing, to begin with, but as he watched, she let her lungs catch up.

"I bought the Sunstrike in 'as is condition,' because nobody was willing to clean it up. That was okay, because they brought the price down." She paused to clear her throat, which he was glad of since her voice had almost disappeared.

"The woodshed had a lot of things stored. So did the basement. Some of the cabins did, too."

He nodded.

"I've gone on cleaning binges occasionally, but only for areas I use. I'm not a clean freak—I just like a sparse feel to where I live."

"So you're saying there's a lot of equipment lying around?" he prompted.

"Yes."

"This kettle could have been anywhere?"

"Well, not just *anywhere*, but one side of the basement is stacked full of the things you'd want for bulk food preparation, and it might have been down there. It's a walk-out basement. There's a nice patio underneath this main deck." She gestured behind them, toward a deck which extended the living space over ground which dropped dramatically. "Old-timers sometimes mention having barbecues down there, and you can see it would be pleasant. As soon as you carried your plate away from where they must have cooked, you'd be right in the woods."

He nodded.

"I don't need the basement space, so I haven't done anything about that storage."

"We'll need to have someone go through it."

"It isn't locked."

"Am I to take that as permission?"

She shrugged.

"I can get a warrant."

She shook her head as if she were tired.

He thought a few moments. "Is it another of these situa-

76

tions that isn't a commune, to you, but to me, anyone goes in there and takes anything they want?" he asked.

If she noticed any irony in his voice, she didn't react to it. She simply nodded.

"People do?"

She gazed at the floor, as if she could see through it into the storage area below. "I guess I hear someone clanging around down there occasionally," she admitted. "Some of the cabins don't have very good supplies."

"Most people would call Nine-One-One if they heard someone in their house."

"I don't think of the basement as being part of the house, because it has only an outside entrance," she said in a voice which had lost its resonance. "The basement was built first. The house was added later, so if I want to go down there for something, I have to go outside just like anybody else."

It didn't sound like the end of the thought, and so he waited.

"Sergeant—" She frowned at him. "Now that you've told me this, I can understand your attitude, but I don't know what to do about it." She sighed as if she wasn't getting enough oxygen. "Anyone could have borrowed Sunstrike equipment, and welcome. But no one from the original Sunstrike would have taken equipment down there to where the boys got into trouble, because that birder cabin's new. When any of the originals come through, they live as if this were still the Sunstrike, and I try to stay out of their way about that—we all do. It's obvious that the stress level is pretty high for them, and so why shouldn't they come here to a time, as well as to a place?"

"What about the people living here now?"

She shook her head. "No one would have taken a kettle or anything else down there, because none of us go to that cabin. It's for the high school."

"You have proof?"

"No. What would proof be?"

He inspected her face a few moments. "Could the kids

have taken equipment themselves, taken it directly?"

She nodded. "Anyone could, if they knew where to look."

"How many of them hang around enough to know?"

She paused a moment before she shook her head, and so he knew the answer. Some of them *did* hang around, and she'd take the fall herself, rather than contribute to their trouble. That made for a complex situation, because it implied anything she said was unreliable if she thought she was protecting someone. Fuller kept saying something of the sort, but he had dismissed it as a student's generosity toward a friendly teacher. He was going to have to rethink, because Fuller's judgment was evidently better than he had given credit for.

He stood up. "Do you know how many of these kids hang around?" he asked as they walked to the door.

"No, but I'm not aware of anyone unless they come to the house." She caught her breath. "Well, or unless we happen to meet on the trails."

"It would be to your advantage, Lindy, if we could prove the kids did this to themselves," he said, pausing at the door.

"My lawyer says the same." She touched the leaves of a geranium on the window ledge. "How much trouble would the boys be in, if it turned out to be just them?"

"That's not yours to choose."

He waited for some kind of an admission, some detail she had been holding back, but she just gave one of her all-purpose nods, and he saw she hadn't really wavered. She stepped out onto the deck to see him to his Cherokee. A loud whir seemed to come from everywhere. He looked around sharply.

"It's okay," she said. "Just a pheasant. They love the blueberries." She pointed to six-foot bushes growing out of giant cedar stumps.

He wasn't used to being protected, and doubly not by someone he had been trying to annoy into spilling secrets.

It took him a moment to focus. "Those are blueberries?" he asked. "The kind you eat?"

"Yes, but I like the pheasants more than I do pancakes, so I don't harvest them."

What could she be thinking? he wondered. If she put the dietary preferences of pheasants ahead of her own menu, and if she reassured cops, where did she think she was going to end up?

All he could see in her eyes was sadness. Those kids are going to *have* to talk, he thought as he started down the steps.

9

As she drove to Bellingham the next morning, Lindy was still worrying about Stash. She knew he prowled the Sunstrike because she had seen him there occasionally, as she had told his mother. He would surely know about the barbecue area, but that didn't mean he had prowled the storage. There was no reason to suspect him more than any of the other boys. After all, Tim had known how to find her house, even without being able to see the trail. And as to the others—how did she know whether they hung around? She hadn't met them, so she didn't know if they were familiar.

She turned off the arterial and drove slowly through the Sunnyland district toward her appointment. She liked the area's unpretentious homes which had been lovingly maintained instead of being replaced. The houses were staggered for privacy, some built close to the street while others, like Max Owen's gray shake cottage, were set toward the back of their spacious lots. As she parked in front of the house, she tried to feel it wasn't wrong to hope for someone suspicious. Her insurance adjustor had liked Max Owen, she remembered as she went to the door, but Lindy didn't know Deb Wayne, so she wasn't sure what her attitude might prove.

When he answered the doorbell, she forgot her hopes. He was a cricket of a man, with fine white hair standing upright as if he sometimes clutched it. His bright blue eyes nested in pads of wrinkles, and his leathery cheeks suggested exposure to the weather. He wore an old-fashioned coat sweater over a white turtleneck, and his tweed trousers looked like part of a suit.

Lindy was glad she had dressed up. Her dove shirtwaist would probably look casual to him, although she wore dresses so rarely that it didn't feel casual to her.

"I feel like I've got to understand, Mr. Owen," she explained as he ushered her into his workroom.

"Everyone calls me just plain Owen, Honey, even family," he said as he settled an easy chair for her.

He sat in an expensive desk chair which gave him wheels in front of a counter seeming to hold everything. At the back was a strip for plug-ins, and every socket was in use. Far enough away from his computer so as not to create a heat problem, he had a microwave, as well as a hot plate, electric skillet, electric teapot, and warming coaster. His radio and TV were on the other side of the computer, along with stacks of books and magazines. Unopened mail lay beside a standing clip full of the window envelopes which suggested bills.

The room wasn't really decorated, its walls being a straightforward blue and its carpet unpretentiously gray, but it looked cozy because it was complete. He owned an entire house, but he obviously lived here.

"It's about this moonshine, Owen," she said. "You hear about people drinking it, and all they get is these hideous hangovers."

Owen dropped teabags into mugs. "Oh, well though, no, it'll give you *less* of a hangover, if you make it right."

"Then I don't understand what went wrong for these kids."

He poured boiling water into the mugs. "I blame myself, Honey. I shouldn't have told Timmy to go along whenever his big brother was headed for trouble. Timmy's sharp as a lemon and I thought he'd keep Karl out of mischief. I never imagined it would flow the other way."

Lindy sensed he would resent automatic sympathy, and so she searched for a more general tone. "It's hard, being a teenager."

"When I saw those boys, I felt like sin." He jigged the tea bags.

"You can't live their life for them, Owen."

"Well I wish that rule would change."

Lindy smiled, and he brightened gamely. He removed the teabags, added milk, and handed her a mug.

"Cops were all over in here," he said, glancing around in distaste. "Acting like revenuers, telling me I set up the still as a way to show off. I wish the lads *had* asked me to help—they wouldn't be in the fix they're in."

"Why do the police accuse you?"

"Oh, well, I used to make white whiskey when I was about as big as a bean sprout. My dad made it, really. I helped."

"So that makes you guilty for life?" Lindy asked.

He answered with an obliging laugh, but he didn't smile.

"I told them I never helped those youngsters," he said in a grieving tone, "and I said I didn't appreciate being called a liar for saying so, but all the good that did was to send them looking for another way to put it."

"Like what?"

"Oh. I'm writing my memoirs."

He pronounced it with the accent on the first syllable, *me*moirs. The look in his eyes told Lindy it was a joke. A joke with his grandson, Tim, she suspected. She grinned.

"Is that what the computer's for?" she asked.

He whirled around in his wheeled chair and touched the keyboard. "Timmy's a computer whiz. He set this up for me and got me going. So the cops think he sneaks in here and reads off my screen all about hooch but gets it wrong."

"Could that happen?" Lindy asked.

"No. Timmy's as honest as a piece of string. And even if he wasn't, it wouldn't do him any good." He turned his screen on and called up a file. "Here's what I say about being eleven, which was the last year Dad and I made po-teen. You can see for yourself."

Lindy hitched her chair closer so she could read. The passage was only two screens long. Including no technical information at all, it simply told of his friendship with his father. Smiling as she got involved in their joking relationship, she touched the page-down key in order to read on.

"Here now, that's enough of that," Owen said at last, "guests are supposed to talk."

"But it's *good*," Lindy said as she sat back and picked up her mug of tea. "Have you got a publisher yet? I'll want to read the whole thing."

"Oh, no," he said, his voice dropping modestly, "it'll take me another year or so to get it all down in the first place, and then, according to my daughter, you have to rewrite every word. I'm just enjoying the doing of it. I don't know who'd read it."

"I would, for one."

He smiled at her, his face disappearing into folds. "Well, you certainly are a polite young woman, but what I meant was, you can see there's nothing there."

Lindy didn't point out that he could have rewritten the passage, after he found himself accused. It didn't matter what he could have done since she was sure he hadn't. He seemed honest as a string, as he had described his grandson.

"How did the kids find out what to do, do you know?" she asked.

"Timmy says this Vance Crayson knew all about it." Owen blew across the top of his tea. "If he's the one, then he deserved to drown, good luck to him."

"Tim seems like a nice person. I can't imagine him blaming someone if they weren't to blame."

"Well, there you are. These cops think so, too, which is why they swear he's lying to protect me." He pressed a finger against his chin. "Timmy *would*, I think, but he didn't need to, because I wasn't in it. Even if Timmy lied to these cops for sufficient reason, why would he lie to me? He wouldn't."

"I'm sure that's true." Lindy nodded several times, holding his gaze. "What was it that Vance got wrong?"

"Now don't you go firing up some mash."

She laughed. "No. I just hope to understand."

83

He flattened his mouth until it was just one more line in the fanfolded lower half of his face. "Well, it's a simple matter, if you do it right." He studied her as if unsure whether she could resist temptation. "You take your grain," he said at last. "Soak it in your hot water. Crush it. Add a little malt and you've got your mash. Now, ferment your mash. Use a pot still, for your best flavor. Do your distilling. Get your temperature right—you don't want to pick up your bottoms."

"Your bottoms?" Lindy asked.

"What's left in your pot after you run through your coil. If you do it right."

"Is that what hurt them? They picked up their bottoms?"

"More than likely. Distilling's an art, and if you buy from an artist, home whiskey's the best beverage God ever made, but any alcohol's a poison, which is why you like it."

Lindy sighed. Owen shook his head.

"Aren't we odd—liking poisons?" Lindy said.

"We're people."

Lindy nodded. He was right, of course, and he was in a far worse situation than she was, so his ability to be philo-sophical made her ashamed of her anxiety. On the other hand, there was nothing he could do about his regrets, so he had no choice but to feel resigned, whereas, was there any hope for her?

"Oh, Owen," she said. "I wish we could just go back and start again."

"Don't you though?"

That seemed to sum it up, and so Lindy rose to go. "I've certainly enjoyed this," she said. "I thought I would—I liked Tim and he takes after you."

Owen chuckled, pride in his grandson overriding grief. He escorted her toward the south side of the room, where the original wall had been knocked out and replaced by a greenhouse extension which drew sunlight inside. Facing the street, double glass doors were propped open to let in the warm, fresh air.

Lindy lingered at the door to shake hands. Owen

watched her go down the barked path to the street. As she reached her car, she paused to wave. Owen had waited for it, not turning back inside until she drove away.

Circling the block to get back on the Mt. Baker highway, Lindy headed out of town, letting Owen's chat turn slowly in her mind. Grateful for the change in the air as she crested Stewart Mountain's shoulder, she wondered if she had learned anything useful. Maybe, she decided.

Leaving the pavement to begin her walking-pace drive through the Sunstrike, she noticed a new flag, which probably belonged to a student since it was cluttered with unconnected symbols ranging from lightning flashes to smilefaces. That left only one flagpole empty. She hoped Faith would hurry and claim it for Stash.

When she got home, she went upstairs and changed to sweatshirt and jeans before calling her lawyer. "Harry?" she said when the receptionist forwarded her call, "apparently those kids may have made a routine mistake in how they produced their moonshine. If I could show how that happened, show it doesn't take bad intentions to get moonshine wrong, would that help me?"

She could hear his chair squeak. She visualized him leaning back, hooking his free arm over the top of his head.

"Are you thinking expert witness? That grandad? To show they got into trouble through their own negligence?"

"Yes, but not if it casts more suspicion on him."

"You'd better think of yourself on this, Lindy. You haven't got room to be concerned about anybody. They're all going to have to look after their own posteriors."

"No."

She listened to Harry breathe. He had stopped smoking since he had defended her against the university, but his lungs still weren't clear.

"What if I asked Owen to help me make a good batch," she suggested, "and then we could make a second batch, a bad one, where he showed me exactly what we did to make it dangerous. And then I could take a sample of both kinds to the university. I know some chemists up there. They'd surely be willing to do an analysis for me."

"Especially if you promise them a quart of the good stuff."

Lindy laughed. "Good idea. I hear it's like drinking a warm cloud."

Harry's gusty sigh was as explicit as a case study. "I don't want you in the moonshine business, which is how the cops are going to view your plan."

"They don't have to know."

"With half the university talking about warm clouds?"

"Oh. Yes, I suppose you're right."

She could hear his chair creak as he spun to gaze toward the university, which he would see as a brick patch among the evergreens of Sehome Hill.

"I'm going to hope we can negotiate instead of going to court," he said.

"Oh, yes, *please*. I'd rather lose than go to court."

"No you wouldn't. So try this. See if the grandad will give the cops a sworn statement. He's already in it, from what I hear, so he might as well go along. He should explain *in total detail* what probably went wrong. Make it look simple, tell him. He can say he's cooperating because he didn't hurt his own grandkids, and he wants them to find out who did."

"It's awkward. I only just met him."

"Well, he's quite a character, so just pour on some charm."

Lindy groaned.

"Don't get your hopes up too high on this, Lindy," Harry said, "because that still really is on your land."

"But the kids say it was the Crayson boy who supplied the information. He was seventeen. At that age, wouldn't he have been covered under his parents' homeowners?"

"Okay," Harry said, "if these accusations against Vance hold up, we might have something to argue with."

"Could you be a little more affirmative, please?"

Harry chuckled.

10

LINDY WENT OUT INTO THE WOODS TO PUTTER ALONG THE trails, for her usual cure. However long it took, she was determined to feel composed before she called Owen. He wouldn't find it easy to make an official statement to police he thought of as revenuers, and so she had to ask in exactly the right way.

Noticing a graceful black mushroom bell which had appeared overnight, she crouched for a closer look. Springing out of the edge of a stony patch, it still had traces of dust on its bell from its struggle to emerge. She smiled.

The pause to admire worked its magic. She wandered on more comfortably, pausing at a turn in the trail to estimate the change in the string of growths which shoved out of the earth as golden knobs and expanded into plush gold rosettes a foot across before hardening and turning as brown as wood carvings.

When she was sure of her mood, she strolled back to the house and called. Owen didn't answer his phone. She grabbed a book and went outside. She spent the afternoon reading, redialing Owen occasionally. When the evening birds began, she went inside.

Standing at the sink in front of an open window, she cleaned the carrots and chopped the cauliflower left on her deck by an anonymous Sunstriker. She added a turkey fillet to her impromptu stir fry and took her plate back outside to eat with the argumentative birds for company.

Owen still hadn't picked up his phone by the time she left for her Thursday group at *Ours*. She could drop by on her way home, she decided, glancing at her watch as she reached the city's ring of malls. It wouldn't be entirely polite, but people who didn't want drop-ins had an obligation to answer their phone.

The members of the Thursday session were very different from the women who gathered on Tuesdays. These wore their jeans like a costume, and their fleece tops were designer items, not sweats. They never stayed beyond an hour. They didn't set themselves a formal topic, preferring to swap hints about dealing with upsets in anyone's week. Much too busy to sit down with the newspaper, they were unaware of Lindy's trouble. Lindy was grateful to be treated just as usual, which hadn't happened anywhere else since Tim stumbled out of her woods.

When the meeting broke up, she drove back to the Sunnyland district, waiting for a line of shoulder-heaving racewalkers to clear the intersection before she coasted to a stop in front of Owen's home. The house was dark, but Owen had seemed as rooted in his place as she felt in hers, and so she didn't think he would be out for the evening. Maybe he had only his reading lamp on. She couldn't see any light, but it wasn't a large lamp. Maybe his computer blocked it. She decided to check, since she was here.

Bypassing the cement front walk, she used the bark path which led directly to his all-purpose room. When she reached his glassed patio, she saw dim lights inside. His computer?

She tapped on the open glass doors. When he didn't answer, she stepped inside the glass addition and tapped on the door frame of the main room. He still didn't answer, but she could see his computer screen's bright blue. He must have forgotten to turn it off, she suspected. It would be damaged if it stayed on all night, and so she crossed the room to turn it off for him. His chair was turned away, but as she approached, she saw that he was still sitting there. He must have fallen asleep over his memoirs, she thought affectionately. But before she could tiptoe away without disturbing him, she realized something must be wrong. The rug felt mushy, and—was there an odd smell?

I mustn't start expecting a disaster over every least surprise, she warned herself. The good advice didn't seem to help, and so she went to the counter and groped for the switch on the flex lamp. She adjusted to the abrupt brightness by closing her eyes a moment. When she opened them again, she saw that the floor was red. It didn't make sense.

"Owen?" she said.

He didn't react.

"Owen? Is something wrong?" she asked more urgently.

When he still didn't turn, she stepped closer, feeling protective as she saw how comfortable he looked, his head leaning against the tall back of his chair, his mouth open in total relaxation. His arms rested easily in his lap, palms down. When she was close enough to see past the arm of his chair, she saw and looked away at once and didn't believe and glanced again, even though the first brief sight had been enough and would be enough forever. His tweed pants had acted like a sponge, stiffening as the fabric filled with red. His sweater had functioned like a wick, drawing red up his sleeves to the elbows. His chair was leather-look plastic, and nothing clung to it, but red had puddled all around its wheeled legs, seeping into the rug, filling it, washing across the bare linoleum into pools where puckery skin had formed.

Lindy didn't believe so much red could have come from one not very large man, but something inside her evidently believed, because she was screaming, she realized. She thought about stopping her noise, but wishing to stop wasn't the same as actually stopping. Screaming as often as she could catch her breath, she touched Owen's cheek. Cool. It seemed too personal, it was taking advantage, but she pressed her fingers under his jaw anyway. No thump.

He doesn't *look* dead, she protested. The realization that she didn't know what death looked like slowed her noise. Marshaling her mind, she grabbed the phone and punched 911. When help was on the way, she didn't hang up.

"This emergency is connected with a case the city police,

Sergeant Richison is working on," she said in a voice which shook. The dispatcher transferred her call before she could think what else to add.

"Richison."

"Sergeant, this is Lindy, I came over here to Owen's house, he's killed himself."

"Stay right there. Don't touch anything."

She hung up the phone and turned to the man she had hoped to make into a friend. "Owen?" she said to him.

When he didn't respond, she leaned closer and called gently toward his ear, "Owen, can you hear me?"

He didn't react.

"Come on, Owen, please hear me."

His partly open eyes seemed to be staring at his computer. She followed his gaze, grateful for anything else to focus on.

"To My Family And Those I Have Betrayed," the formal farewell began. In a paragraph short enough to fit on the screen, he had taken full responsibility for everything that had happened to his grandsons and their friends. He asked everyone's forgiveness. He said good-bye.

The wording was stiff and cumbersome, not like his memoirs. Lindy couldn't believe so warm and spontaneous a man could have written such a lifeless thing. She gave in to sobs which shook her body with every attempt to breathe.

Richison came in the side door and stopped. "Stand still, Lindy, crime-scene is on the way, and they'll want to know if all these footprints are yours. Are they?"

"I guess so," she said vaguely.

"Are you okay?"

"I guess so," she repeated.

He gazed at the blood which had flowed toward the glass doors, proving that the old house had settled unevenly. He moved around to the other side of the room, staying beyond the edge of the blood. When he reached the clean area, he crossed the gray rug and looked at Owen.

After a long inspection, he reached down and gently

90

picked up one of Owen's index fingers in order to lift his hand. Owen's lap was full of blood, but the flow had stopped. Richison rotated his hand.

"Thank God," he said fervently.

Lindy looked at him.

"They slashed his wrist."

"What did you think?"

He tenderly put Owen's hand back where it had been. "You find blood in the crotch area, you expect a torture killing. But here, they just laid his hands in his lap so he wouldn't spurt all over. A *lot* better. I hate *kinky*. But whoever did this never even thought about games."

"Games?" Lindy asked in a remote controlled voice.

"Torture," he explained.

"He killed himself," Lindy said.

"No, he didn't." Richison looked surprised. "Suicides will slash their wrist inside a garbage bag and tape the bag shut, or they'll settle themselves in the shower and leave it running—whatever they can think of to keep things clean. At-home suicides are considerate because a friend or family member is going to have to find them, and they think about that. People say suicide is selfish, but generally not, unless you've got a loner, which Owen wasn't."

"It isn't selfish of him to want to end here," Lindy protested. "This room was his place. It's where he was comfortable."

"Come on, Lindy, didn't you look at his wrist?"

She gazed blankly at him.

"The deepest part of the cut is on the little-finger side of the wrist. If you do yourself, the stab part of the cut is on the thumb side." He closed his right hand around an imaginary knife in order to stab and slash his own left wrist.

Lindy closed her eyes in order not to see the demonstration.

"If you're going to pass out, don't do it into that blood," he said.

"I'm okay," Lindy whispered, opening her eyes.

His intent look told her he thought she wasn't, but she

91

ignored it. "I thought cops don't tell you when something's not what it looks like. I thought they like to keep secrets so they can spring out of the bushes when you give yourself away by knowing something you shouldn't."

"Yeah, well, to a certain extent that's true. But it's also true that very few crimes are solved without the assistance of the community." He spoke the stilted phrase in a formal way which showed it was quoted from staff training programs. "I prefer to talk, myself," he added more genuinely.

"Well, then, that note," Lindy said as she pointed to the computer, "surely he didn't write it, if you think he didn't kill himself."

"Hang on a second, I'm going to record this," he said, pulling out a hand-size tape recorder and identifying the situation. "Okay, now," he went on, "Tell me what you're seeing."

She caught her breath and held it a moment. "He showed me what he called his *memoirs*." The joking pronunciation made her start to cry. She pressed her hand hard against her lips.

Richison didn't react.

Finally she went on in a clogged voice. "He has a folksy style. Not like that." She nodded toward the screen.

"Okay, professor, we aren't grading themes here."

"People have a personality when they write. He's free and easy about spelling and nonstandard usages. It's charming. Not like that."

Richison sighed. "Okay, I'll have someone see if there are earlier drafts in his computer's memory. Maybe that's a statement he was working on," he said, frowning at the screen. "Maybe he was working himself up to suicide. He'd have had to cooperate for someone to kill him this way, because he sat here waiting to bleed out."

Lindy pressed her hands against her eyes. She could hear a radio faintly from a neighboring house. It seemed impossible that anything so normal could still be going on. She tried to focus her thoughts on it.

"Do you pray?" Richison asked.

"I could." She cleared her throat. "Would you like me to?"

He shrugged. "I just wondered what a doctor of philosophy in the history of comparative religions does in these situations."

"Oh." Lindy wondered, too. "Well, I could pray that I'd never again be so overly involved with the mindless routines of polite manners that I'd fail to follow up on an inkling of something wrong."

"Which means what?"

Lindy looked at the computer, its blue screen full of white words. "I came over to meet him this morning." Laboriously, she told about her visit. "I should have come back immediately when he didn't answer, this afternoon," she added, "but I just kept trying to call. He kept not answering. I should have come over. I could have stopped this."

"What time was it?"

She tried to remember. "I don't know."

"Estimate."

Her entire memory was a blank. What had she done before coming here? She wasn't sure. She tried to start with the other end of the day. Morning. She couldn't remember.

"I'm sorry."

"You said you came over here earlier."

She nodded.

"Did you have an appointment?"

She nodded.

"When did he invite you for?"

"Eleven," she said as memories began to form through a smoke screen.

"How long were you here?"

She groped for detail. "Maybe an hour."

"Then what?"

She shook her head.

"Why were you calling him, if you'd just visited?"

"Oh. That's right," she said, brushing her hair off her forehead. "That's right," she said again. "I went home, and then I called my lawyer with this theory. Not theory," she corrected herself, "just hope."

When Richison opened his mouth, she explained her theory without waiting to be told.

"So, by one o'clock, you were calling and Owen wasn't answering his phone?" Richison summed up.

"One o'clock?"

"You tell me."

"Oh." She visualized her home phone. "No. I went for a walk after I talked to my lawyer. I didn't want to sound nervous when I called Owen."

"How long was the walk?"

"Just out to that biggest Douglas fir."

"Ten minutes?"

"Well, and then over to that oldest black cottonwood. It's bark is a different color, sort of mauve, and I like it."

"Half an hour?" he asked patiently.

"I looked at fungus along the trails."

"An hour?"

Lindy tried to imagine a clock. "By three. I called him by three. Or maybe a little after."

Richison nodded, apparently satisfied, but he watched her face intently. "Okay, this morning, you had your chat here in this room?"

Lindy nodded.

"What's different. Anything at all that's changed. Moved, disappeared, added—anything."

"I'm sorry." Her eyes filled with new tears.

"Come on, Lindy, be some help. I grant you most witnesses aren't in any state to identify what they're looking at if you hand them a mirror and tell them how it works, but you're a professor. Now show me some brains."

She tried to concentrate. "I turned on that lamp myself."

"Okay."

"He hasn't changed his clothes."

"Okay."

"Everything was neat."

"Okay."

"I guess he's moved his mail. It was sort of scattered around that bill clip, and now it's shoved aside."

"Making room for lunch?"

"No, he put his tea on the other side, and he'd have his plate over there, too, if he was eating and working. Anyway, is that a dried water ring? Your lunch plate wouldn't be wet."

Richison looked. "You're assessing his housekeeping?"

"I know men who are good housekeepers," she said.

"Yeah, I probably do, too." He sighed. "Anything else?"

Lindy shook her head but under Richison's insistent gaze she went on looking, feeling useless. The arrival of the crime scene crew called a halt. Richison clicked off his tape recorder and crossed the room to stand talking softly as police both in and out of uniform poured through the glass doors. After a few moments the techs spread through the room, opening their equipment packs while the photographer was busy.

"Why don't you just take your shoes clear off," one of them said to Lindy. "Step out here first." He indicated an area which was free of blood.

"I'll make tracks."

"I'll know where they came from," he assured her.

She used long steps, to keep the disturbance to a minimum. When she stood beside him on the unstained part of the rug, she bent and untied her walkers.

"Just leave them there," he said as she stepped free.

She started toward the glass doors, skirting the blood and equipment.

"Wait for me in your car," Richison said as she reached the door.

She walked down the path in sock feet, grateful for the mundane reality of splinters from the woodchips. Reaching her car in a dream, she rolled down the window and sat leaning back against the headrest. She closed her eyes. Her mind was useless, but she couldn't seem to make it numb.

She saw Owen, sitting at his ease in his comfortable chair as if he were a portrait of relaxation, a work of art which had achieved permanence inside of her.

Why would he sit there so peacefully while his heart pumped him empty? she protested silently.

"I have to go talk to the daughter," Richison said.

Lindy startled at the sound of his voice at her window.

"Sorry," he said.

She looked up at him, tears tangling her eyelashes and blurring her vision with silver. He stood beside her, his face shadowed, his head seeming bowed in the spiritual sense. Finally he walked around the car. When he stopped beside her passenger door, she reached across to unlock it. He stepped inside and stared through the windshield for a while, his jaw clenched.

"Were you close?" he asked at last.

"No." Lindy sniffed. "I didn't know any of these people before Tim landed in my pond. But I liked Owen. I met him this morning. I was going to try to make a friend out of him."

"Yeah, I liked him, too. He wouldn't give me the time of day, he was sure I was bound to hurt somebody he cared about, but even so—"

Lindy was surprised to hear loneliness in his voice. The painful sound roused her.

"Do you *really* think it's murder?" she asked. "I know what you said, I followed your logic, but how *could* it be?"

"I don't know." He reached up to cling to the grab bar above his door while he thought it over. "Murder doesn't make sense to me, even though I've listened to the explanation I don't know how many times. Murderers are just like anybody else. When you finally catch up with them, they want to tell you about their day. Their point is, something must be missing from the rest of us, if we don't understand."

Lindy wiped her eyes. "I can't believe he's dead."

"Yeah." He released the grab bar and turned to look at her in the light reflecting in from the corner streetlight.

"It's an infraction to drive in socks," he said.

Lindy tried to analyze his unexpected announcement. Finally she remembered leaving her shoes for the tech. "There are some hiking boots in the trunk."

"Okay." He continued to watch her. "We have this ride-along program, for compassionate situations. The official participants I've been exposed to so far irritated me, but you come across so gentle, even I respond. From what your student says, that's just a mannerism. You're tough, he says, but what you seem is soothing."

Lindy drew a ragged breath. "I hate being discussed."

"Yeah, most people do." He searched for words. "What I'm saying is, you're not on the official list of cooperating ministers, but I want you with me regardless."

"I'm not a minister."

"You're a spiritually concerned workshop leader," he paraphrased irritably. "I'd appreciate it if you'd run a compassionate workshop for me. According to Owen's wallet, his daughter is his next-of-kin, and I don't look forward to telling her about this."

Owen's daughter would be Tim's mother, Lindy thought. If it only meant talking to a stranger, she could face it, she decided, but if Tim happened to be there, she would start remembering how Owen had loved him. She would think about how gallant Tim had been, floundering among her small-mouth bass. She would be no use to anyone. Her tears began again.

"Okay, if that's how compassion hits you, let's try the truth," Richison interrupted. "Owen showed you what he's writing, so you got more out of him than I did. Can you do the same with the daughter? When I tried to talk to her about the moonshine, she threw me out of the house."

"Owen said you were accusing him. She probably felt protective."

"And you're saying she'll feel better about me now?"

Drawing a long unsteady breath, Lindy said, "All right." She reached for her keys. "That's your car there, isn't it? That Cherokee? I'll follow you after I put on my boots."

97

11

OWEN'S DAUGHTER, ELLIE PATRICK, KEPT HER HUSBAND'S name when he left her, along with the riding academy he had encouraged her to start. The site of her arena was pleasantly rural twenty years ago, when she chose it. Her property tucked up against the edge of Cornwall Park, making it easy for advanced riders to use the park's well-tended public trails. On the property's other side, there had been acres of undeveloped woods as a source for a pleasant creek which ran through Ellie's pastures and fields, watering her horses effortlessly.

But then the hospital beyond the woods decided to expand. Like a cancer relieved of chemotherapy, it popped up in widening rings of surgi-centers, pharmacies, homes for radiation therapies, doctors' centers, helipads, substance abuse dormitories, psychiatric shelters, daycares for sick children, and relief-care centers for the helpless old. When the whole hill beyond the woods was paved and built so that it drained too rapidly, the pleasant creek turned into a scabrous sewer. Ellie Patrick saw the transformation as symbolic of her life.

When Lindy and Richison walked into her indoor arena, she was watching a class of adult professionals who used riding for exercise after long work days. Two appaloosas, a Morgan, and three quarter horses circled the brightly lighted building in trotting pairs, their dust rising head-high in the chilly air. The riders were dressed for Western style, their plaid shirts topping color-coordinated turtlenecks, their picturesquely tattered jeans tucked into cowhide boots which were paisley stitched. Ellie wore a goose-down vest over her costume because the huge arena lost heat sharply through its single layer of boards on unmasked framing.

"Mrs. Patrick?" Lindy called from the truck entrance which stood open for ventilation.

"I'm Ellie," Ellie answered, but when she turned and saw Richison, she shook her head. "This is my last class, and I go to bed after it, because my day starts early. So forget it."

"I'm afraid we really do need to talk with you," Lindy said. "I'm Lindy. I don't know if Tim mentioned?"

"Oh, yeah. Thanks for helping him." She called, "And reverse," watching the ragged column untangle itself before she added, "Okay, go ahead. But seriously, make it quick."

She was standing about thirty feet away. Lindy decided she couldn't shout her news.

"I guess we really do need to talk privately," she said.

"Privately," Ellie echoed, jamming her fists into the belly pockets of her down vest. "That usually means trouble, but there can't be trouble, I've already done trouble."

Lindy was very aware of Richison standing beside her. She hoped he wouldn't decide the conversation was going too slowly and muscle in to speed things up. He had agreed to leave it up to her, but she hadn't seen anything to suggest that he was richly endowed with patience.

Ellie got tired of their silence. "It can't be Tim," she told them. "He's spending a few days at his dad's, where all he can get hold of to drink is fruit-flavored seltzer. And it can't be Karl because his girlfriend came over and picked him up for dinner. She drinks, but she was on her way home from work so she was sober. I doubt she'd drink today, anyway, as mad as she is. She's trying to sell Karl on blaming his grandad. 'Even old men have to process their failures' is how she puts it. She was hoping to talk Karl into going over there later on so they could gang up on his grandad." Ellie shrugged. "Not that it matters. No one but a total jerk would think of Dad as old, and Dad's seen jerks before."

Richison stepped closer to Lindy. She nodded slightly without looking at him.

"If they went to see Owen, when would that likely have been?" she asked.

"They probably didn't go. Karl knows better than to blame his grandad. But he might give in on it because they have to go somewhere, and Dad doesn't use most of his house. I don't let them get into it here. If Karl wants a woman, he needs a job first. May Anne lives at home, too, so she's got the same rules," Ellie said. After a moment, she said, "Oh God."

The greenish arena lights distorted colors, but even so, Lindy could see the utter whitening of Ellie's face, and so she began talking at once.

"Did you talk to your dad today, Ellie?" she asked. "I was over to his house around noon, and he seemed like a perfectly wonderful man. I hadn't met him before, but Tim told me what a fine friend he was, and I was glad to see how right that was. He was so full of the future, but he wasn't too optimistic to the point of idiocy, so you could follow along with him because of all the common sense strung through the cheerfulness. What impressed me was how he was dealing with this tragedy for your boys. He was sad, of course, and he wished he could go back and fix it, naturally, but he knew better than to get into guilt. At least, I thought so. Do you know for sure what he felt?"

"Has something happened to Dad?"

"I'm afraid so."

"*And* walk," Ellie yelled without turning to see if her class would do as they were told.

Lindy watched the horses slow gratefully, taking their cue from Ellie rather than from their riders.

"What happened?" Ellie asked, moving toward Lindy at last.

"I truly don't know," Lindy said, speaking softly to encourage Ellie to draw closer. "I couldn't reach him by phone, around suppertime, and so I dropped by." She

100

paused. "I was the one who found him."

Ellie stood too close, but Lindy didn't step back. She looked up into the large dark eyes which Tim had inherited, and her heart broke all over again.

"It isn't always hard to die," she murmured. "I wish he hadn't died, but I believe it wasn't hard for him."

"I don't want to know."

Lindy nodded.

"Take care of your mounts," Ellie shouted into Lindy's face. "Do you know what happened?" she added quietly.

"Not really. There's a suicide note on his computer screen, taking the blame for everything, but—"

"He'd *never* do that," Ellie interrupted. "He *loved* Timmy, he'd *never* do that to Timmy—make him feel guilty for the rest of his life. Never."

Lindy nodded.

"Did he shoot himself?"

"No."

"Then *what?*"

"His wrists are cut."

Ellie grabbed her by the upper arms and began to shake her. Richison reacted automatically, but Lindy lifted a warning hand where Ellie couldn't see the gesture. She relaxed her body and gripped Ellie's arms to minimize the effect as much as she could without seeming to reject it.

Ellie finally stopped. "How *could* he?" she asked, not releasing her bruising hold on Lindy's arms.

"I don't think he did."

Ellie stopped breathing.

"Who was angry at him, do you know?" Lindy whispered.

"Nobody!" Ellie shouted. "Everybody loved him," she added more quietly.

"I can believe that. I sure did."

Ellie's eyes were abruptly bloodshot. Lindy was relieved. She stopped struggling against her own tears, stepping closer so they could cling and give in to it together.

Richison moved to the aisleway where the riders were

brushing their horses and storing their tack. "Leave by the side door," he said when they stared at him.

He stood watching so they felt obliged to stop glancing past him toward the grief which filled the usual exit.

Lindy drove slowly across town toward South Hill where most of the faculty lived. Richison trailed her in his Cherokee. A cop on her tailpipe gave her an excuse to be offensively correct about every gesture, but what she really wanted was the extra time to get her feelings organized. Richison's view was that she was on a roll. She had gotten Owen and Ellie to talk, which they wouldn't do with him. He would have liked her to be there while he talked to Karl and his girlfriend, but they had left May Anne's about half an hour ago, her mother said. Tim and his father were next on Richison's list.

It had been a shock to find out who Tim's father was. Lindy had noticed Tim's last name, but she hadn't thought about it—not until Richison complained that Professor Patrick had stone-walled him in an earlier interview. He wanted Lindy along since she knew how to deal with campus types.

For Lindy, Greg Patrick wasn't just a campus type. They had served on enough university committees together to feel like friends. It made the compassionate element of this visit far more painful. Teachers tended to maintain networks based on interest rather than family. She suspected Greg would have liked Owen. He must have ignored divorce and kept in touch, not with a former father-in-law but with a man he valued. He shouldn't have to hear this news from a cop, but it was almost midnight—an awkward time for a friend to drop in.

The sprawling old view house on Fourteenth Street blazed with light. Lindy parked beside it, and Richison pulled to the curb behind her. When they got out of their cars, he walked at her elbow like a date. He held the yard gate open for her like an escort. When they approached the house, he reached around her, friend-fashion, to lean on the doorbell. The courtliness reminded Lindy how long she had been treated either as a totem victim, by people on campus, or else as a totem healer, by everyone else. She explored the novelty in order to occupy herself as they waited.

Footsteps began inside and grew louder. The door swung open, drenching them in light.

"Lindy! Hello," Greg Patrick said. He was tall and thin, like Tim, with dark hair, and startling hazel eyes which devastated women students. Wearing a nondescript sweatshirt, tight jeans, and thick red boot socks inside dark Birkenstocks, he looked very faculty.

"Hi, Greg, have you met Sergeant Richison?" Lindy asked.

Greg turned a cold look. "Yes."

"Could we talk with you a little while?" Lindy asked.

"Both of you?"

"I can leave if you insist on it, Professor Patrick, but I'd rather Lindy has backup, whenever she's basically doing police work," Richison said.

Greg narrowed his dramatic eyes. "You're a *cop*? Jesus, Lindy, surely jobs aren't *that* hard to get."

She shook her head. "They've got this ride-along program."

"I've heard of it," Greg said, "but you're no minister."

"That's true, but—"

"She knows what people believe," Richison interrupted. "That works better in compassionate situations than laying out what she believes, so I like working with her."

Greg looked at Lindy rather than at Richison. "Compassionate?"

She simply looked at him, her eyes showing enough familiarity with grief to do the job.

"Christ, Lindy."

"Yes, I'm sorry."

Greg grasped Lindy's shoulder in a defeated gesture. After a moment, he nodded. "Well, come on in."

He gestured toward the breakfast L and opened a kitchen

cupboard to set out three glasses. He poured sherry before he sat down with them.

"Your eyes look like you've been crying, Lin."

Lindy rubbed her eyes. She picked up her glass for a tiny sip so the men would follow the gesture.

"It's about your son's grandfather," she said softly.

"Owen? I saw him, what? Few weeks ago, down at the co-op. Wonderful old geezer. Has something gone wrong for him?"

Lindy hesitated. "He supposedly committed suicide." She cleared her throat. "I think somebody helped him."

Greg set his glass down with a slam. "Oh Christ," he said.

"I know."

"This'll kill Tim."

"Is he here?"

"Yes, he's asleep. Morning's soon enough for him to face this—I'm not waking him."

"Okay," Richison said.

Greg gave no sign of hearing the permission.

"Can you think of anything that might say either way about suicide?" Lindy asked after a moment.

"Jesus, Lindy."

"I feel the same. But could we pretend for a minute here that we're convening the Grade Inflation Oversight Committee so as to get to the bottom of it once and for all?"

He looked at her, desperation gradually giving way to memory. At last his body shook with laughter in the way his women students so admired. Lindy knew it was half hysterical, but she was relieved by the change anyway.

"They're still at that, you know," Greg said. "The faculty senate passed a rule last spring. Now, you can't give more than one A per class."

"So everybody started giving everyone an A?" Lindy said.

"You got it."

Their tension eased in the grip of a discussion which was safe, familiar, orderly, academic in all senses of the word.

The softening made tears possible. Lindy imagined how Greg's students would react to the glitter in his expressive eyes.

"You know, Lin, I hope it *was* murder," Greg said, clearing his throat. "Think how you have to feel, first, while you're working up to suicide."

"If it was murder, Professor Patrick," Richison interrupted, "have you any ideas as to where we might start?"

Greg frowned at him. "I assume the other kids are out of it since they can't see well enough."

"According to the doctors, the situation isn't all that bleak, except for one of them," Richison said as if he were merely discussing their health.

"I won't debate it," Greg said in a flat voice. "It isn't the issue. What's real is, they couldn't possibly think Owen deserves something from them, however well they see."

"Do they all know that?" Richison asked.

"Christ." Greg frowned at his sherry. "Well, you tell me—it's your question," he said in a classroom tone, which emphasized his intellectual's automatic resistance to police assumptions of a power which was merely physical.

Richison didn't answer.

"What about your sons' friends?" Lindy asked. "Would any of them decide to set things straight?"

"Set *what* straight?"

"Could they have gotten interested in moonshine because Owen talked about it?" she asked.

"No," he snapped. "He'd never have let them do it wrong, if they copied him."

"That's what he told me," Lindy agreed. "I'm willing to go with it. But would any of the kids want to shift guilt onto someone in easy reach?"

Greg closed his eyes to ponder, an habitual gesture which made his students think of beds. "The guys are all playing it tough—what a *man* to drink yourself blind. But you might talk to girlfriends. I'm not sure about the others, but as to my kids, if anyone's in love with Tim, he appears not to know it. Karl's involved, but I can't stand the woman, so I don't know what she thinks on any subject except Karl."

"Would you know how to make moonshine, Professor Patrick?" Richison asked.

"If ignoring what I said reflects a categorical assumption that women don't kill, that attitude is illegal in this state, Officer," Greg said glacially. "When we talked at my office, you said you're new here. You may not know we have equal-treatment laws, state-level. You're out of line."

"Thank you, Professor," Richison said, "I'll interview not only the girlfriends, but their woman-buddies as well, so we can be sure nobody has decided to protect someone. Your suggestion is a good one. I assumed you'd know I'll act on it. But since we're here with you at the moment, I'd like to get back to what I asked you."

Lindy was shocked that anything could amuse her in such circumstances, but she saw that Richison must have been analyzing her behavior. He must have decided wordiness led Northwesterners to talk.

Greg sighed. "Can I make moonshine?" he repeated as he gazed thoughtfully at the ceiling. "Yeah, I suppose so. I'm a biologist, not a chemist, but— I'd have to go into it to get the ratios right, but—"

He thought a while and finally looked at Richison as if he were a student who had been flunking already, even before arriving late for class. "You're working it up that someone blinded the kids, and now they must be looking for a fall guy so you'll stop running around with your hands full of question marks? You'd do better to shed that kind of big-city attitude. It's entirely too drastic for here. No one would kill that good old man, just over the jitters."

"He does seem to have been a good man. It makes motive a problem," Richison answered. "I wouldn't connect his death with his grandsons' difficulties, except for the suicide note."

"The note's almost certainly fake, Greg," Lindy said. "But it says Owen's to blame about the moonshine, so the police have to connect it."

Greg sighed. "Which means you aren't really asking about moonshine, you're asking about murder. So, let's see. I'm a biologist, right? so I'm going to depend on that." He launched into an appalling, annotated list of blood-altering agents and their effects, heart inhibitors, nerve paralyzers, stroke inducers, and deep-muscle-group relaxers which he might have recourse to, as a murderer. "If they used any of those," he concluded, "I'm righteously in your cesspool."

"They slashed his wrists," Lindy murmured.

"Oh Christ."

12

DAN WAS VERY AWARE OF HOW LITTLE SLEEP HE HAD GOT-
ten last night. His eyes burned and he couldn't stop narrowing them in spite of knowing what that looked like. His
redhead's skin displayed his state of health even though his
hair had long ago darkened to brown. If citizens didn't assume his gray-smudged lower lids meant a hangover, they
were sure to conclude the purpled sockets meant a fist
fight. He had shaved with extra care, so at least he wouldn't
seem like a gutter all-nighter, but he knew he wasn't looking the best for knocking on neighborhood doors.

He started at the far end of Owen's block, hoping to get
his routine together before he reached the neighbors who
were most likely to know something. The shellacked front
door of the corner house opened almost before he finished
his knock. A woman stared out at him, her white hair in
rollers, her ancient chenille robe topping puffy slippers. He
displayed his shield and got no further than saying his name
before she cut in.

"It's about Owen? Poor soul," she said.

"I'd like to hear what you know about it," he said, tossing out his planned introduction, which was to have gently
broken just enough of the news while omitting all the details.

"It's why I haven't had time to dress—we've all been on
the phone. Janeece, two doors down, she's got that conference calling service so we can all talk at once," she said,
stepping aside as if cops were welcome visitors. "Come on
back, I'll pour you a cup of coffee."

He followed her through an immaculate front room into an equally neat kitchen. "No, thanks," he said as she reached for the coffee pot, "I drank coffee to keep going—I was up most of the night."

"You look it," she told him.

He sat down at her spotless kitchen table and listened to her account. She had heard all the theories and crossed them off one by one. No one believed in the suicide note, she told him. Owen wouldn't kill himself, because of his beliefs, not that he talked about his beliefs. And not that he would want to die—he had everything to live for, and his health was good. On the other hand, no one could have wanted to kill him, because all anyone had to do to love him was to meet him. If he was dead, it had to be by mistake or by accident.

Dan thanked his hostess and went back outside. As he walked next door to try again, he seemed to hear the overhead phone lines humming. He interviewed his way along the street of small homes, gradually losing his temper, although he didn't allow it to show. It was bad enough that the whole neighborhood had already gotten together on what they believed. What made it worse was the Northwestern accent. To his California ears, this local speech sounded like babytalk. It was modulated sweetly, with great use of flexible lips and an exaggerated rising and falling cadence, which in his experience no reasonable adult would use to another adult outside of bedroom talk. It made him feel jeered at. The local police used the same speech, so he knew he wasn't being patronized, but he felt it anyway.

Still, putting up with it paid off at last, two houses past Owen's. The daughter had been sitting in her upstairs room, staring out the window because she hated math. She had signed up for a correspondence course at the university because there was no point in wasting the money to enroll if she couldn't pass Math 101. Her older brother's university experience had proved that. She had spent yesterday deciding what kind of a life she could have if she just gave up on school.

"I might be able to help you," Dan offered cautiously, propping his elbow on the arm of the pillow-laden couch in order to rest his jaw wearily on his hand.

"You know someone at the university?" she asked.

"No, but I know math."

Her gaze hardened so abruptly, he wondered if he had made a mistake. Like everyone else in the neighborhood, she hadn't seemed to resist police, but math was a different matter, evidently.

"How come?" she asked.

"I majored in it," he said. "I thought it would be more under control than politics or history or any of those."

"I'll be right back," she said without any change of expression.

Her feet thumped up the stairs.

"She's always like that," her mother apologized, straightening the music on the piano rack.

"She's the only family member who might have seen something?" Dan asked.

"Yes. My husband's out on a fishing cruise, he's going to be just sick when he finds out. And my stepson lives on his mother's brother's farm, down in Oregon. I volunteer over at the hospital, and wouldn't you know yesterday would be my day."

Dan nodded. He glanced through the side window, which gave a clear view of Owen's house since the home in between had been built closer to the street. If the daughter had been watching, she could have seen everything.

She thundered back down the stairs to sit beside him on the couch. She opened the math text on her lap and handed him the workbook. She pointed to a problem which was almost obscured by pencil markings which had been incompletely erased.

"Yeah, well, this is a mess, but you can get it," Dan said in the sympathetic tone he used with his brothers and sisters. "Look." He reached for her textbook and used its index briefly before turning to a table of formulas. "You just want to pass the course, right?" he verified, looking into her angry eyes.

She nodded, drawing her mouth down in disgust.

"Then what I'd do . . . memorize these." He studied the list of formulas for a moment. "From here to here," he said, showing the crucial formulas with a spread hand which carried the scars of an active childhood. "Then, whatever the problem asks, pick one of these formulas and use it."

"You're kidding."

"No. You'll guess wrong, sometimes, but you'll be right often enough to grab a C. I've got two brothers in college, and this is how they're surviving it."

She grinned and reached for the workbook, shoving it into the text to mark the place before she slammed it shut and tossed it to the far end of the couch.

"If this works, I'll buy you a beer," she said.

"Sounds good. Tell me when you're twenty-one."

"Oooops," she answered, playfully covering her mouth with one hand.

Her fingernails reached an inch past the ends of her fingers. Obviously fakes, but expensive ones, Dan decided. He realized he hadn't seen anything except plain hands since he had come north, but he couldn't decide whether he missed it.

He smiled, hoping she would respond.

"Let me tell you what I saw," she said.

"I'd appreciate it."

"Owen doesn't have tons of company, but his family's around a lot, it's not like some of these houses where they might as well be sealed. One grandson's a jerk, but one's real."

"Which is which?" Dan asked.

"Karl's worth looking at. So naturally I watch, which I can do out my side window. Yesterday, Karl never showed. I guess he can't drive?"

"You're sure he didn't drop by?" Dan asked.

She rolled her eyes. "Do you think I'd miss it if he did?"

Dan grinned.

"So anyway, there was this woman coming back over and over. Dressed *up*, like she was making an impression, or something. And I guess she did, because Owen walked her out to the door, the first time."

"Who was she, do you know?"

"Never saw her before."

"Can you describe her?"

She nodded vigorously. "Middle-aged—"

"I'm not sure what that means to you," Dan interrupted.

"Thirty?"

He nodded.

"A dress, not quite black. Skirt too long, clear to her knees. Jacket over it in the afternoon. Plum, I guess."

"What about her, herself," Dan asked. "Hair, skin, height, weight, that kind of thing."

"Dark hair, covered up by this floppy hat to match her jacket, in the afternoon. Pale skin." She inspected his tan. "Not as tall as me. No weight problem."

"Did you see her car?"

"Didn't look."

"Did she stay long?"

"Yeah." She nodded. "Every time. And they must have gotten it together in the afternoon, because when she came back in the evening, she was wearing jeans."

"What time was that?"

"Just a few minutes before all you cop cars came."

He smiled slightly. "What about the other visits? Do you remember the times?"

"Before lunch, the first time." She ran a fingernail along the edge of her lower lip, beneath the gloss. "And it must have been about two, the second time because I was giving up on studying. And then I saw her from down here, the time she came over in jeans."

They all looked out the window toward Owen's house.

"You're sure it was the same person?"

"Yeah. Nobody else came, and Owen wouldn't be seeing

different strangers all in one day. He hardly met strangers."

"You didn't talk to him? To ask about it?"

She shook her head.

"He wasn't really that kind of a neighbor," her mother said. "If you saw him out at the mailbox, cordial as could be. Outside gardening, always a story to tell. But no coffee, no inside visiting."

Dan nodded. He stood up and thanked them on his way to the front door.

Continuing with the canvass, he finished the block and came back along the other side. He crossed the alley and introduced himself to all the households behind Owen's. By midafternoon, he had located two more witnesses who said much the same thing. Obviously they knew what he had already heard, but they seemed such solid citizen types, he couldn't imagine them following a teenager's lead unless they had to in order to tell the truth.

It meant Lindy was outnumbered. She admitted to only two visits. That made the third visit interesting.

13

ELLIE PATRICK CALLED LINDY ON SATURDAY MORNING AND asked her to conduct services for Owen that afternoon. Tim had taken a liking to her because she helped without lecturing, and he was hoping the ordeal would be less awful with her in charge.

When Lindy murmured her respect for Tim's gallantry without really answering the request, Ellie hurried on. Owen had treated everyone's kids as if they were his own, and so there had to be a memorial service, according to the counselors assigned to the boys. They were wrong, Ellie believed, because all of the survivors had been horribly cut up by the funeral for Vance. The counselors claimed they were processing, but Ellie said no, they were having a hard time, which was why anything for Owen had to be totally simple. All the parents were cooperating, in order to avoid charges of neglect from the counselors, but they agreed with Ellie that a small, private gathering was the most any of them could face. Greg was offering his house since the personal touch might help his sons.

The arrangement made Lindy wonder about their divorce. Was this tragedy causing Ellie to set her anger aside? Lindy was sure it wasn't a problem for Greg, because he had never considered their divorce to be traumatic. She remembered how he had described it at the time. After a committee meeting one day, as they had walked to the library together, Greg had said out of the blue that educational changes had destroyed his marriage. He and his wife used to have everything in common because of his interest in biology and her interest in horses, but now, he worked with computer simulations, whereas she was still involved with the living product. Not that she favored using animals to experiment on, he had explained fair-mindedly, but she called him a fool for acting as if a computer simulation of the internal structures of a worm was any preparation for going out into the garden to find one.

It had seemed a very academic conflict to Lindy, since in her experience, divorce came from an increasing unwillingness to be handled by someone whose body no longer seemed ambrosial and instead had become a mere casing for the lungs and larynx which discharged unending insults. Still, she remembered how real it had been to Greg.

But now, with this, maybe they both regretted the past. In case tragedy was bringing them together, she felt obliged to help. On the other hand, the damaged teenagers would be there. She dreaded seeing the blind parade which was going to ruin her life, even though they hadn't meant to.

Oh, what difference does it make? she asked herself, they're there whether I see them or not.

Getting set for the ordeal, she wandered outside, where she always felt most comfortable. She crossed her home clearing and stood by the pond where Tim had floundered. Why couldn't the whole episode have been as unreal as it seemed to her?

Footsteps approached on the path behind her. She turned. It was like seeing into a past she hadn't lived herself. The Sunstrike had been in love with yellow, and so Lindy knew what to think about a barefoot visitor wearing an ankle-length straight gown of a gold geometric print on yellow cotton. Her dark hair had begun to go gray—a moving reminder of how much time had passed since the Sunstrike's glory days.

"Lindy?" she said in a spacey voice.

"Hi."

"I feel awful, asking such a favor. I'm Sunny."

"It's okay, Sunny, do you need something?"

Sunny tucked her hair behind her ears. "I feel so guilty."

"No, don't bother with guilt."

"But I didn't mean it to work out so bad."

Lindy looked at the barely focused gaze. "Did you want to tell me?"

"See?" Sunny said. "I like to sit on top of the riverbank and think about how it was in the old days."

"There's nothing guilty about that."

"But I mean—" Sunny gnawed the inside of her lower lip, a gesture which distorted her worn face. "I sit beyond one of those blackberry thickets so you don't have to know I'm there and be disturbed when you like to stand there, looking."

Lindy's heart sank. She knew residents were all around, but she hadn't carried the thought out. It was an effort to nod encouragement.

"What I mean, I *know* how stills smell because we used to have one when all of us here were Sunstrike. I *knew* it was a still down there. I didn't say anything because Sunstrikers don't say anything. But now— With all this— I mean—" She brushed her hair behind her ears again. "These modern people don't know much, and so maybe I should have said something."

Lindy sighed. "Don't blame yourself, Sunny. Even if you'd told me in time, and even if I'd asked them to stop, they'd have just moved somewhere else to get into trouble."

"I wish I'd said."

It was a huge concession for a Sunstriker even briefly to consider interfering, so Lindy nodded. "We all wish we'd done it differently, I'm totally sure of that."

"I want to go to the service for this grandfather. To show I feel bad."

As always, Lindy was surprised by the Sunstrike's information network. "I'm going," she said. "Would you like a ride?"

"No!" Sunny said with an instinctive recoil from anyone who took responsibility. "It's just—" She looked down to tug at the handmade seam of her long skirt. "I don't have the kind of clothes the family would probably think I ought to wear."

"We're about the same size," Lindy said. "Why don't you go upstairs and pick out something? You're more slender than I am, but if you grab a tie belt, I'll bet something would fit you."

"Thanks." Sunny drifted toward the house, looking so mentally dilapidated it was hard to believe she was well enough organized to plan her wardrobe and allow time to hitch a ride to town.

Lindy lingered by the pond, but the interruption seemed to have driven away all hope of the serenity she searched for. She trailed back to the house in time to see Sunny emerge wearing Lindy's only long skirt—a navy wool. An unconstructed jacket minimized her flatness. She had chosen heeled pumps and brushed her long hair up into an attractive twist. The transformation was surprising. Except for her drug-grayed skin and soft-focus eyes, she might have been anyone.

Lindy smiled. "Looks good!"

Sunny waved and started down the two-track, walking easily in the borrowed heels. Lindy wondered what her former life had been, to teach her such normal skills.

She went inside to shower and put on her best dress—a stone silk tunic over a straight skirt. She kept her mind focused on Owen as she headed for town. By the time she reached South Hill, both sides of Greg's street were parked full. She walked the last three blocks to Greg's house. His kitchen door was standing open. She went on in. A central hall led to a wide, curved front room which embraced the south view of the Fairhaven district's docks, the west view of the San Juan Islands beyond Bellingham Bay, and the northwest view of the city filling South Hill's face.

She paused in the doorway to orient herself. All the furniture was occupied, and the floor was full of people murmuring in clusters. Sunny seemed to fit right in, her head bent as she listened to a trio of women leaning against a cedar planter holding a weeping fig. Richison sat on a straight chair by the bookshelves which filled the only solid wall. On another straight chair beside him, Brent Fuller sat. They were surrounded by an empty space which declared them quarantined.

The teenagers at the center of the disaster huddled together, although Stash was missing. Lindy looked them over carefully, wondering if she had seen them around the Sunstrike. Except for Tim, she didn't think so. But that proved nothing, she reminded herself, because she hadn't recognized Tim, that first morning, yet he had known his way around her property.

The three who were present held their heads at odd angles, as if just the right slant might help them focus. Their clothes set them apart as well. Their friends had shown respect by wearing dark spiderweb prints over baggy jeans, for the boys, and gigantic dark sweaters over black tights, for the girls. But the boys who were having some trouble coping had been dressed by their mothers, and so they wore un-stone-washed black jeans with straight legs and no pleats. Their gray dress shirts fit them, and their jackets were man-tailored. Lindy had a wild impulse to laugh. The way they looked, it was no wonder their girlfriends weren't sitting with them.

"Thanks for doing this," Greg said at her elbow. "Nothing fazes Karl, but Tim's going through hell, and I'm not much better."

"I feel a little awkward about it," Lindy admitted.

Greg flattened his mouth in the abashed smile-gesture which was so effective with women in groups. "I won't listen."

Lindy smiled faintly. "It'll be just Celtic Christianity 405. I'm not going to save anybody. The Gaels tended not to."

Greg patted her shoulder.

Lindy looked toward the far end of the room, where Ellie sat in a bow window which gave a view of the Michaelmas daisies in the yard's lovingly tended border. She had dressed up by wearing her English riding costume, com-

plete with hard hat. When she touched the empty chair beside her, Lindy picked her way among the groups filling the
floor, nodding when people glanced up at her.

"Are you okay?" Lindy asked as she sat down.

"More or less," Ellie said.

They both looked at their watches. The room fell silent.

"I liked Own," Lindy said conversationally. "I expect
everybody did, and we all still do."

There was a brief murmur.

"I feel like it's right for us to tell each other."

The murmurs spread. Eyes began to glitter as people remembered, but as they told about it in lengthening detail,
they found nostalgic smiles behind the tears. Lindy
watched.

When the room quieted, Lindy described her meeting
with Owen and explained how special it had been. She told
about his memoirs and paraphrased one of his yarns about
his dad. And then she paused, gazing through the window
at the sky which was stacking full of the heavy clouds which
formed only over the edge of salt water.

"I'd like to describe this situation the way Owen saw it,"
she said, urged by their longing to feel reconciled. "I don't
know if Owen talked to you about it, but he was part of one
of the oldest of our faiths. I'm glad, because it's a lovely
faith, which seems right for a man like him, a wonderful
man."

She looked at their eyes.

"The basic thing about Owen's belief is that everybody's
best is good enough. From that, you get how to deal with
problems. If you're crosswise with someone, you don't
seethe or lash out. Before it gets that far, you ask the person
causing you trouble to meet you in front of a witness. A
spiritual thinker, not a cop. With this witness watching,
you remember to keep your better nature up front—that's
the point."

She smiled at them. They softened their mouths obligingly.

"You work it out, whatever it is. You don't try to *win*,

119

because that would mean someone else loses. If someone were to lose, that might be the end of them."

She paused. It was a way of thinking that did away with anyone's need to murder, Owen would have said, but if murder happened, it dealt with that, too. She wondered if they were taking it in.

"That part matters a lot, because Owen's faith says nothing ends," she went on. A few of them looked doubtful, and Lindy was silenced by the vision of Owen's empty body. But it hadn't seemed empty. She had still felt him, somehow a presence in his chosen room.

"If you're Owen, how you divide up the year reminds you. During summers, long days—that's the light half of the year, where you're walking around doing your best."

Oddly, Richison and Greg seemed to be listening most intently. Of course Greg was used to hearing her committee reports. And Richison's mind never seemed to wander, when a witness spoke on any topic. But for the rest of them, she wasn't sure what they heard.

"It's during the winters, the long nights, that you have your dark half," she went on. "For people who believe like Owen, the dark half is as good as the light. It's when you recharge, get ready. Each year *begins* that way—with the dark half. And life's the same, in Owen's faith. You end up in the walking-around part, the light, but you begin with the dark."

Most of the watchers had begun to weep or else struggled not to, so Lindy brought it to a close. "That's what's going on with Owen, now—he's getting set for his fresh start."

"Oh, Lindy, make him come back," Tim said in a voice which rose and broke like a boy's.

Lindy moved to crouch beside him. "He *is* back, Tim, don't you see? You've got him *forever*. It's what he believed, and he had the right to believe it, and he loved you," she said. "He *admired* you, don't you know that? He told me you're sharp as a lemon and honest as a string."

The watchers smiled damply, and Tim made three convulsive noises which were more laugh than sob. "That's

120

Grandad," he said, but he made a fumbling grab for Lindy.

She put her arms around him. He clutched her as if they were once again stumbling on the steps up to her deck. She was relieved when she heard people moving around behind her, bringing the painful, formal situation to an end.

Greg ceremonially opened the double leaded-glass doors to the dining room. Tim drew away, crumpling into himself. Lindy took hold of his hand so he would stand up and stay beside her as people came forward. He endured it with her for a few moments and then he moved away, awkward with tears or damage, she wasn't sure which. Ellie came to join her, sharing the vague murmurs people wanted to offer before they drifted toward Greg's student-catered buffet. Lindy watched the teenagers being shuffled out of the room hand-over-hand like buckets on a fire line.

"Tim really can see, can't he?" Lindy asked as she watched.

"Oh, yeah." Ellie sighed. "The doctor says he'll get good enough, if he cooperates with his therapy. And as far as Karl," she paused to shake her head as she watched her older son, "he says as long as he can see his girlfriend's—"

"Well. That's good," Lindy said, even though she wondered if it was. She watched Karl enter the dining room with his head tipped back sharply as if he could see best out of the very bottoms of his eyes. Shorter than his parents, stocky, he seemed to have come from a different world. His arrogant gestures and smirk also seemed better suited for life on ancient Mars.

"Which one is his girlfriend?" Lindy asked.

"May Anne. She didn't come." Ellie sighed. "I suppose I don't blame her. She feels like we don't respect Karl, and so she refused to be a guest in Greg's home."

Lindy looked at her. Was that really a good enough reason for May Anne to skip the services for a man she had blamed? she wondered.

"You know how it is with parents, especially overachieving ones, which is May Anne's view of us," Ellie said as if Lindy's silence had reproached her. "Karl's been sitting around one house or the other since he got out of high school. He uses this tough job market for an excuse to not look for work. There are plenty of entry-level openings, but he says he'll work when he finds something interesting."

Lindy smiled faintly. "At that age, I was working in a library, shelving books."

"Yeah, I'm sure, and I was mucking out stalls," Ellie said grimly, "everybody starts at the bottom. Everybody but Karl."

They fell silent as a somber group approached, the public expressions on their faces labeling them as teachers. Lindy found herself shaking hands with the history teacher, the shop teacher, the journalism teacher, and the coach who had helped the high school bird-watching club build the birder cabin.

"I never dreamed it would be such un-fun," the history teacher told her.

"Kids," the shop teacher agreed.

"We're really sorry for your trouble," the coach added.

"You do a nice presentation," the journalism teacher said.

They left together, using the front door in order to circle the house outside, rather than pass the dining room without pausing for ceremonial food. It was kind of them to attend even briefly, out of loyalty to the boys, Lindy thought, since they couldn't have known Owen personally.

As the room cleared, Stash's mother came to stand beside her. Like everyone else, Faith had dressed to show respect even though her clothes looked recycled. A blue and green scarf filled the throat of a black shirt which topped her jeans.

"Do you know Faith, Ellie?" Lindy asked.

"Yeah, we've met. Over these kids," Ellie said as they shook hands.

"You did a good job with this, Lindy," Faith said. "I'm going to leave instructions for when I croak."

"Thanks. But don't croak."

122

"I *feel* like it. Listen." Faith glanced around. "This isn't the time or place, but we need to talk."

Ellie stepped back politely and half turned away, greeting people and accepting their comments for Lindy as well as herself.

"Sunday's always crazed, with everybody processing their Saturday night," Faith said, lowering her voice, "but could you come to the rescue house on Monday? I know the polite thing is for me to come to you, but you're so far out, and the rescue house is jammed, right now, with school starting, and—"

Lindy shook her head to interrupt. "Not a problem. What time's good?"

"Whenever you're up and around, Monday. I *really* appreciate it."

Lindy smiled. Faith touched her arm before turning away.

Ellie came back to stand like an informal receiving line, and the two women watched Faith go down the hall toward the back door, rather than lingering at Greg's buffet.

"Stash is the one I worry about," Ellie said. "The background he comes from, he needs everything else going for him."

Lindy nodded. "I think his father—"

"Jail, I know." Ellie sighed. "It turns the cops against Stash. Faith attended for him, today, which was the best we could do. He's stuck in this state home which wouldn't let him attend because he'd be associating with his partners in crime."

"Oh God."

"Yeah," Ellie said. "Greg promised no one would speak to Stash, if they'd just let him attend, but they still said no."

They both sighed.

"I suppose you can see how case workers confuse themselves," Lindy said after a moment. "There's been so much publicity about situations where they didn't intervene when they should have, and then something horrible happens, and everyone blames them."

"And so they make up for that by intervening when they shouldn't. Two wrongs, you know—" Ellie said.

Lindy nodded. "It must be hard for them, though."

"Right. Name anybody it isn't hard for."

"That's true."

"About the other kid, Al," Ellie said, "I hardly know him. The doctor says Karl was fortunate enough to chug-a-lug, proving what a man he was," she rolled her eyes. "So he threw up most of what he drank. But Al really is a serious drinker. He's been at it since he was in middle school, is what I hear. So he just drank a whole lot without trying to outdo the world, which let him keep it down. Unfortunately. So he's blind for real, they're saying. I don't know if they actually know."

Lindy looked toward the dining room, where a thirtyish woman stood beside Al in front of an antique china cupboard. She was holding a plate and feeding him and herself with alternate bites. An attractive woman with long silver earrings and loosely floating hair, she was making a game of it, and Al seemed content. Each time she steadied her little finger against the edge of his mouth, he lunged against her hand to snap up the bite she offered, his blond hair flying.

"Is that his sister?" Lindy asked.

"Noooooo," Ellie said, "that's Opaline. She was his high school history teacher, to start, and then she decided he needed private tutoring, on top of the regular class work. Nobody realized exactly what she meant to tutor him in. Now that he's graduated, they don't feel like it has to be a secret anymore."

Lindy looked into Ellie's eyes.

Ellie snorted. "Join the modern world."

"I guess. Is that why she wasn't with the other teachers? There was a scandal?"

"Believe it."

Standing alone a few feet away from the playful couple, watching them tensely, was a beautiful woman about ten years older than Opaline. It was easy to guess why she was so intent, because she had Al's blonde hair and sensual mouth, and something in her posture—ready, alert—also echoed Al's.

"That's Al's mother?" Lindy asked.

Ellie nodded.

"She's really brave."

"Yeah, she is," Ellie said. "She boards her jumper at the arena, so we've gotten acquainted. She's *very* talented. Rides hunt seat. Takes *any* risks."

Lindy was grateful for the detail which suggested strength. What would it feel like to have an attractive son who resembled you and who also got into such irreversible jams? she wondered. Belatedly, she wished she had attended the services for Vance. No matter what that funeral might have cost her, it couldn't have been as hard as what Mrs. Crayson was doing, appearing here in support of Al. To lose one child, and to see a second child struggling—how could you go on? she wondered. For the sake of the remaining child, you would have to. But how could you not be torn to shreds by all the conflicting loves and loyalties, before you even reached your own needs?

"Is Mr. Crayson here?" Lindy asked.

"No. He told me he'd be bound to cry, which would make people lose confidence in their taxes—he's an accountant. He does my taxes, is why he could be frank about it. I said it wouldn't shake my faith in him, but he claimed he was sure."

It didn't sound like a real reason, Lindy thought, since his family surely needed him here. "Let's go talk with her," she said.

They crossed the room together.

"You didn't pay last respects to Vance," Mrs. Crayson said as Lindy faced her.

"No," Lindy agreed. "I was afraid I'd seem out of place, or be a sad reminder, or be inconvenient somehow."

"I suppose you think I'm out of place here," Mrs. Crayson said.

"No, how could anyone think that?" Lindy asked.

"It's good to see you Alice," Ellie said soothingly, "I

125

need someone here who knows what I'm going through."

Mrs. Crayson turned to Ellie, grief making her stare seem almost blank. "I prefer seeing you at the stables."

"*Yes*," Ellie said, "I wish we were there right now."

Sensing that Ellie might comfort Mrs. Crayson, while she obviously just provoked anger, Lindy stepped back. "I'd like to catch Brent Fuller," she said.

"Thanks for doing this," Ellie said, reaching out quickly to touch her elbow. "It gives me things to say to Tim. I knew Dad believed *something*, but I could never get it out of him."

Lindy nodded and turned away. Brent and Richison stood at opposite ends of the buffet, clearly eavesdropping on as many conversations as possible.

"Could I talk to you in the kitchen, Brent?" Lindy asked.

"You bet, Dr. Adair."

Richison watched as they left the dining room together. Lindy ignored it. She led the way to the breakfast nook where she and Richison had told the news to Greg. When they were both sitting down, Lindy drew a long breath.

"Would you tell me about Sergeant Richison?" she said. "If it puts you on the spot, obviously just act like you can't quite hear me."

Brent frowned. "I'm not supposed to talk to the public about a fellow officer."

Lindy nodded. "That's what I was afraid."

"So if you'll remember you didn't hear it from me—"

Lindy smiled.

"What did you need to know?" he asked.

"Maybe it's nothing," she admitted, "maybe it's just that he seems so California I can't see why he came up here. Even if he's running from something, I realize it might not matter, but if he isn't quite what he should be, I'd like to know. He's hanging around and I can't prevent it. I don't even mind, if he's just working on this case, because I want it solved, and he seems intelligent, so maybe he'll succeed. But I'm not willing to get worked over by someone with a past he needs to hide."

126

"Is he annoying you?" Brent asked so sternly she was startled.

"No, no, not like that. It's just that sometimes I start to trust him, and other times, I don't know."

Brent nodded. "I wondered the same thing, so I put off that first visit out to your Sunstrike until we got a report back from San Diego on him. I wasn't willing for him to work around you if there was any question."

She smiled softly. "Thanks."

"San Diego says he's okay," Brent said. "He's a native of the city, so they should know if he's ever been in trouble. They say he hasn't been. They know they have to give a fuller report, now, than they did before California cops got such a reputation, so they filled it in. Why he left, he's burned out on big city crime, they said, and it makes sense of what I've seen of him. When I drove through the Sunstrike to visit you, he thought we were using logging roads."

They both laughed.

"He's not married, so it would be easy for him to leave on an impulse," Brent went on. "But the force down there says he's got all these brothers and sisters to help raise—it's why he doesn't marry—so they were surprised when he left. It might be true, because he really is overboard about protecting kids—it's getting in his way, on this case about you."

"I'm glad of your judgment on it, Brent."

"I've been wanting to talk to you about Stash," Brent said after a brief pause to mark a change of subject. "Richison's so dead set against blaming any of the kids."

"I sort of am, too."

Brent frowned. "Let's just talk about understanding what happened, leave blaming out of it."

Lindy nodded, bemused to hear her own methods used against her.

"Stash is in the worst spot, of all those guys, because he hasn't got any family to fall back on. There's no one to listen to his anger, which leaves him no way to get over it."

Lindy nodded.

"His dad is in jail on an habitual charge, which means Stash grew up with no respect for the law."

"I'm not sure how much contact he has with his dad," Lindy said.

Brent nodded. "Which makes him search for a substitute."

"I suppose."

"So he chose Owen for that, looked up to him."

"I guess they all did."

"Owen made moonshine sound like fun, when it definitely isn't," Brent said. "You don't want that from your hero."

"I've never understood how men feel about heroes," Lindy said hesitantly.

"You feel betrayed by their mistakes."

He stated his rule so firmly, Lindy suspected there must be a story behind his knowledge, but she didn't want to hear it. "Even so," she insisted, "what happened can't involve Stash."

"He was in control of the still because he lived in the cabin, so he has guilt to deal with, on top of revenge."

"No." Lindy shook her head, over and over. "No, please, Brent, no, truly, no. I can't stand it. Stash has had enough trouble, and his life hasn't even started yet."

"You can't want him running around thinking death is a responsible way to solve problems."

Lindy sighed. "I hadn't thought of it that way."

"Okay, and you don't have to, because I am."

14

Lindy left Greg's house in a daze of worry. When she reached the street, she saw Richison standing beside her car. She wasn't prepared for it. Would Brent be in trouble for talking to her? She wasn't sure. Working herself up to resist, she approached briskly.

Richison greeted her with a social half-smile. "Is it true, what you said about dividing the year?" he asked.

"Yes." She stepped into the street.

"You believe it?" he asked as they looked at each other over the roof of her car.

"Owen did." She studied his face, thinking about Brent's assessment of him. "Why do you keep asking what I believe?"

"Cops are curious, I guess. And I don't know anybody else but you who can be confronted by a murder and still make this sound like a pretty world."

He *had* been listening, Lindy realized. Why? she wondered, what did he want? His shadowed eyes told her he wanted something. Maybe he wanted a prettier world.

"The world is just the world," she told him. "There are different ways of looking at it."

He grinned. She simply met his gaze.

"Do you have somewhere we could talk?" he asked. "We probably shouldn't sit here in your car where people will see us, and I'm assuming you don't want to go down to headquarters."

"Very perceptive." Lindy's gaze drifted down the visible part of his body. He had dressed to show respect, his gray tweed jacket matching his Oxford gray pants and dark tie. Maybe he had liked Owen and had attended the service for normal reasons—was that possible? she wondered.

"What about Post Point Park?" she asked.

"It's going to rain."

"Northwesterners don't notice rain, but I suppose Californians do. Where would you rather?"

"Park it is. I'll follow you."

She stepped into her car. He started for his Cherokee but stopped abruptly.

"Lindy?"

She leaned out of the window in order to hear.

"About the other night, on our way over here. I'm not a traffic cop and never was. You don't have to trust me—what you can count on is, I don't have any blank tickets on me."

It took Lindy a moment to understand. Finally she laughed. His face brightened.

She pulled out and headed down into Fairhaven, a natural sun pit cupped between professional, high-budget South Hill and even higher-budget middle-class Edgemoor. Fairhaven had always offered an easy life, no questions asked, and since the Sixties, it had emphasized its off-track appeal by accommodating wanderers as if "street-people" weren't a word. Its narrow, uncurbed streets and tiny houses radiated a funky charm which was repeated in a casual population who walked everywhere.

The loose but strongly felt community had been briefly threatened by the arrival of the Alaska ferry, which built a gigantic pipe-and-green-glass terminal. Community meetings had been passionate, but outrage had faded when actual Alaskans began to arrive. Booted, jeaned, packing their all, they fitted into Fairhaven's unpretentiousness.

The only important loss was Post Point Park. In the old days, it had been a charmingly untended grass plot above granite riprap which restrained winter storm tides. People from all over the city drove down to clamber over the rocks and admire the kelp caught in barnacles thriving between the tide marks.

A railroad right-of-way skirted the edge of the park, offering a level but sharp-graveled path south to Post Point, itself. Walking the right-of-way was technically trespassing, but Fairhaven didn't believe in that. Besides, sharing with an occasional train lent excitement, and so people continued to stroll down to the Point—a wedge of golden sandstone, pocked and scoured by salt water and carved by love-sick teenagers. The buoy off the Point clanged and groaned for added romance.

When the ferry arrived nearby, the Port Authority upgraded the park, hoping overnighters would feel out of place and stay away. Using designer logs, designer hawsers, designer benches, and designer roofs, the Authority turned the once delightful space into a standard unit which could have been found in any city in the West.

Thinking about urban change, Lindy stood on the recently blacktopped park path. When Richison joined her, she stopped looking at the storm-whitened bay.

"You get used to all this cold and wet, I guess," he said as he shrugged into a parka.

She nodded, waiting for him to stop studying her tunic, flattened against her body by the storm wind. As always in such situations, she acted as if she didn't notice his primal gaze.

"The service was good," he said. "I've been to a lot of funerals. They're usually appalling."

"I suppose you do go. I hadn't thought of it."

At last he looked at the white-caps, stacking noisily against the riprap. "With an acquaintance killing, whoever did it is almost always there. Maybe from guilt, or they need control. But what it looks like is a thrill."

"It might be just their reality needs," Lindy said.

"Meaning?"

She shrugged. "If it's the first time they've killed someone, they probably can't quite believe it happened. They want to hang around and see what other people think about it.''

He smiled. "Are you really that forgiving?"

"I'm not forgiving at all. I *terribly* resent it about Owen. But you have a better chance of figuring it out if you understand the person.''

He watched her face intently. "You're playing detective?"

Lindy nodded as if the question were sincere. "I'm interested in people.''

"Plus the civil suit."

She nodded again. "Yes, unfortunately."

"You were right about the suicide note," he said after a pause. "There were earlier versions of everything else in Owen's computer memory. But not the note. Whoever killed him must have written it at home and copied it into his machine while he was bleeding to death.''

Lindy shuddered.

"They evidently wore gloves," he added.

Lindy bowed her head.

"We canvassed Owen's neighborhood," Richison went on, watching an almost pure white gull balance into the wind above the edge of the bank, its black eye piercing as it studied him. "Canvasses are time-consuming, but they're usually worth the effort, because people sometimes saw something, or they heard shouting, or something wasn't quite right but they didn't call the cops, and now they're ashamed they let it go, so they don't come forward unless we ask.''

"Someone saw something?" Lindy asked.

"Yeah."

His voice was edgy. She looked at him.

"They saw you."

"Well, you knew that," she said. "I told you myself."

"Yeah." He stopped watching the gull.

"There's more, isn't there," she asked in a discouraged voice. "Tell me the whole thing all at once, so I know what I'm facing.''

"I can't." His eyes were shadowed as expressively as if he weren't a cop. "You'd better tell me about your day."

Lindy could feel her face and throat flush. It was a useless reaction—anger—and it hurt her sense of herself, but she wasn't sure what Richison would think. When she realized it might *matter* what he thought, her nerves rebelled.

"I already told you, there at Owen's."

"Yeah, but you were in shock, and at that point, I didn't have witnesses with other ideas."

Lindy waited for the surge of outrage to subside. "Thursday?" she said as moderately as she could manage.

He nodded.

She thought a while. "You're going to think I lead a brutally unexamined life, but I have trouble remembering, once a day's gone."

"Don't go academic on me, professor. Just tell me your day. Start with 'I got up.' "

Maybe it wasn't meant to be rude, she thought, maybe it was meant as a kind of appeal. Reminding herself of Brent's description, she wondered if Richison was having a hard time, too. Owen's death wasn't big-city crime, but it was murder. If Richison had burned out badly enough, maybe any murder dismayed him. Could that be?

She began a slow stroll to the end of the blacktopped walk, recalling as well as she could. At the end of the blacktop she paused, looking blankly at the woven-wire enclosure for outdoor storage which hemmed in the park's north edge. Interrupting herself to add details, rearranging her timetable when she saw she should, she turned back to stroll toward the railroad right-of-way which blocked the south edge of the park.

When she finished, Richison hunched his shoulders forward as if he were cold even inside his parka.

"Try it again," he said. "And this time, don't leave anything out."

Lindy stopped walking. Running back over what she had said, she stared across the bay at the high hump of Lummi

133

Island, which had grown vague in the developing storm. Finally she sighed and turned to him.

"If you think there's something I'm not telling you, that must mean someone saw someone doing something else at Owen's house, and whoever it was looked enough like me to be confusing. Is that it?"

He watched her face.

"So let's see," she said, as if she were willingly thinking aloud. "I'm five-seven. After dark, or twilight, you wouldn't know whether I'm a man or woman—I'd be just somebody in jeans and sweatshirt and shortish hair. Those teenagers are all bigger than I am, but after dark, I don't know how accurately you judge size. Anyway, it probably depends more on how big the people are who watched me, how big are they?"

"Try midafternoon," Richison said.

Lindy rubbed her upper arms as if the beginning spitter of rain distressed her. "It was a nice day, so they must have seen clearly," she said unhappily. "Did they identify me by name?"

He didn't answer.

Lindy closed her eyes a moment. When that didn't really help, she decided enough was enough.

"I'm sure there must be millions of cop rules about this," she said, "but why don't you at least glance at how it is for me. I was a teacher for four years. At a hundred students a term, three terms a year, that's a lot of people to know. Or at least to be known by. If somebody saw me and knew who I was, that's one thing. But if all they did was describe a stranger, I need to know it."

"All you *need* is to tell me the truth."

She pressed her lips between her teeth in an effort to control her anger. Or was it fear she hoped to control? Once the idea suggested itself, she couldn't seem to shake it. It was fear.

And so she pretended anger. "I did tell you the truth, and here's another part of the truth," she said aggressively. "You can't include teachers on your suspect list. Teachers

134

don't do crimes. They're too well known by too many people to risk it."

"No, it works the other way—a public figure gets so used to being stared at they forget it matters."

"It matters to me."

"Evidently." He thought a moment. "You aren't batting a thousand for honesty, you know. Outside Owen's house that first night, you tell me all heartbroken that you don't know any of these people. And then Professor Patrick greets you like a long-lost friend."

She rubbed her eyes. "When you asked, I hadn't realized who Tim is. I guess I may have been told his last name, but it isn't that unusual of a name, at least not around here, so I didn't connect it."

"Maybe. But you sounded like buddies, which means a divorced man is going to have explained his private life to you, including introducing you to his kids."

Lindy sighed. "Greg has an interesting mind. He's a sincere teacher. That's the kind of thing you know about your colleagues. You can get quite fond of them without knowing the least detail about their home life."

He gazed at her eyes noncommittally.

"I wish you would believe me," she said.

"Okay. When possible."

"I'm going to pretend you aren't hostile," she said after a while, wondering if she dared to trust Brent's information about Richison's personality.

His mouth eased slightly.

"I probably have proof about where I was, midafternoon, if it matters," she said.

"I'd like it."

She refused to look at him. "I went to see Owen late morning. I went back after my group meeting. In between, I was home. I've told you that twice, and it's true, and it'll be true forever. There might be a witness."

"Meaning there is, but he may not be willing to come forward, because of conflicting commitments?"

"She."

He was silent. "What *exactly* are you telling me?" he asked eventually.

She turned away from the wind to watch the park's small, designer trees whip wildly. "Leftovers from the Sunstrike hang around. You don't necessarily see them, but they see you."

"One of your communards saw you?"

"I call them residents."

"One of them knows you were home?" he repeated.

"I think so." Speaking carefully, leaving out any detail which might identify Sunny, she told him about Sunny's watching the still.

"Let's go talk to her," he said as he cupped one hand under Lindy's elbow.

"No!" She freed her arm and stepped farther away from him. "I'll ask her if she's willing, but I won't give her away."

"You tell me which resident you're talking about, or else I interview everybody you've got."

"*Not* without warrants, Sergeant. Laws apply, even to cops."

"Laws apply especially to cops."

When she didn't budge, he sighed. "Okay. I'll follow you out to your place. You get hold of this woman. Ask her to talk to me. You of all people ought to cooperate, with the noose your neck is in."

"Being at risk is all the more reason not to do to others what's being done to me," she insisted.

Looking irritable, he stalked off toward his Cherokee, but he didn't pull out first. Lindy was annoyed. He intended to follow her, making sure she went straight home. So she couldn't run from him? So she couldn't stop at a public phone in order to call and set up a story with one of her residents?

Or, maybe just habit, she admitted, trying to believe it. I mustn't start feeling guilty, she warned herself. If I do, I'll act guilty. It was far too easy to see where that might lead.

She drove out the Mount Baker Highway, steaming at

the gunmetal Cherokee in her rearview mirror. She rolled slowly through the Sunstrike and parked in her usual spot. He pulled in beside her. They walked toward the house in silence.

"Don't you lock up?" he asked as she slid the glass door open.

Since the answer was obvious, she didn't even glance at him.

"I wish you'd lock your doors at least until this case is settled. We won't know who might be next on someone's list until we figure out whose list it is."

"If someone wrecks my life, there's nothing I can do about it, but I'm not going to wreck it myself," she said.

He sighed.

She stood in her book-lined entryhall and dialed with Richison watching. Sunny didn't answer.

"A two digit number?" Richison asked.

Lindy rubbed her forehead. "If I explain, you'll use it against me."

He drew a chest-expanding breath. "I personally don't suspect you of anything, Lindy, but there's evidence. If I'm going to insist you're not who we're looking for, I have to contradict what we've got, because it's *all* we've got."

She wondered if the reaction was genuine. It might be. Or it might be an interview technique. She shrugged.

"A telephone lineman lived here for awhile," she said. "He had fallen off a pole. They wouldn't let him work on just buried cables afterwards, even though he was sort of busted up. By the time he was out of the hospital, he saw he was tired of his family anyway, so he went on the road. We were his first stop. The accident was a blessing in disguise, he said."

"It doesn't sound like a blessing."

"No. But sometimes people get their values in order when they hit a snag."

They both thought about it.

"So, anyway," Lindy added, "he stayed a few months and set up this private phone system, in exchange. He had everybody out there digging to lay underground wires—he was a good manager. All you do is punch in the number of the cabin you want."

"Nothing communal about that," Richison said neutrally.

When she shot him a cranky look, he grinned.

"I'm hanging around until this witness shows up," he warned her.

Lindy decided not to struggle with it. If she sent him away, he would simply wait at the entrance to the Sunstrike, questioning everyone as they tried to get home.

"Make yourself some coffee if you want some," she said not quite graciously.

She went upstairs to change out of her official wardrobe. She took her time, showering before putting on lime sweats. She came back downstairs to find Richison pouring boiling water through freshly ground coffee beans. Wearing a sweater the same vibrant blue as his eyes, he looked surprisingly domestic.

"Do you keep a change of clothes in your car?" Lindy asked.

He glanced over his shoulder with a pleasant look which wasn't quite a smile. "I did today. I didn't want to stay trussed up, and I had an idea I wouldn't get home before who knows when."

He had placed three mugs on the marble sheet beside the stove. He filled two of the mugs while Lindy tried calling Sunny again. When there was still no answer, she followed Richison to the living room. He had built a fire and pulled easy chairs close to it. Lindy suspected the homemaking activity was supposed to lull her off her guard, but she responded to it anyway.

Before they had finished settling down, an ancient VW bug labored into the clearing. As they watched through the broad glass windows, a black door opened on the basically tan vehicle and Sunny stepped out.

"Well, that was easy," Richison said, getting up to go back to the kitchen to fill the third mug.

"Don't hassle her, Sergeant," Lindy said, following him.

He shrugged. "You're the hostess, you handle it. Provided that works, I'm satisfied."

Sunny came in without pausing to knock or call out.

"This is Sergeant Richison, from the Bellingham police, Sunny," Lindy said as Richison held out a mug of coffee.

Sunny turned away without the slightest pause for thought.

"He's not after the Sunstrike," Lindy said.

Sunny stopped but she didn't turn around.

"I wanted to ask you about that still, Sunny," Richison said affably. "I figure there must be people living here who aren't quite as clueless as Lindy, and usually I wouldn't know where to start, but you came in to that service, today, which tells me you can handle people, along with what's more real."

Sunny bent her head as if she were pondering.

"I'm from California, and so I know how it is with a commune. There was one out in the valley beyond the city where I grew up, San Diego. We all knew about it. So when my brother disappeared, my mom insisted I had to go out there and try to get him back. I found him, all right. They had this nice thousand acres with their own lake stocked for fish and their own henhouse for eggs and their cows for cheese and this field for hay, which is what my brother was in charge of, hay. He'd already gotten out there with a scythe and cut it. I helped him turn it so the sun would dry both sides. We're city people, so it was an adventure, but I don't know if you've worked hay? It gets into your hair and between your toes and everywhere. On you, you can get rid of it by jumping in the lake, but let it get into your clothes and you're never rid of it. So we worked stripped, which gets you real. My brother talked all about it and was glad to. I could see his point and so I didn't mess with him and ended up staying two months, myself."

Lindy watched him in astonishment. He looked sincere. Do they send cops to acting school? she wondered, or is it just California?

"What has you wired up?" Sunny said in a near whisper.

"Well, to start, I'd like to hand you this cup of coffee so we could all sit down together," Richison said, "at least, that's how it would be on my brother's commune."

Sunny turned as if she had forgotten how, but she took the mug. Richison led the way into the living room and waited to sit down last, as if they were playing ladies and gentlemen at a courtesy workshop.

"Would you tell me everything you can about that still?" Richison said after a sip of coffee.

Lindy struggled with a deepening unreality. He had said he wanted to check her alibi, but he seemed to have forgotten that.

"I'd need to know your curiosity structure," Sunny said, looking at his ostrich boots.

"Owen was murdered," Richison said. "Someone blamed him for what happened down in the river here. I figure one question's going to answer the other."

"He never came to their cabin," Sunny said in an absolute tone which seemed out of keeping with her vague eyes. "A lot of people did, but not Owen."

"That's it, that's exactly what will help," Richison said.

He and Sunny sat nodding at each other so empathically Lindy began to wonder if he really had spent time on a commune. It would never have crossed her mind to encourage Sunny's shambling style of talking, and yet Richison seemed to have all the time in the world. It could mean he knew her life. Lindy looked at him with new eyes.

"If we co-counsel, you'll have to gentle up on Lindy," Sunny said. "She really doesn't know."

Richison nodded. "I'd about concluded that."

"She's scheduled, so invisible is easy," Sunny went on. "She comes out to the bank every day, always after eleven. The deck of the river cabin has a whole row of mooring rings, but after one-fifteen, she'd never see a boat."

Lindy sighed.

"Good to know that," Richison said.

"So. Who was there, not Owen," Sunny asked herself like a topic sentence. She began a list, explaining each name. A lot of them were people Lindy had never heard of—locals, evidently. But some of them were from the high school, and others were a surprisingly flexible circle of friends.

Lindy wanted to ask how Sunny knew them, but Richison seemed to have forgotten that cops were curious. He didn't interrupt the flow in any way, only nodding at the end of each item. He didn't take notes, Lindy noticed as she realized she was forgetting the names as fast as she heard them. Did he really have so accurate a memory? Or was he listening for a single name? Or was he just waiting for discrepancies?

His face told her nothing because she couldn't believe what she saw. His blazing blue eyes were sad, and his mouth was sympathetic. He had scooted down in his easy chair and propped his feet on the hassock, and Sunny was responding as any woman would to the sight of such a man stretched out almost supine beside her, one deeply tanned hand dangling gracefully over the chair arm, his ring finger suggestively bare.

Did he know how he looked? Lindy wondered. He might be just getting comfortable, to help Sunny feel comfortable, but what he looked like was a very physical man supremely ready to take pleasure in whatever any woman might willingly do to him.

Lindy turned to Sunny, trying to see her as a man might. It was hard to judge. She was gentle, and a man might think she was yielding, as if she had no self. But Lindy knew the Sunstrikers better than that. In reality, women like Sunny were secure in an individuality which had been so thoroughly tested they never needed to consider who they were. They *knew*. It was easy to envy them their final peace, even though their road to serenity didn't bear thinking of.

Lindy tried to imagine Sunny in either of the bookstore groups, but it wasn't possible. Sunny wasn't questing. She didn't think of feminism, she simply lived her independence. Would a man know that?

She couldn't decide. The two of them were talking intimately, as if no one else were in the room with them. It was a jolt to remember they were discussing murder.

15

SUNNY AND RICHISON STOOD UP TO LEAVE AS IF THEY WERE A couple. Sunny stopped in the entry, seeming unselfconscious as she stripped to her briefs. Bare, her thin body showed surprising touches of grace. Lindy politely looked away, but Richison didn't.

"I'd wash these for you, Lindy, but I don't do dryclean," Sunny said, folding the borrowed garments neatly and stacking them on the walnut table which held the phone.

"Don't even think about it," Lindy said. "I'm just really glad you came to the service."

Sunny nodded and headed for the door. Richison smiled at Lindy before following. Lindy watched them down the steps—like a willing hostess, she told herself, although that wasn't what she felt. They stopped at his car. He reached inside and retrieved his jacket, draping it around Sunny's bare shoulders solicitously. Sunny looked at him with no trace of coyness. The tableau made Lindy's heart hurt. She had long ago concluded there had been no room for courtship on the Sunstrike. When people talked about that past, they referred to needs, not even to passion, and certainly not to love. It seemed joyless, to Lindy, but they thought of it as staying with their own center.

What was happening now must be what Sunny wanted, she decided, because she had left her Sunstrike shift upstairs in Lindy's dressing room. She could have gone back up to change, if she had wanted to. Or, she could have gone with Richison as she was and returned Lindy's clothes later—along with the borrowed heels she was walking off in. Would Richison know, or at least suspect? Would he jump to conclusions?

He opened the passenger door for Sunny but didn't linger to close it. It looked like a compromise—respecting her ability to shut her own door but being cordial also. It seemed to work, but how did he know? she wondered, was all California like that? Or did he just know communes, as he claimed? That didn't seem likely, since he kept accusing her of being one.

She watched him get into his Cherokee gracefully and brace one hand on the back of Sunny's headrest in order to look through the rear window as he backed around. The posture exposed an appealing curve of bare throat.

Was that staged? Or was he just safely maneuvering his car? She decided she couldn't tell.

And that wasn't the only thing which annoyed her, she realized. It wasn't fair of him to stroll off before she had a chance to ask him about some of the points the interview had raised. Watching them drive away at walking speed, she wondered what they were talking about—both of them were smiling.

Suddenly she realized what it was to be a cop. People like Richison were granted the perpetual right to pin people down. They could ask in friendly mode, as Richison seemed to, or they could be disgusting about it, as movie cops usually were, but regardless of the method, they always had the right. Richison could stop anyone, anywhere, to ask even the most point-blank of questions. And people had to answer, no matter who they were. Or at least, they were safer if they talked in the neighborhood of answering. Even Sunny.

Wishing she could stop thinking about it, Lindy plunged into housework. Saturday morning was her usual time to tidy, vacuum, launder, shop. Preparing for Owen's ceremony had interrupted her schedule, but as she got out the vacuum in order to catch up, she paused. Sunny thought

144

she was horribly tied to her routines. Her life had sounded dull, in Sunny's summary.

On the other hand, using routines meant she accomplished boring necessities, whereas if she had to choose, each time she cleaned, she'd probably never get around to it. She turned on the vacuum. Disliking the noise, she wondered what Sunny's house looked like.

Catching up to her schedule kept her busy until bedtime, and a rollicking storm woke her around two o'clock. Branches swept her roof. Trunks groaned. Dislodged cedar needles drove against the windows in occasional gusts. In the distance, a major tree fell with a crackling of torn branches leading up to an earth-shuddering thump. Lindy smiled, liking to feel part of a larger world. She didn't know exactly when she fell asleep again, but by morning the woods were breathless, and so she spent the day picking up after the storm. Branches were down in all the trails. She carried them to her clearing to stack beside her firepit, not willing to risk burning until the rains had settled in to stay.

Only one tree had gone down across a trail—a ten-inch alder which had been a standing snag before the storm hit. She got her chainsaw from the toolshed. Bucking up the long-dead tree, she carried firewood segments back to the woodshed. By dark, she felt luxuriously exhausted and wholesome, as she always did after outdoor work.

She was grateful for the physical interlude, because it helped her make up her mind. For Richison, this trouble was just his job, she reminded herself, taking it step-by-step as if she were back lecturing in Logic 202. That meant he would figure it out or not, with no special worry either way. But for her, if every least part wasn't resolved, she was back to zero. She couldn't believe she was seriously a suspect in Owen's death, and in spite of everything, Richison hadn't seemed to treat her like one. But the police investigation would focus on the deaths. The still wouldn't matter except as an interview technique for a pair of murder investigations, or possibly a murder and a wrongful death. She thought about Sunny's uncensored talking, as she was maneuvered into pouring out her thoughts without realizing exactly why. Richison was skillful, and so he might solve these deaths, but his ability didn't help her. If the moonshine claims ran on unchallenged, she would end up broke. No job. Not even technically unemployed, so no benefits to bridge her over. She hadn't been beaten up, so the rescue house wouldn't take her in. She could car-camp down on the low bank side of the river, as other people did when they had nothing else, but she would feel she really was a derelict if she let lawyers and cops make that choice for her.

That's not the point, anyway, she added, turning away from the selfish thoughts. The point is the forest. If developers are given the Sunstrike, the trees don't get a second chance.

She hoped it was only her fierce determination which brought back her familiar nightmare. During the anxious time when she had struggled with the university, she used to dream every night that she was on the run without being equipped to travel. In the dream, they were always gaining on her. Who "they" were was never specified, and she never seemed to know what they would do when they caught her.

She had had the dream so many times, during that long struggle, that she had become comfortable with the city where the dream ended. It wasn't a place she had ever been, awake, but it was beautiful, she realized when she could separate it out from her dream feelings of emergency. A long row of golden poplars lined a narrow road climbing out of a basin onto a high tableland. She always woke somewhere in the white city which filled the basin. What woke her each time was the struggle to get to the lovely road. This time, she tried to remember the dream city instead of the fear as she planned her day. She would have liked to wear jeans to the rescue house, but she had other appointments planned, and so she compromised on a wrap skirt in royal cord over tall boots. She topped a cream cotton shirt with an oversized blue sweater and headed for town.

146

The rescue house was in the Lettered Streets behind her lawyer's office. Its three floors of bedrooms had sheltered happy families for almost a century, but by the time the last of the final generation moved away, the neighborhood had changed. Surrounding homes had converted to student co-op housing and home-shares. It was a tolerant context, where a group home full of bruised women and wailing children was perfectly acceptable.

Lindy knew no one used the front door, and so she parked on a side street and walked along the alley past a separate structure at the back of the lot. It was hard to tell how it had started out because its broken-pane windows were in no particular order, and its gables were the wrong height to be either attics or lofts. Remodeling depended on donations of labor and materials which looked like scraps. The process turned the section under construction into a patchwork, but the labor was ungrudging, and so finished sections were appealing.

Lindy stopped to admire the work with a lone carpenter who was laying floors. There would be a dormitory eventually, in the other half, he told her, but this gameroom was almost ready to keep the rain off homeless children. He told her about his own children, who played in his converted garage. They loved being outside whenever they wanted to, and he was pleased to be giving the same freedom to the rescue-house kids.

The carpenter's confiding chat put Lindy into a cheerful mood as she climbed the leaning wooden steps to the rescue house's enclosed back porch. Inside, a note taped to the old spiderweb door said, "come on in."

"Hi, Faith," Lindy said as she stepped through onto a worn linoleum cluttered with tracked-in damp maple leaves.

Faith looked up from a battered desk tucked into a small space beside the door, where most people might have put a stand-up freezer. She huddled in a shapeless wool sweater, her feet warmed by a whirring milkhouse heater.

"I was going to take you to my room," Faith said, glancing around, "but my assistant had to drive a new arrival to the hospital, and somebody's got to be here where people can find them."

"It's okay."

Faith sighed by blowing through half-open lips. "Coffee." She pointed. "Mugs." She pointed again.

Lindy slipped out of her shoulder strap. Taking a dollar from her wallet, she hung her bag on the kitchen chair nearest Faith. She poured a mug of coffee and tucked the money under a notepad holding the beginnings of a grocery list.

"Why I asked you to come over here, I've got this awful, *awful* problem," Faith began as Lindy sat down beside her.

"I'll do whatever I can."

"I'm used to *helping*, not needing help."

"Everybody needs help someday," Lindy said. "I've gotten my share. It's time I passed it on."

Faith dug the blunt end of her pen into the line beside her mouth. "It's about Stash."

Lindy nodded.

"You don't have kids, do you? so I don't know if you realize they usually decide they're adopted when they turn teenage and can't be*lieve* how embarrassing their parents are, so the obvious answer is that they aren't really theirs."

Lindy smiled.

"But in Stash's case, it's sort of true," Faith added soberly. "He isn't adopted, but he's not mine, and I thought it was better to admit it to him. It never gets in our way, between the two of us, but it's killing him with the cops."

"I'm sorry, Faith, I missed something," Lindy said, setting down her mug. "What do you mean, he isn't yours?"

"He was born on a commune. That's the story of my life—that damned commune." Faith sighed. "You live on a commune so you ought to understand this, but you keep saying you don't live on one, so maybe you really don't know."

"I don't know," Lindy agreed.

148

"Here's how it works. Everybody's doing it, but nobody bonds, so you're never sure who the fathers might be, when you get caught. Then after the birth, you have group care so the kids can explore peer relationships, as healthier. I don't know if it really is healthier, but what I *do* know is, you put your kid in this playroom and go on with other things. Every so often, everybody comes back and picks up theirs. My kid had black hair and blue eyes. This once when I went back to pick him up, there was only one child left— this spindly blond. I told the nursery helpers, but they just said, oh, no, this one was mine and when their real hair comes in, it isn't anything like their birth hair. I told them somebody had swapped because my kid didn't cry much and this one had colic, but they said don't be silly."

"Did you look around for your own boy?"

"Yes, but three women and two men left the commune while I was looking. They all took kids with them. Everyone has only a first name which isn't the one on their birth certificate, so how can you trace anybody?"

"So you took Stash."

"I felt sorry for him."

"He grew up to be a nice person," Lindy said, refusing to think of Brent's theory about him. "You've done a good job."

Faith shrugged. "Yeah, he's a good kid, tries to be. We're friends most of the time. Why he swears to the cops I'm not his mother is, he wants to live on his own, be legally emancipated, now that I can't keep him here with me. We talked it over, and I could see his point, but it backfired."

Lindy was interested. Most people would have said something sentimental. Or else angry. Faith's honest assessment sounded surprisingly affectionate, in comparison.

"I don't know what you mean about the backfire," she said.

"Cops want parental supervision, so if I'm crossed off, they look for a father. This guy they've got in jail—King— really is Stash's dad, probably. King and I were together when we went to the commune, and maybe the nursery people figured your husband's baby is yours, whether he *is*, or not."

"A commune must be hard on marriages," Lindy said.

"Believe it." Faith nodded several times. "King joined the commune so he could sleep wherever anyone was already lying down. I mentioned not liking it. He pointed out I don't live up to my marriage commitments, either, because I promised to take him as he was, and now I was setting limits." She fussed with the papers on her desk. "I loved him though. So when I said it was over, I figured that does it for men, as far as me."

"It's hard," Lindy said soberly.

"So anyway," Faith said, "I wanted you to know plans have changed. I asked you about letting Stash crash out there on the Sunstrike, but the social workers say no, now that Stash says I'm out of it and I can't claim I'm not."

"Is that the only reason they refuse?" Lindy asked cautiously, "just that he claims he doesn't belong to you?"

"Yeah. What other reason could there be?"

"I don't know—I don't really understand much about government types," Lindy said.

"Lucky you."

Lindy smiled. Faith obviously believed what she was saying, and so maybe Stash wasn't in as much trouble as Brent hoped he would be. Brent hadn't seemed to identify Stash as the one who contributed the Sunstrike's copper kettle to the still, and Faith's behavior suggested there weren't any special accusations against Stash. On the other hand, Stash was still in custody, even though the other boys had gone home as soon as their doctors released them. The discrepancy worried her.

"If I get a chance to help, I will," she promised as she carried her mug to the sink, "but I'm not sure what I can do."

"I'll appreciate it." Faith adjusted her paperwork. "Trying's all anybody can ask of anybody."

"I guess that's true."

150

16

LINDY LEFT THE RESCUE HOUSE FEELING EVEN SADDER THAN before she went. Everything she learned seemed to extend the grief, and the interview coming up might make that worse. So, get it over with, she told herself as she drove to the All Perils office in the nearby Fountain District. A slowly spreading commercial area beside the Lettered Streets, the Fountain District basically resembled a Western town, with false fronts and unused display windows. However, some new arrivals had moved into rezoned homes, changing nothing but the paint, and a few neglected houses had been replaced with utilitarian mock-stucco strips set sideways to the street on narrow lots.

All Perils was halfway along a strip squashed between a veterinarian hospital and a shoe repair. The office manager—Ted, according to his desk nameplate—had a bare-temple haircut which labeled him as a student, at least part-time. He smiled nervously when Lindy gave her name.

After staring at the intercom a moment, he stood up and disappeared down a short hall. During the pause, Lindy read the credentials wall. Certificates framed under glass told her Deborah Coffman Wayne had earned merit awards from an independent crash school and a forensics seminar run by the state medical examiner.

"Lindy?" Deb said behind her.

Lindy turned. "Looks impressive."

"Fights off boredom." Deb pointed to one of the green plastic conference chairs and sat in another, keeping the magazine table between them.

Lindy hesitated. "Forensics? Maybe you can help me more than I thought."

"Sing your song. I'll do what I can."

"Max Owen died. The grandfather of two of the boys. Did you hear about it?"

Deb nodded. "Your cop reported, your Richison. Surprisingly cooperative. California, I guess. Must be a friendly place."

Lindy decided not to discuss California. "There was a suicide note that takes all the blame to Owen," she said instead. "I was wondering if that could help?"

Deb sighed and recrossed her legs, her tight skirt slipping even higher on her firm thigh. "Your claimants against you are pointing out that the grandfather's statement is just one opinion, and although you're looking at a deathbed confession, it's still just one opinion as to proportional blame. Plus, your cop says the suicide note's a fake."

Lindy pressed her lower lip between her teeth.

"I'm talking it up, believe me. If we can get an agreement that nobody's as much as fifty percent responsible, which maybe with this death, we might, you're in a much better position to say you won't even listen to a pain and suffering claim. It isn't true—you have to listen even if you don't have to hear—but it would give us something to bluff with, while the opposing attorney makes his speeches about liability and social responsibility and so on. He doesn't believe in that kind of thing, in fact, but he has a speech about it anyway."

"What if we went around lawyers and talked to the parents directly?" Lindy asked.

Deb shook her head, her dark hair flying. "Once a client's represented, I'm not allowed to talk to them."

"But what if I do?" Lindy asked.

"Not wise."

"But is it against the law, or anything drastic?"

"No," Deb said, drawing the word out slowly. "Not quite."

"Well, then, I feel like I should try. Dealing through lawyers, I feel like I'm just asking what the worst possibility is and then choosing it."

Deb sat motionless.

"I *have* to feel like, if we talked it through, just as people, it would make a difference."

Deb didn't react.

"You see me from the outside, as a stranger," Lindy said. "Do I seem like someone who deserves to be totaled?"

Deb's energetic gaze panned Lindy's face. Finally she lifted one hand and rocked it back and forth. "Even money," she said.

Lindy sighed.

"Don't tell me if you do this," Deb said. "And don't tell them you told me."

She scanned Lindy from rumpled crown to damp boot soles. "If you go, don't make threats."

"I never do."

"Don't offer a bribe."

"I wouldn't know how."

Deb sighed.

When Lindy stood up, Deb offered a firm handshake. It seemed like a bon voyage gesture toward a person on a suicide mission. Lindy hoped it was simply Deb's brisk way.

She returned to her car, thinking about Mrs. Crayson in order to keep her mind off Deb. She should have made this trip before, she realized. She hadn't been looking at the whole situation in the right way, hadn't been visualizing the parents' grief in terms of how utterly individual such a feeling was. Since she wasn't a parent, her lapse was understandable, but she wished she had thought of this before.

The Craysons lived in an older lakeside neighborhood. Their home would have been described as lovely by anyone, Lindy thought as she parked in the sloping driveway. It was dug into the top of a four-lot cluster which ran down to the lake. Surrounded by a designer version of a snake-rail fence, it looked like a child's storybook model of a homestead.

As she rang the doorbell, Lindy admired the firethorns

bracketing the front step. Since she had prepared herself to speak with Mrs. Crayson, she was disconcerted when a man looked around the corner of the house. Comfortably middle-aged, wearing a brown coat sweater with his jeans, he gazed at her over half-glasses.

"You're not Avon," he told her.

She smiled, thinking of her lack of makeup. "No. I'm Lindy. I was—"

"Oh, yes," he interrupted. He shifted his trowel into his left hand and wiped his right hand on his jeans before holding it out as he walked toward her. "I'm sorry about all this legal stuff, and I'm glad to meet you so I can say so."

"Thanks."

He smiled ruefully. "I know what you're thinking. Al's the spit of his mama, and they tell me you never met Vance. He was the one who looked like me—darker hair, darker eyes, darker skin, the works. It's funny about kids, you go through all that agony, raising them, and you think at least you'll have the pleasure of looking down and seeing them cry at your funeral. You don't expect to cry at theirs."

The words sounded confidently public, but his dark eyes were wet.

Lindy nodded. "I feel just terrible for you," she said.

He cleared his throat. "Well, I'm going to take that as a benediction. Al says you're a preacher. I've never held much with God, myself. I'm more interested in His Footstool, if that's what you Bible-thumpers call this." He swept his trowel around his carefully worked side yard as he led the way toward the back.

"I like land, myself," Lindy agreed.

"That's what Al said. Do you mind if I go on working while we talk?" he asked. "Vance used to hang around, get into everything. I miss it."

Lindy nodded. "I've never had that kind of family."

"Only child?"

"Yes."

He shook his head as he knelt beside a cold frame. "That

sounds lonely. Of course, everything gets lonely if you wait around for it.''

Lindy watched him trowel organic material into a ridge. "I didn't know celery grows in this climate," she said.

"It's more trouble than it's worth, and they say you oughtn't to mound it, for nutrition's sake, but we like it blanched," he said. He rocked back on his heels to inspect the sturdy, dark-green celery plants which he hadn't yet covered up to the level of their leaves. "It's funny how you get into things," he said, scratching behind his ear with the point of his trowel. "When Al was in first grade, he came home one day, showing his seat work. They were supposed to draw a picture of food. He had this row of ferny tops, like he'd seen in stores, but his carrots were these orange triangles sticking up into the air like an Iris bloom."

Lindy smiled.

"It rocked me back. I thought—what sort of father am I, good for nothing but earning money while my boys don't know a carrot is a root? Our first little garden, all we raised was bugs and worms." He chuckled.

But his smile faded as he looked out across his urban farmstead. "That's when I started working just the tax year so I could be at home doing things to include the kids. I was never an accountant like all those jokes about accountants, I just got into bookkeeping because it's orderly."

"Gardening looks orderly the way you do it," Lindy said as she looked at neatly tended pumpkin vines. She decided not to mention the subsistence plots near some of her cabins, where residents let garden seeds fight it out with weeds.

He followed her gaze. "Yes, your kids outgrow it, but by the time they do, you've gotten interested for the sake of the thing itself. We buy our meat, of course, but as far as vegetables, we're self-sufficient on just about an acre."

"That's wonderful."

Taking her interest for granted, he explained his version of rotation. Last year's garden supported an alfalfa patch where bees were busy. A carefully turned space showed where this year's summer vegetables had been. Mulch surrounded squash, cabbage, a late potato crop. Grapes covered an arbor extending a separate building which looked like a miniature barn. Raspberry canes marked the east edge of the property, and the north side was taken up by string frames for hops. Logs wired together surrounded a floating patch of cress in the edge of the lake to the west.

"We make our own beer," he said. "Talk about microbreweries." Smile lines ran into his sideburns. "Minimicro is more like it."

"It sounds like fun."

"It can be." He sighed. "I wish those kids had asked about their darned distillery. I know it's stupid to wish."

"We *all* wish," Lindy said. After a pause, she asked, "do you know what happened?"

"No, they never said a word to me, and of course now Al's so defensive, with his brother dead. I asked him why they didn't talk to me about it, but he says I'd have told them not to. Which is true." He paused to nod. "I looked into it, way back when. It's illegal, but the law's no more than the law, and you get curious, if it comes from vegetable materials."

Lindy nodded.

"Well, whiskey turns out to be an *ordeal*, which is what I could have told them. You can raise the grain, but that's hardly even the beginning."

"How did you learn?"

"The best way to learn anything is from a book."

"Could the boys have borrowed your book?" she asked.

"No, I trade books in whenever I'm through with them." He sighed. "Alice doesn't like the clutter. She says they catch dust, which of course they do. Anyway, I guess they got their information from this grandpa who died."

"I did wonder where they learned," Lindy said, trying to make the comment sound as if it didn't matter.

"Everybody likes to talk about their past, make it interesting, but it's hard to understand a man like that grandpa, not stopping to think about how some things oughtn't to be discussed."

"He told me they didn't learn from him, though," she said.

"And you believed him, did you?" Mr. Crayson said in a friendly way. "Let's see how many tall tales I can tell, to take you in."

Lindy felt disloyal to her memory of Owen, leaving such a theory uncontradicted, and yet, what could she say? She had believed Owen, but Mr. Crayson had already discounted that. She could add that it made her uneasy to blame only the dead—Owen, Vance—but she knew a feeling about fair play wasn't any answer to Mr. Crayson's logic.

"I wish we could just go back and start from the beginning and get it right, this time," Lindy said.

"Yes. Yes, that sounds like a good plan." After a moment he squinted up at her as if it were only the light which bothered his eyes. "I expect you came out here to discuss something, and it appears I haven't given you the chance."

Guiltily, Lindy realized she couldn't go on with the questions she had intended to ask. She couldn't bear for Stash to be under suspicion, and so she wanted some of the adults to look guilty instead. In theory, Mr. Crayson had seemed like a good possibility, since his sons had suffered the most. But meeting him canceled that. Or was all this family-style affability just put on? Could anyone really be so charming, in the midst of such grief? She had to find some way to ask.

"Mostly I wanted to meet you," she said. "I wanted you to know I feel sorry. My insurance and my lawyer—I don't know if they remember to say that."

"Oh, I know." He leaned the point of his trowel into the earth. "Speaking of lawyers, it's my wife who wants this lawsuit. I don't hold with it, beyond expecting whoever's responsible to make good on whatever our health insurance doesn't cover. Our family lawyer tried to tell Alice drawing up a suit now is premature, seeing that the police haven't yet said what really did happen down there, but she has her own life, of course, and anybody faces it however they can."

Lindy nodded. "I understand."

"She can't bear what's happened to Al."

"Who *can* bear it?"

"Well, yes, but her case might be a little worse." He looked into the distance awhile. "I tell her—money isn't going to change a thing. If money'd change anything, it would already be changed. I'd go back to work full-time. Anything that would change it." He looked up at Lindy with a wry smile. "Join a church, even, maybe, if that would do the job."

Lindy smiled sadly.

He nodded and sighed. "You know, poor Alice, that boy—named for her. Looks like her. Takes after her— they're both athletes, you know, even though he was into team sports whereas she rides. The point was, he was going to *be* her, in her view—her answer to everything she hates about being a woman."

"Did she grow up in a hard way?"

"No more than anyone, so far as I can see, but she says a man can't know, and maybe you can't."

It sounded feminist. It might be a good sign—maybe they could talk. Lindy tried not to let herself hope unduly.

"How do you feel about that woman's stuff?" he asked.

Lindy looked out across the dark lake. "Maybe none of us really understand what anyone's life has been. We all have to take each other on faith."

He laughed like a cough. "There's the preacher coming out."

Lindy smiled at him. "I'm not really a preacher."

"Whatever you say, Sister."

Lindy laughed.

He smiled nostalgically. "I can't tell you how long it's been since I heard anyone laugh." He looked into the air above her head. "Well, no," he corrected himself, "I can tell you *exactly* how long it's been. Do you have kids?" he asked as an afterthought.

"No."

"Smart," he told her. "Stay with that. What they're for is to break your heart."

Lindy touched his shoulder.

He drew a long breath. "I don't know why I'm sounding like this. It's been a long time since the boys hung around home, so how can I claim to miss them?"

"Where did they go, if they weren't here?"

"Oh—" He smiled at her. "Out to that cabin of yours, obviously."

Lindy looked distressed.

His smile faded at once. "I used to think they went to happier homes than this one." He glanced at his house. "Their mother says no to loud music. You can see her point. It probably isn't actually music to the kids, it's more like a pile driver, talking back." He smiled again, shaking his head. "And I'm probably much too likely to find something for them to do. I kept trying to draw them in to family life," he admitted.

"But surely that's true of everyone," Lindy said.

"No, a lot of parents don't act like us, I guess. That horse barn *wants* loud music, according to the boys, and their football coach is living alone, these days, so he likes kids around, even if all they do is sit."

Lindy tried to remember her visit to Ellie's riding arena. Had there been loud music? She didn't remember any.

"Your sons might just be saying that," she said, "but even if it's true, you have to be yourself, and they've got to deal with it."

"Can't change your spots, I guess," he agreed. "You might go talk to Alice, if you could face it?" he went on. "Maybe nothing helps, but you might help, it seems like. You got *me* to cheer up, anyway. And poor Alice, she's shopping down at Nordstrom's, trying to forget."

17

IT WAS EASY TO FIND MRS. CRAYSON BECAUSE THE AFTER-math of the region's downturn had sent most of the shop-pers to the discounters, leaving the more expensive stores in peace. She was leafing through a wall rack of tops featur-ing blacks and whites when she caught Lindy in her periph-eral vision.

"You're that lady preacher, aren't you?" she said with-out interrupting her search. "I hardly recognize you in those clothes."

Lindy looked at her reflection in the mirror alcove. "I guess not. I dressed up for the funeral."

"It wasn't a funeral."

"That's true," Lindy said, reminding herself of the very structured church which had performed the funeral for Vance. She hadn't stopped to think, before, how her ap-proach at Owen's service must have appalled Mrs. Cray-son.

"My husband told you where to find me?" Mrs. Cray-son asked.

Lindy nodded. "I stopped by your house. It seems like we're all in this together, and I wanted to say how sorry I am about every part of the whole tragedy."

Mrs. Crayson took off the loose jacket she had tried on and held it up to Lindy's face. "You're right not to wear black. Makes you sallow."

Lindy nodded. She recognized the symptom—people locked in the first terrible grip of grief usually had difficulty following a line of thought very long or very consistently.

Mrs. Crayson's abruptness made her heart ache.

"I suppose I shouldn't wear colors," Mrs. Crayson added, tossing the jacket over a nearby round rack.

"Of course you should, if you like them," Lindy said. "There are some pretty colors on the other side of the mirror," she added, determined to follow whatever topic Mrs. Crayson offered.

Mrs. Crayson went to the rack Lindy had pointed out. "Do you wear teal?" she asked as she chose a jacket and stepped in front of the mirror to try it on.

"I haven't," Lindy said. "It looks good on you, but I don't know if it will last."

Mrs. Crayson ran a neutral inspection over Lindy's sweater and skirt.

"I noticed you were years out of date," she said as she held her teal-clad arm up to Lindy's face. They looked at their reflections a moment, and then Mrs. Crayson slipped out of the jacket and held it for Lindy. Lindy pulled off her sweater, aware that she didn't deal with clothing as gracefully as Mrs. Crayson did. She thrust her arms into the slightly warmed sleeves of the jacket Mrs. Crayson held. The secondhand feel of the garment was disconcerting, as if they should have been friends before they wore each other's clothes. But maybe that was the point—maybe Mrs. Crayson was making friends. Lindy was glad to encourage her.

"Turn around," Mrs. Crayson said. "Yes. Looks good."

Lindy smiled. "I didn't really come to shop."

"I suppose you mean I shouldn't be shopping."

"No. Why shouldn't you shop?"

Mrs. Crayson stared at her.

"I think you're right to do anything active, anything that helps the time pass for these next few weeks, few months. What you're facing is just too hard. Hard beyond imagining."

Mrs. Crayson turned so she could study Lindy's reflection in the mirror. "Haven't you been told I'm suing you?"

"Yes." Lindy took off the jacket, arranging it tidily on its

161

hanger, giving herself time to stop feeling caught off guard.

"That *is* why you're here, then—hoping to talk me out of it. Don't bother," Mrs. Crayson said as she pulled an orange vest off its hanger.

"I hoped it might help if we talk everything over, just as ourselves. Lawyers can't help about feelings."

"Indeed they do," Mrs. Crayson said, inspecting the reflection of her backline in the orange vest. "When our lawyer explained what you win in a civil suit, I felt better for the first time in who knows how long."

Mrs. Crayson's mouth drew down in an honest bitterness that was painful to watch. Lindy wondered if anything could help. Thinking about the almost empty store, she remembered how her mother used to love to shop, as a form of social life involving only women. Back before two-income families were the norm, and before mail-order was the usual source, stores were jammed. Lindy remembered lingering as a child, bored and unwilling, while her mother drifted among racks of clothing, commenting to nearby strangers who offered something friendly in return, everyone smiling, content. Mrs. Crayson was old enough to have enjoyed that ritual. She must have felt betrayed, when the stores emptied of everyone but tourists. And now, her own arrival here must have provided a nostalgic moment, Lindy realized.

Could Mrs. Crayson be coaxed to join a women's group, as a replacement? Lindy wondered. She could arrange an invitation to the Thursday group—not right away, but maybe in a month or two. And for now, was there any way to help?

But Mrs. Crayson didn't wait for help. "Let's go look at shoes," she said as she tossed the orange vest onto a round rack.

They wove a path through the racks of separates and sat down side-by-side near the boots. As Mrs. Crayson frowned at the display, Lindy realized how this process must seem to her. At home, there would be no escape from her husband's frank wrestling with regret. Her son's defensive rage would be even more disturbing. And behind everything else would lie the silence where her other son should be. But here, relationships were financial, without undercurrents or needs.

A clerk strolled over to them.

"Professor Adair!" he said, his face igniting in a grin.

Lindy inspected quickly—sandy hair cut short all over, no sideburns, pale eyes, high, freckled cheekbones, a long jaw above a flexible neck and lanky body. She didn't remember him.

"No," he said in answer to the survey, "you don't remember me. It's my brother. He pointed you out to me one day on campus. He was in your Logic 201, and he's never stopped talking about you."

Lindy smiled. "Well, maybe I return the favor and talk about him. What's his name?"

"Judson Dade."

Lindy's smile brightened. "Oh, yes, I remember Judson. He sat by the windows and kept them open no matter how cold it got, which was fine with me because I prefer it cool."

"He used to work nights. He didn't want to miss a word, but he was scared he'd fall asleep."

They both laughed.

Mrs. Crayson interrupted with her shoe size and asked to see all their top-of-the-calf boots. "Do you get tired of that?" she asked as the clerk disappeared.

"I liked my students," Lindy said instead of answering directly.

"I've never held a job," Mrs. Crayson said.

"It's fun," Lindy said, "but you give up your privacy."

"Having a blind child takes away your privacy," Mrs. Crayson said as she leaned over to remove one shoe.

Lindy had been thinking about Judson. Being dragged back to Mrs. Crayson's trouble left her feeling as if she had been punched. "Will rehabilitation help?" she asked softly.

"Who knows." Mrs. Crayson straightened up. "There's

a school in Seattle. I want Al to go, but it's a boarding school, and he refuses to leave town. His father backs him up, which he shouldn't."

"His friends are here," Lindy said, "he probably thinks about that. I know I would."

"Friends? No—just the one." There was an edge to her voice which alerted Lindy.

"His girlfriend?"

"She's no girl."

"She seemed nice, at the services," Lindy said. "I haven't met her, of course."

"Don't," Mrs. Crayson agreed.

When the clerk returned with an armload of boxes, she held out her stockingfoot. "What's your size?" she asked, looking at Lindy's feet.

"Same as yours," Lindy said, quite sure tact required her not to proclaim her half-size smaller feet. "But I don't need anything new at the moment," she added as she stood up.

"I'd enjoy showing you things, to see if that would change," Judson Dade's brother said optimistically.

Lindy smiled at him. "I'm trying to watch my budget. I know that's not good news." She turned to Mrs. Crayson, to add, "it was good of you to talk to me."

Mrs. Crayson lifted one hand in a small wave without looking up from her foot.

Lindy wandered out into the mall, feeling depressed. Mrs. Crayson was dealing with her grief in a way that was hard to watch. Probably it would be better for Al to get out of the house, she decided as she returned to her car. If you had made a mistake as important as Al's, it would be dreadful to face your mother's despair every day.

She puzzled over family life all the way home. When she went into the house, she was stopped by her phone's red message light. She punched the reply reluctantly. Richison's open-throated California voice poured into the room.

"Lindy, Richison here. I'm sure you assume your alibi held up, but I'll say so to start with because I want to follow it up by asking a favor. I'm trying to assemble everybody involved in Stash Sonner's situation so we can resolve this thing. I want them to come out there to you, where nobody's going to walk in and give them an excuse to think of something else, or drag them away to a so-called emergency. Stash is still in what amounts to detention, but the other kids aren't, which doesn't sound fair to me, and I'm assuming you feel the same. Is your calendar clear at ten tomorrow morning?"

He could have been anybody, Lindy thought as she dialed the number he had left, an uncle, anybody. If you didn't see his frozen face, you wouldn't think of him as a cop.

When she identified herself to the police switchboard, she was patched through to a crackling voice that said, "Richison."

"Ten's okay," she said.

"Thanks. I'd appreciate coffee for six people. But no food. It's *amazing* how these people can distract themselves."

Lindy laughed.

"Yeah," he said.

When they hung up, Lindy went outside at last. Mist silvered the meadow grass, but in the woods, falling moisture lodged on the higher needles and leaves and didn't reach the ground. She stood at the edge of an open space where ivory-rimmed peach ruffles of fungus lined every seam in the crumbling bark of a downed fir trunk. She gazed a long time, grateful for the renewed beauty which rain was bringing to the forest.

At early dark, she went back inside. Knowing Brent's attitude toward Stash, and his conflict with Richison over it, she dreaded tomorrow's meeting. She didn't want to eat, but she dug a portion of chicken stock out of the freezer and added rice and slivered spinach to provide a low-stress meal. She didn't want to go to bed, but she went anyway, lying sleepless. Sometime after three, she realized what she feared. They might be going to draw her into the social ser-

165

vices structure. Stash had asked to live out here. Richison must have scheduled the meeting here so they could see what Stash was requesting. Would they insist she qualify as a halfway house or group home or foster family? And if they did, after Faith's appeal, and knowing Stash's need, could she refuse?

When the sky lightened, she got up bleary-eyed and arranged chairs in front of the fireplace. She built a fire, for cheerfulness, using *fully* aged and *totally* dry wood so the smoke would have less than the twenty percent opacity rating allowed by law. These people weren't wood smoke enforcers, but if they took a dislike to her, they could complain to people who were. She didn't have a party coffee pot, but she had a spare family size carafe, so she dripped a second batch as soon as the first was ready. She was glad the preparations took a while, because she didn't want to seem worried, and she knew her feelings would show, if there was time to think.

At ten o'clock, the stamping of a single pair of feet brought her to the door.

Richison stepped inside onto the tiles. "I gave us a few minutes before the rest of them get here," he explained as he brushed rain out of his coffee-colored hair.

Lindy took his parka, giving it a practiced shake outside the door before she hung it in the kitchen alcove which also housed the microwave and chainsaw. Richison filled two of the mugs she had set out on the marble slab beside the stovetop, adding milk to both before he went to the living room in an at-home way. By the time Lindy followed him, he had arranged their mugs on a small table in the middle of the half circle of chairs facing the fire.

"I thought you'd want to know what happened the other day with Sunny," he said as she sat down beside him.

Lindy nodded.

"You pretend you don't have an established system going, here, but your residents came to your rescue loud and clear."

Lindy tried to judge his eyes, but their blue depths held a

feeling she couldn't assess. She waited silently.

"I'd hate to go into court with your people as my sole support, especially facing those solid citizen types over there in Owen's neighborhood. But these witnesses out here make sense and they know what they saw. You were home all afternoon, and they're ready to go through fire about it."

"It sounds as if Sunny introduced you around," Lindy said.

"Yeah, she did. Very helpful. Determined to protect you, just like you tried to shield her. Nice for the two of you. A little negative toward me."

Lindy sighed. "You're a cop."

"Yeah."

"It makes me angry, but I see why you have to suspect me," she said in response to the hint of loneliness in his eyes.

"I didn't suspect you, I told you that," he said. "But I had to check this out for your student's sake. If Fuller had questioned you, and you answered the wrong way, he'd have had to put handcuffs on you, and I don't think he could have done it."

She stared into the fire. "No, I suppose he couldn't."

"I wanted to clear it up."

"It doesn't matter," Lindy said. "You did your job."

"It matters," he said. "You're trying to be tolerant of me, and even if you were succeeding, which in my judgment you aren't, even if you were, that's not good enough. I want you working with me."

She looked at him for a long, stressed moment. "You didn't hurt Sunny, did you?"

"No. Absolutely not." He met her gaze. "But I can see why you had to question me about it," he added.

When she finally managed to smile, he grinned disarmingly.

"Now that I've got an alibi, will you tell me what your witnesses said about me?" she asked.

If he recognized it as a challenge, he gave no sign. He

tipped one hand over to show his palm, as if they had always enjoyed each other's total trust.

"Somebody visited Owen in the middle of the afternoon. They swear it was the same person as the morning visit. They're a little less sure about the evening visitor."

"They saw a stranger? I mean—I look like anybody else, provided they didn't recognize me by name," she reminded him.

He laughed. When she flushed, he toned it down to a wide smile. "The descriptions we're working from won't pick one person out of a city full of strangers, but they don't have to. You're the only possibility, unless we can expand the list."

Lindy rubbed her eyes. "Do I look like anyone to you?"

"No, but you know more people than I do, so you're the one to figure this out. We need to talk to whoever they saw. At the least, they can narrow down the time we're concerned with."

Lindy brushed her dark hair off her forehead. "In books, the autopsy says when someone died."

"Yeah, that works in Bellingham, too," he said. "If our witnesses are right, your look-alike got there maybe an hour or so before Owen died." He shrugged. "She may not know a thing. But the fact that she doesn't come forward makes you suspect probably she does."

"Not necessarily," Lindy said. "She could be just scared. I know I am."

"Maybe. But whatever, she's got to say it to me."

18

THEY BEGAN TO HEAR CARS LABORING UP HER DRIVEWAY. Lindy went to the door as a caravan entered her clearing. Brent parked in the edge of her meadow and got out of his car to watch the rest of them fan out and park without a thought to the tracks they were digging into the grass. When Brent turned and saw Lindy, he smiled. The rest of them stepped out of their cars without a glance and hurried toward the house, hunched against the light rain.

In the entryway, the state employees introduced themselves but didn't hold out their hands. Their business suits seemed painfully out of place on the Sunstrike, making Lindy glad she had taken trouble with her appearance—she had matched her most expensive wool slacks with a silk shirt. She gestured them toward the living room, where they looked surprised at the hominess she had achieved in the lodgesized space.

Richison poured their coffees as if he were the acknowledged host. Lindy realized Brent was watching him speculatively. She smiled at Brent to ease the situation, if it could be eased.

"I'd like to run this like any case conference," Richison began. "Everybody has their say, but we're not leaving here until we have a plan everyone can accept."

Lindy thought it sounded like a long day, but maybe cops were more efficient than academics, she reminded herself. On the other hand, only two of these were cops, she thought as she scanned the half circle of frowns.

"The Sonner child has an environment which is hostile

169

in every way," the friend of the court said, cradling his coffee mug in both hands, "we're not releasing him."

"He isn't a child," Stash's caseworker said. "If he were, he could live with his mother."

"She isn't his mother," a state appointed lawyer said. "I'm representing his father, who's in the county jail as a farmer raising the best cash crop he can find. But try to tell that to the prosecutor's office."

"What is the best cash crop?" Lindy asked, thinking about Mr. Crayson's carefully tended celery.

"Marijuana."

Lindy laughed.

Everyone stared at her.

"I just was thinking of it from his point of view," she said.

No one answered.

"Will the court go for that? Can he be retrained to farm something else?" she persisted.

"Hard to say," his lawyer said. "But he's in custody now and can't supervise his son—that's the point at the moment."

"The boy insists he belongs out here in the county," Stash's caseworker said. "He wants to be on his own."

"He's proved it doesn't work, living there with that still," the friend of the court said. He turned to Lindy. "Were you aware he was living down there?"

"No. A member of someone else's family mentioned it, after all this happened, but I don't know it for myself."

"Are you willing to take responsibility for him?" Faith's lawyer asked.

The whole thing *was* a trap, Lindy realized. She was afraid her irritation would keep her from thinking clearly, and so she took her time, waiting until she felt ready, and then speaking slowly.

"It might seem to you that I have a lot of space for one person, but I haven't been into house-sharing," she explained. "I like people, so I tend to adjust and think of them, when they're around. But my work focuses on val-

170

ues, and I think about theoretical issues more clearly when I'm alone."

"I notice there's nothing on your walls," the friend of the court said. "Is that one of these 'values,' or are you moving out?"

Lindy gazed at her walls. They were real boards, not paneling. To her, they were beautiful and deserved not being covered up. But that wasn't why they were bare, and she decided the truth might prevent a digression into esthetic systems.

"My former husband was artistic," she said. "I haven't been able to stand paintings, ever since my divorce."

Richison and Brent looked at her, but the rest of them stared at the walls.

"What about letting Stash be supervised by this writer he keeps talking about?" Brent asked. Feeling Lindy's curious gaze, he shrugged.

"I'm glad you're thinking along those lines," she said.

He smiled.

Everyone watched them.

"What writer?" the friend of the court asked.

"Rascal Dunn is what he writes under. Nicodemus is his birth name," Lindy answered.

"Never heard of him."

"You should have," Brent said. "Stash doesn't talk about much else. Identifies himself as a Leemunterstrock, which appears to be some kind of a nonhuman I don't really know what, from, is it an asteroid?"

"Nick writes science fiction," Lindy said to the shocked friend of the court.

"You know him?" Stash's caseworker said.

When Lindy hesitated, Brent cut in, "He lives here on the Sunstrike."

"It isn't really the Sunstrike anymore," Lindy said.

They all stared at her.

"The guy's a published writer?" the friend of the court asked after a moment.

Lindy nodded.

"You have residents who aren't on the edge?" the case-worker asked.

Lindy folded her arms. "For one thing, people come out here according to their own decision. They don't pass a needs test. And for something else, writers make less than you think. At least, most of them do. They seem to live on nothing. Shoe strings."

"This writer of yours is broke?" the friend of the court persisted.

"I've never asked, and he isn't exactly mine."

"What difference does it make, if Stash can't read?" the state appointed attorney asked.

"Who says he can't read?" Faith's lawyer said. "He's performing above grade level, according to his school reports."

"His eyes," the state appointed attorney said.

"He's capable of living on his own," Richison said. "Haven't any of you people checked with his doctor?"

Silence fell.

"This writer, then," Stash's caseworker said. "Who knows him?" He looked around the circle.

"Would Nick join us, Lindy?" Richison asked so expansively Lindy realized it was what he had planned for.

"I could call and ask," she said, trying to feel resigned.

"Do."

From the desperate glance Brent shot toward Richison, Lindy suspected the conversation wasn't like any case conference he had ever attended, but it seemed to be working the way Richison wanted, and so she got up and went to the entryhall. As she punched in the local network code, she could hear the men begin to murmur, in the other room. She wondered if they truly thought they had to work behind her back. Probably they were simply expressing conspiratorial personalities, she decided.

"Dunn," a voice finally said in her ear.

"There's a gathering of public service individuals over here, Nick," Lindy said, aware of the abrupt, eavesdropping silence in the next room. "They're discussing a seventeen-year-old kid who needs a place to stay, and since he's an ardent fan of yours, they might let him crash somewhere under your wing, provided your wings look terrestrial enough."

Nick's reverberating laugh rang down the phone line. "On my way. I gather fatigues are out?"

"Sort of."

His phone crashed into its pad. Lindy took a coffee pot with her when she returned to the silent living room. Brent thanked her for his coffee, and Richison smiled up at her meaningfully, but the rest of them simply accepted the service as if it were due. No one moved but her, and when she returned from putting the pot back on the stove, everyone was staring into the fire.

"Lindy," Nick called as he came through the back door, stamping himself free of the rain.

Lindy wasn't sure it had been a good idea to call him. When no one else was around, she didn't think about it, but now, compared to these state employees, he seemed to fill the room as if he really were a space hero. It wasn't just that he was taller than anyone else. He seemed to have been constructed on a more universal scale, seeing sights beyond the limits of this globe, thinking thoughts wider than the limits of this galaxy, entertaining feelings more profound than merely human sensibilities.

Even so, he had taken time to be cooperative, putting on an elegantly distressed suede jacket over a camera-ready blue shirt. His gray slacks fitted smoothly over a flat stomach and athletic legs. Booted feet made him seem ready to embark a space capsule at any moment.

He quickly surveyed the watching faces, nodding and saying "Fuller" noncommittally when he spotted Brent. When she started to pull another chair into the half circle, he sprang to help, smiling as if everything amused him.

"This is Nicodemus Dunn," Lindy said as she went back to the kitchen. "I'll let you say your own names."

When she returned with a mug of sugared coffee for Nick, the men were just sitting down again.

"Do you know Stash Sonner?" the friend of the court asked Nick.

"Not knowingly."

"You ought to," Stash's caseworker said. "He can recite every word of every book you've ever written."

"Well, that's good," Nick said soberly. "A writer needs fans, so there's my start, there's my one."

Lindy smiled. "You're the object of a constant parade of fans, and you know it. You cause traffic jams."

He cast her a meek-eyed look. "I'm always afraid they'll change their minds when they see me in a good light, or they've gotten me mixed up with someone else, or they're new immigrants and their English isn't very good yet."

Richison laughed.

Nick gazed at him interestedly.

"I'm trying to set up a bargain," Richison said. "If Stash's lawyer pleads him guilty-but-naïve, I can get him off with time served in shelter care, plus probation, but he's got to have somewhere to be, where there's at least a hope of having him supervised but not nagged."

"Guilty!" Lindy said. "No! He doesn't even slap mosquitoes—I've seen him just brush them aside!"

"Guilty of participating in a still," Richison said, his face a warning. "If you remember, Professor Adair, an illegal still is what this investigation started out to be."

"That's true, Dr. Adair," Brent said.

"I forget." Lindy drew a long breath. "The other seems so much more important. Part of the time I forget the first."

"Have you met this kid, Lindy?" Nick asked.

She nodded. "He hangs around," she admitted, since Stash seemed to have said so himself. "I suspected you're the magnet even before people started telling me so. He's fascinated by computers, but he hasn't got the money for them. I've wished there could be some way to get him going. Into college early, or *something*. His mother's a good person and does her best for him, but it's hard since they aren't related.''

"Well, assuming I pass muster, I could have a coke with him, afternoons, play father, or whatever men do.''

"Mr. Sonner is in no position to provide a home for the boy, but he does *not* relinquish his parental rights, and I'm here to see those rights enforced," the state appointed lawyer said. "I'll remind you that Mr. Sonner *is* the boy's guardian.''

"It's well and good to claim this inmate's rights," Stash's caseworker said, "but Stash is living in shelter care, which makes the house manager his temporary guardian.''

"*Temporary* is *right*," both lawyers said.

"Maybe we can solve this by saying I'll talk to the kid just one-on-one without saying exactly what I am," Nick said with the quick tolerance of a man who daily dealt off-world with aliens. "And maybe Genevieve would take care of the rest of his routines. I'm assuming he's wholesome, if you're interested in him, Lindy, and Genevieve would probably enjoy having somebody lug wood in exchange for whatever he needs.''

"Genevieve?" all the state employees asked.

"She's the woman across the trail and down from you, Nick, is that right?" Richison explained. "Grandmotherly? Offered me a gingerbread square—is that the one?''

"Right. She makes great gingerbread," Nick said.

"She certainly does," Richison said. "Sunny introduced us. Genevieve seems to know everybody, so probably a teenager wouldn't mind having to let her know about him, too.''

Lindy smiled at him.

"You know," Nick said. "If one of you social service types can get this kid an early admission to the community college, it might turn him around, from what you just said, Lindy. And I'm sure we could get a ride for him.''

"Terry's still driving down to the tech school, isn't he?" Lindy asked.

"He was the last time I saw him at the grocery store,''

Nick said, "but some of the ones going to the university have more reliable wheels. They could swing past the community college, couldn't they?"

"Yes. And talking to them would get him thinking about transferring to the computer science program at the university, as soon as he has a record at the community college."

"Well," Richison said. "This is resolved, then? Good."

"Absolutely not," the friend of the court answered. "If neither Professor Adair nor Mr. Dunn is appointed as resident supervisor, then I need to meet the person who is to serve in that capacity."

"Would that be Genevieve?" Lindy asked.

"I don't want to see her over here," the friend of the court said with a patting motion to hold Lindy back. "I want to inspect *in situ*."

"Would that be a problem, Lindy?" Richison asked. "Genevieve didn't seem to mind when I dropped in with Sunny."

"Okay, but I want to call her."

Richison nodded. "That's fair." He surveyed the closed faces around the half ring. "Lindy's going to call," he announced.

No one answered.

Nick laughed.

19

LINDY WATCHED THEM DRIVE AWAY, NICK RIDING WITH RIchison to lead the caravan. Grateful to have it over, she went upstairs for jeans and spent the rest of the day with a maul and wedge, splitting wood beside the grapevine which shrouded the woodshed. Taking her time, enjoying it, she self-indulgently saw a power-tripping face on the head of the wedge every time she swung the mall down on it with whole-body effort.

She stopped early, so she could shower and microwave a frozen serving of chicken lasagna before she headed to town for her Tuesday bookstore group. Languidly relaxed from the physical day, she decided her feelings had retreated to a manageable level. It ought to mean she could trust her reactions, and that was good because of what she hoped to do.

As usual, it was raining harder on the bay side of Stewart Mountain. In the city, she splashed toward the mall. Water several inches deep clogged the parking lot where the new drain hadn't yet been installed. She left her Subaru under the nearest light and dashed through the downpour, grateful not to dodge sawhorses now that the rebuilding had moved beyond *Ours*.

"It's a mess out there," the bookstore owner told her cheerfully when Lindy stripped out of her light-blue foul weather jacket and reached outside the door to shake it over the sidewalk.

"*That's* true," Lindy said as she dropped her jacket onto the pile of wet clothing just inside the door and headed for

177

the meeting room. When the convener asked for urgent topics, Lindy held up her hand.

"My values are in conflict," she said, "and I'd like to hear what everyone thinks about a problem I haven't solved. If that's okay—I know it's interrupting our schedule."

"Of *course* it's okay," the convener said. She looked around the group. When she had collected unanimous nods and murmurs, she gestured to Lindy.

"Here's what's worrying me," Lindy said. "I don't know how you're supposed to feel toward someone who's suddenly got a serious handicap, if they caused it themselves and broke the law to cause it. I mean, a drunk driver plows into a family—you know *exactly* what to think. Or you fall off a trail on Mount Baker and by the time Search and Rescue reaches you, your broken leg has to be amputated—you know what to think. But say a friend or family member makes illegal whiskey and gets it wrong and drinks it anyway and goes blind—what's all right to feel? Should you blame them? Blame somebody else? Say 'oh, sorry, bad luck,' no responsibilities mentioned? Or what?"

They spent three hours debating it, defending all possible sides. Faith arrived late. The women she sat beside whispered to catch her up, apparently not realizing she was involved.

When the meeting broke up, the convener walked out of the backroom at Lindy's side. "Was that helpful?"

Lindy nodded soberly. "I've been needing to know what normal feelings are," she admitted. "It seems like I feel something different, every time I meet someone else who's tangled up in this. I'm just so tired of being confused, on top of everything else."

"Well, *that's* normal, anyway," the convener said.

They both smiled gamely at the not-very-amusing joke as they stepped out into the driving rain.

Faith was waiting by Lindy's car, water cascading off her navy windshirt. "Talk a minute?" she asked, as Lindy dashed toward her.

Lindy unlocked quickly. Once inside, they sat gasping and brushing at themselves, half-laughing at their hopeless state.

"That detective of yours came over this afternoon," Faith said at last. "I don't really like cops hanging around the rescue house, but he seems sincere. Is he?"

"I think so."

"He says he worked out this situation for Stash, because a whole bunch of you there on the Sunstrike came to the rescue. He says I owe you, and I do, but I don't know how to pay."

"You don't owe me," Lindy said. "All these years, you've been raising a kid who wasn't yours. Now you're getting a little help at last. How does 'owe' get into that, unless it's what the rest of society owes you?"

Faith shook her head, raindrops flying. "Try it this way. If Stash had lived with me, he wouldn't have been crashing in your cabin. If he hadn't been down there to watch it, they wouldn't have been able to use that still. If they hadn't used the still, you wouldn't lose your property. Your cop says it's beautiful out there."

Lindy tried not to notice how casually Faith assumed her property was lost. Hearing it said made it seem more real, an omen.

"Those kids were going to build their still," she said. "If not there, somewhere."

"Probably." Faith sounded grudging. "Knowing them."

"Do you know what drives me crazy?" Lindy asked. "What happened wasn't *meant*. I know there was that call to the tip line, but it can't be right. So why do we all feel guilty?"

Faith inspected her face gravely. Suddenly she laughed. Embarrassed by the tactless reaction, she covered her mouth with one thin hand, but she went on laughing.

Catching it, Lindy smiled. "What are you thinking?"

"You shouldn't be saying no one's to blame. What you ought to be is so angry *you're* the one going around killing people," Faith said. "It's *weird* to hear you talk like this."

Lindy's smile disappeared completely.

Faith touched her wet shoulder. "I'm just saying what you should. I'm not saying you did."

"I wonder how many people think that?"

"So what if we do?" Faith persisted. "Anybody'd call it justified."

No, I wouldn't, Lindy answered silently, and neither would Richison. But—could Faith be right about everyone else?

LINDY WAS GLAD the next day was Wednesday. During her life as a teacher, she had become friends with a university counselor, Maggie Anderson. When Lindy lost her job, they didn't see each other casually at work anymore, and so they agreed to meet for dinner twice a month, in order to stay in each other's life. Making it ceremonial, they had a standing reservation at one of the recreational port's restaurants, *The Visitor Dock*.

Since she was meeting a faculty member, Lindy wore campus clothes—jeans tight enough to suggest stirrup pants under a sweater big enough to pass as a tunic. Maggie was already at the restaurant, sitting beside the window at their usual table, watching private boats parade down the channel toward the open Bay. Seeing her, Lindy smiled. Maggie didn't brighten her straw-colored hair. She wore no makeup, and so nothing interfered with the mild look which seemed so appropriate to her gray eyes.

It was also appropriate to a counselor who dealt almost exclusively with strangers. As the university's front-line crisis counselor, Maggie had an enormous caseload. Lindy knew how often she worked after hours, but she never mentioned it, never looked frazzled, never allowed herself to seem absent.

As Lindy joined her, she smiled a welcome. Their usual waitress brought their iced teas without asking, said "your usual?" without listening for the answer, and cleared away their menus with a friendly flourish. Lindy joined in watching the boats, discussing them idly, sipping her tea, relaxing. Maggie told a campus story so they both could laugh.

"Are the newspapers getting this chaos right?" Maggie asked at last.

Lindy watched their waitress arrange their crab and grapefruit dinner salads. "I haven't been reading the papers," she said when they were alone again.

"I thought you'd call if you wanted to talk," Maggie said as she picked up her fork.

Lindy nodded. "But I wouldn't have known what to say, beyond '*help!*' "

"There's nothing wrong with 'help.' "

Lindy smiled.

"Greg Patrick talked to me," Maggie said after a bite of crab. "Officially he wants advice on helping his sons face things, but from the way he sounded, I got the impression you were more of a concern."

"This cop asked me to be his ride-along," Lindy explained. "I'd been crying when we went to see Greg."

Maggie nodded noncommittally.

"Maggie—" Lindy stopped.

When Maggie seemed prepared to wait all night, looking pleasant and undisturbed, Lindy realized she was on the receiving end of Maggie's professional mode. Maggie had the extreme quietness which most counselors cultivated, but it seemed natural, from Maggie. Even so, Lindy hated to turn into a client instead of a friend.

"I'm afraid there's something wrong with me," she admitted. "One of the mothers said I ought to be going around killing people, but I don't *feel* angry, or cruel, or at least I don't think I do. I'm afraid, whenever I think about being sued, but even then, I don't feel like killing anyone. Or am I just kidding myself?"

"No," Maggie said softly, "what you think you feel really is what you feel, I'd say, from knowing you all these years."

When Lindy couldn't stop frowning, Maggie sighed. "People have all different ways of dealing with what they can't bear. We've done so much talking about the grieving process, we forget the people going through it are individuals."

Lindy studied her salad.

"I can't imagine you killing anybody, or even thinking up how to accomplish something like that," Maggie said.

Lindy brushed her short temple hair.

"When you lost your job, you weren't into hating, even then, were you?" Maggie went on.

Lindy shook her head without looking up. "It hurt. But so? Hating wouldn't have changed anything."

"Exactly. And the same thing now. You always just go with the feeling itself and don't cover it up with anger. That's your pattern. Your nature."

Lindy rubbed her forehead.

"When people say you should be angry enough to kill, they're thinking of the grandfather's death, of course, but what they're really doing is just going through it with you, saying what they'd feel, themselves," Maggie insisted. "They'd feel trapped, if they'd been caught in the aftermath of the birder cabin tragedy, the way you have been. They know they'd lash out. They assume anyone would. That's all they're saying."

Disconcertingly, Lindy remembered Richison's claim that she lived in a pretty world. He ought to meet Maggie, she thought wryly, if he wants to confront a pretty world.

"*Do* people lash out?" she asked.

Maggie meditatively ran a long finger down the side of her ice tea glass. "Usually they just talk."

"And go to their counselor."

Maggie smiled.

"I've talked with all the families," Lindy said after a while. "The one suing me, the father seemed sympathetic, but how do you know? The mother has this really abrupt manner, but who wouldn't?"

"It didn't go well?"

"No." Lindy sighed. "Her lawyer's trying to draw her out of herself by getting her interested in this civil suit they're bringing against me, and maybe that's working out for her, at least a little bit. But her husband says he doesn't care about the suit because he blames Owen instead of blaming me. How do you know which version to believe?"

Maggie toyed with a breadstick. "Maybe you should believe them both. They're bound to have mood swings if they disagree."

"I hadn't thought of that." Lindy's voice trembled and so she gazed across the channel at the moorage for a few moments.

"How dangerous is the suit?" Maggie asked as she picked up her knife.

"I don't know. My lawyer says they're asking for the moon, but that's assuming I'm guilty of this 'controlled substances homicide,' which I'd never even heard of, had you?"

"Oh, it comes up once in a while," Maggie said. "Is there any reason to think it applies to you?"

"I'm not sure. Apparently they built their still partly with equipment from the Sunstrike, and it seems likely they borrowed the things themselves, but it's hard to know what a jury might think, if it gets that far."

"No it isn't, is it? Owen's death puts you in the clear, doesn't it? Whoever killed Owen must have been involved in the first tragedy, surely, from what the papers are saying, and this second tragedy doesn't relate to the Sunstrike."

Lindy watched Maggie butter her breadstick. "It might. The Bellingham cop, Richison, has a witness to my being at Owen's house at the wrong time."

"Eyewitness reports aren't reliable," Maggie said absolutely. "We've run tests. If twelve people witness an event, you'll get fourteen contradictory descriptions of it. If the witnesses talk among themselves before they file statements, the strongest personality—not the best observer—is the one who gets everyone to say the same thing."

Lindy had heard the data before, and so she let it go. "He says a person's history doesn't really matter because we're all killers when we want to be," she answered instead. "It makes me nervous to know he thinks that."

Maggie set down her bread. "He's in trouble, isn't he? Shall I talk to him?"

"No, I've got contradicting witnesses."

"I didn't mean that, because he can't be applying his general principle to you." Maggie looked past Lindy, smiling slightly and shaking her head to keep the waitress at bay. "I was thinking about him. If he really does believe everyone is a potential killer, he may be dealing with stress not very effectively."

"Oh. Well, or this might be just something he says. He wants me to start locking my door."

Lindy had expected her to smile, but Maggie looked thoughtful, instead. "I wonder if maybe you should."

Lindy sighed.

"Would you eat, if we talk about something else?" Maggie asked.

Lindy picked up her fork. "I'm just so scared, is all."

"So there's two of us," Maggie said, "I'm scared for you."

20

DAN WAS PUZZLED BY LINDY'S BEHAVIOR AT THE CASE CON-
ference. As a teacher, she would have to be used to groups,
and yet she had seemed uncomfortable. Or, no, not uncomfortable exactly, he decided. Remote was more likely
what she had seemed. She had smiled easily at Brent Fuller—that was to reassure him as a former student. And she
had smiled confidingly at Nick Dunn—to reassure him as
one of her communards. And she had smiled easily at
him—probably to forgive him for intruding on her. But she
had been just this side of invisible with everyone else. Did
she have a reason for freezing state employees?

The smiles were a problem in themselves. They seemed
as asexual as a child's. She was very definitely a woman, but
she never gave the least hint of realizing what that seemed
like to a man. He had to know why. People who masked
their reactions were sometimes just very courteous, and
that was fine, especially in a public figure. But in his experience, self-control could sometimes mean that, if you ever
got inside, you'd conclude you'd jarred the lid off the
devil's cauldron.

Talking to Lindy in a variety of circumstances hadn't let
him make up his mind about her. She had the ability to
speak frankly without seeming intimate, and even when she
cried, she made anyone feel it was something she preferred
to do alone. He was going to have to ask what she really
was, and he could think of only one person who would
surely know.

And so he drove to the Fort Bellingham area, where most

of the houses were built of weathered wood, appropriate to a sandy low bank overlooking the tangle between land and water where the Nooksack River had built its delta while dumping into the bay. The house owned by Lindy's former husband was different. It belonged in a desert. Its orange tile roof was disconcerting under heavy skies, and its cement walls didn't resemble stucco since they weren't cracking and absorbing destructive moisture in the steady rain. Its arched doorway guarded by a wrought-iron grid protected a bright blue front door which couldn't possibly need shelter from the pale, local sun.

Dan stood in the entryway, coping with surprise as he rang the doorbell. The door swung inward while he was still frowning about it. An anorexically slender man with sepulchrally dark hair and eyes stood watching him, a trio of paint brushes clenched upright in one hand.

"Nathan Adair?" Dan asked, showing his shield and giving his name and rank.

"It's Lindy you want, no doubt, she doesn't live here," Nathan said in a light, flexibly modulated voice.

"I wanted to talk *about* her," Richison said.

Nathan stepped back, flinging the door open with a generous gesture. "Parka, if you wish," he said, pointing toward an old-fashioned brass-and-oak pillar rising out of an umbrella stand. Without waiting to see what Dan would do, he walked across tan tiled floors scattered with Navajo rugs toward a kiva-style fireplace which blocked the view.

Dan stripped out of his parka and shook it outside the door, as he had seen locals do. He hung it on the coat tree before following Nathan.

"I haven't seen a place like this since I've been in Bellingham," he said, glancing at the cream walls which were covered by nonrepresentational paintings under glass.

"Carmel," Nathan said. "I just returned last night."

"I've never been to Carmel," Dan said.

"Ah," Nathan said.

Dan sat down on the unpadded chair of black-stained pine beside the similar chair Nathan had selected for himself in front of the small fire. He decided discomfort wasn't a means of shortening visits, since all the furniture was artistic. Instead of cupboards, there were ornately carved Spanish armoires and black pine chests. Instead of couches, there were monastery benches. Instead of occasional chairs, there were these wooden seats. There was no sign of comfort anywhere. He began to understand Lindy's mostly built-in furnishings.

"I realize you and Lindy are divorced, but I can't find anyone else who knows her well enough to talk about her."

"Yes, well, a trip to the past," Nathan said.

"What's she like?"

Nathan gestured with both hands. "What you see is what you do not get."

"Okay, but here's my problem," Dan said. "I've talked to some of her former students and former colleagues, and you can see their mouths zip."

"She endears herself to strangers. That's what she likes, strangers."

Dan shook his head. "She isn't making any effort to endear me."

Nathan chuckled.

"Strangers," Dan repeated. "Does that mean she has trouble sustaining friendships?"

"No, no. A puzzling number of our mutual acquaintances chose sides when we divorced." Nathan paused thoughtfully. "She's totally lacking in standards regarding people."

"What kind of standards?"

Nathan breathed in noisily. "To her, everyone is delightful. It can be an inconvenience."

Dan nodded, wondering if there was any way to turn Nathan anecdotal. "What's she like to live with?" he asked.

"You're asking about sex?" Nathan gazed at the ceiling. "A seven. Or eight, I suppose. *Maybe* nine. On a scale of ten."

Dan sighed. "You're doing the same thing I get from everyone else. Polishing up her image. I thought an ex-husband would surely give me the other side."

"Ah."

That seemed to be the end of it. Dan wondered if a less direct approach might work.

"What's her background?" he asked. "Her speech doesn't sound local."

"Oklahoma," Nathan said. "She's lived here a while. Doesn't lose her accent. Has no ear."

Dan nodded to encourage any kind of fault-finding. "I'm not too familiar with Oklahoma types."

"Sweet. Agreeable. Passive on the surface. Lures you with all those promises in all that southern talk. Do you take this man? Ah dew. She wanted a man who wouldn't be some mindless head of household telling her when to breathe. Or maybe I should put it the way she did—she wanned a mane who wooden be a mahnless hade of how-sole. And so on."

Dan grinned. "Her accent's apparently lightened up since you were married."

When Nathan didn't comment, Dan urged him back to the real topic. "Head of household—was that a problem?"

"The reverse," Nathan said. "I wanted a career woman who understood a man may prefer an unstructured life. She said fine with her."

"You discussed it prenuptial?"

Nathan nodded. "*And* in the divorce decree. She had promised to be the partnership income. When she lost her job and thought we might both start scrimping, hiring out for minimum wage—not my problem."

Dan glanced around at the glorious home. "You're doing all right, evidently."

"At the moment, yes. On the basis of community property, to begin with—I got it all." He indicated the room with his long-handled paintbrushes. "The judge saw that was fair, given our original agreement. And now this arts grant." Nathan looked less uninterested as he described the wing of studios which were to be attached to the city museum. Since the studios would be free to artists who could win the grants which supported them, they would serve as a magnet for the most gifted individuals in a region which collected talent because of its unregimented community style.

"With the university connections I keep up, I have the inside track to become director for the grants program," he summed up.

Dan nodded. "Sounds good for everyone."

"She's discussed this with you?"

Dan shook his head. "No. It's all news."

"Her finances are what interest you?"

"No. I suppose you haven't seen the newspaper, if you just got home last night."

"That's accurate," Nathan said.

"Well, there's been some difficulty out in the county, on her property. She's offering a defense that she doesn't supervise the property and refuses to start."

Nathan smiled with his mouth closed. He held the smile well past any suggestion of humorousness. "And so you're to 'whistle up a stump,' is the way she'd put it, if I remember."

Dan grinned. He was grateful for the information because it showed him how to judge. If Lindy ever relaxed with him, apparently her speech would get down-home. It was one of the things he had wanted to learn.

As if knowing his former wife was in trouble made it easier to talk, Nathan's face grew slowly grave. "What you need to know, to make sense of her relationship to crime, is that she's totally, offensively confident underneath all that please-let-me-please-you manner. It comes from where you wouldn't expect. She's Bible Belt, and her Sunday School teacher when she was eight years old told her she was damned. Did it settle her down? Trust Lindy. She took it that she had nothing else to lose, so why not do exactly as she wanted, until the Devil comes for her?"

Dan imagined Lindy as a stormy-eyed grade-schooler, offended at being judged. It was intriguing to know she had always been defiant. Maintaining her feistiness over the years must have cost.

"Did she tell you this Sunday School story?"

Nathan nodded. "It was during one of our noisier marital negotiations. You don't realize how important it is, until you're looking at it. You truly can't compel behavior, because the worst has already happened, so she thinks."

Dan took it a step at a time. It seemed wrong for anyone to compel Lindy, and yet a husband probably wouldn't think so. He was glad she was divorced.

And did she really believe the worst had happened already? Thinking about the behavior he had seen, he decided Nathan was wrong. He was fairly sure she thought her present situation was one more disaster in a long sequence of horrors, each of which seemed like the worst, until the next exploded in her face.

"Maybe you can give me a reading on this situation," he said. "There are several teenagers involved in this present mess. Their parents ought to be blamed for failure to control their kids, but Lindy won't say so. She stands to lose everything, but she won't use any defense that casts a shadow on someone else. She says that's her plan, and she's acting on it. Now. Are you saying that's because she thinks she's damned?"

"No, no, she very well may mean it, she quite possibly accepts losing everything," Nathan said. "Look at the mind you're dealing with. She's highly theoretical, so in some senses she hardly notices possessions."

He paused to consider, rearranging his brushes so the red, yellow, and blue paint on their bristles would blend and degrade. "Of course, she's always had plenty of everything," he said.

"Probably makes a difference," Dan agreed.

Nathan nodded. "Also, normal people, when they're damned, they feel guilty. But with my former wife—" He shook his head. "When someone tells you you're a hopeless sinner, it's not supposed to leave you free."

"What religion are you speaking from the vantage point of?" Dan asked.

Nathan sighed through his nose. "I grew up in the Methodist church, where a person can reform their behavior at any point, and pay their spiritual debts." He glanced at the west wall of his living room.

Dan looked, too. Since the room was overwhelmed by paintings which covered every scrap of wall space, he hadn't noticed any theme. But guided by Nathan's gesture, he saw that the one wall was entirely religious.

"Lindy calls it a prayer wheel," Nathan said.

Dan studied the artistic wall which should have interested her, comparing it to the bare cedar boards she used as a defense.

"You must know her story," he told Nathan. "Has she ever been involved in this kind of thing before? Trigger for disaster? Provocative bystander?"

"No police record."

"No, I know, we checked that. But a lot of people have a history, even if it isn't on police computers."

Nathan scratched one cheekbone with his paintbrush stems.

"Any episode showing what she might be capable of?" Dan asked.

"She's capable of anything."

"Because of being damned?"

Nathan glanced toward the prayer wheel wall.

Dan studied the rapidly moving gaze, which never seemed to perch. "This reprimand in Sunday School was a lot of years ago," he said, wondering if it was the source for her interest in religion. "Is she still concerned?"

"She only tells the story. Doesn't comment."

"In your opinion?"

Nathan watched the fire. Dan sensed that it was genuine thought, not stagecraft, which occupied him, this time.

"She still feels free," he said eventually.

21

THE PHONE RANG THE NEXT MORNING AS LINDY WAS ON HER way out the door. "Nathan, here," an all too familiar voice said. Light, flexible, it was a voice which had interested her before she knew what its studied modulation implied.

"Hi."

"You're at it again, I see." Nathan paused to draw on his cigarette, making the small, continuing noise which notified his listeners that he wasn't ready to be broken in upon. "Mmmmm, I've been out of town for a couple of weeks. I come back to find my name smeared all over the newspapers. I don't appreciate it."

"I don't like it, either."

"It was bad enough when you were making that stink at the university," he went on. "Crime is worse."

Lindy closed her eyes and hoped for self-control.

"Your cop was around, wanting to know the negatives. I obliged him, which should be a lesson to you."

"I don't have any control over that."

"You would have done better to take your birthname back during the divorce," he said.

"No. Adair is my professional name, no matter where I got it. It seemed better to just go on as I was."

"Not to me."

"Well, why didn't you say so at the time!" Lindy said, angry at last.

"How could I anticipate? You've *changed*."

Lindy pressed her forehead against the wall beside the

cork board which held phone notes. I'm not going to get into it, she thought, I'm *not*.

It was true that she had changed. Mercifully true, she amplified. She had used to think their marriage was her responsibility because Nathan was a free spirit. She had been grateful, at first, to find a man who was willing to be a faculty spouse. By the time she realized he just wanted access to the university studios, she had been listening to his explanation of his ego-needs for so long that she had begun to see herself as being in the wrong on almost any topic, as being an impediment to every life she touched.

Nathan had considered himself too much an artist to quarrel. Instead, he brought up topics which he discussed in terms of her deficiencies. When she had tried to negotiate, he hadn't heard. If she simply repeated herself, he still didn't hear. Only when she had rephrased a couple of times would he consent to answer. She had been slow to see the pattern because admitting he was having fun forced her to take a bleaker view of human possibility. At first she hoped his behavior might be an unconscious response to stress—after all, hers was—but finally she asked him if he was deliberately making her say everything three different ways before he would respond. His satisfied smile was dazzling.

That was when she lost it.

In the long divorce, she had thought she fought clear of her reactive anger. But now, with only a couple of sentences, he had undermined her again. She was amazed at his skill.

She was also blazing mad. *"Yes Nathan I have changed,"* she said, stomping on each word. "For one, I don't listen to your hassling anymore."

He drew on his cigarette lengthily. "You're listening," he said.

She slammed the phone down. When it rang almost immediately, she left the house. By the time she reached her car, her skin burned, her heart pounded, her hands shook.

I mustn't risk driving like this, she thought. Tossing her

shoulderbag into the car, she dived into the woods. She walked the trails until her knees stopped trembling, and then she stood under the boughs of a cedar and watched a tiny natural clearing where wildflowers were taking hold. Occasional raindrops pushed down randomly on individual buttercup leaves, making the open spot look festive, as if small animals were underneath, tugging at the plants.

When she could trust herself, she came back to her Subaru, but leaving the woods exposed her to her subsiding fury, as well as her uncertainty over her upcoming interview. With nowhere for her mind to rest, she tried to concentrate on the road.

She took the midtown freeway off-ramp and drove the half block to the Hotel Friendly, where Karl's friend worked as a maid. She drove slowly through the U-shaped parking lot surrounding the three-story buildings, looking for service carts. She spotted five of them.

Still fueled by her anger at Nathan, she parked and began her search. Since Karl's friend hadn't attended Owen's memorial service, she didn't know who she was looking for, but she hoped the other maids wouldn't be the right age. Both ground-floor workers were white-haired, but one of the second-floor women was probably a teenager. Tall, muscular, working vigorously, she looked capable of the aggression Ellie had described.

"May Anne? Could we talk while you work?" Lindy asked from the doorway.

"It's against the rules," May Anne said, barely pausing in her swooping toss of bedding onto the floor. "Unless it's urgent."

"It sort of is. I'm Lindy."

"I know who you are and I've got nothing to say." May Anne stripped sheets off the bed and nudged them aside with one foot. Her hightops left a granular smudge on the white cloth.

"I realize the guys must have agreed on a story and I can see their friends are going to back them up, but I need to talk anyway."

May Anne shook pillows out of their cases onto the floor. "If you think someone tells me what to do, forget it."

"I didn't mean it that way. I meant friendship."

"For friendship, I know what Karl's family thinks of him," she snapped, "and I won't listen to it from you just because you hang out with his dad."

Lindy shook her head. "I used to work with Karl's father, but I can't remember that he ever mentioned his family."

"I believe it."

Lindy wondered if May Anne's behavior was just normal teenage hostility. Turning every sentence into a separate mistake seemed extreme. She wished she knew more about teenagers.

"They're wrong," May Anne added abruptly, bending over straight-legged so her tunic didn't help the white tights which strained to cover her bum. Lindy wondered if she had been deliberately mooned.

"His folks are *dead wrong* about Karl," May Anne went on as she finished stripping the bed. "If you're so into helping others, you could try talking to that *sheriff*. He's been listening to these stupids so he can hassle the rest of us."

Lindy wasn't sure what to say, since she had wondered, herself, to begin with. May Anne had intended to visit Owen, the day he died. She had intended to accuse him. Her mother said that hadn't happened, but had Brent doubted her alibi?

"What does he say, to hassle?" she asked.

May Anne's prominent light eyes narrowed. "He claims I killed Owen just because I hated him."

"Hated? I thought all of you visited Owen because you liked him."

"I *did*." May Anne's eyes abruptly filled. "I *loved* him. We *all* did."

Lindy rubbed her forehead. "May Anne, would you go a little slower with me? I'm really confused."

"It's not your problem," May Anne told her, unfurling the bedspread over the floor in order to clear it of soiled sheets.

"Well, yes, it sort of is."

May Anne brought a stack of clean linens in from her cart and dropped them on the counter. "Forget it," she said, "I didn't talk to the sheriff, and I won't talk to you. And as far as that city detective, if he wants a date, fine, let him say so, but if he just wants to ask questions even dumber than the sheriff, he knows what he can do."

"He is attractive, I guess, isn't he?"

May Anne looked at her in disbelief. "You *guess?*"

She picked up a sheet and strenuously flapped it open.

"Please help me, May Anne," Lindy said. "I don't want to end up in court. I *hate* courts. I'll *never* get used to them."

May Anne glanced up from tucking a mattress corner. "Cops accuse everybody, I wouldn't take it seriously," she said in a disconcertingly sisterly way.

"Thanks," Lindy said. "That police sergeant questioned even my ex-husband, so I'm afraid it might be serious."

"He's just an asshole, no matter how he looks."

Lindy watched her smooth the sheet. "Insurance laws might crunch me, even if the police don't. Insurance covers a lot of things that aren't your fault. That sounds nice, but actually, no, because you look guilty if your insurance pays."

"I don't get that," May Anne said as she tucked a pillow under her chin and grabbed a case.

Lindy explained in great detail. She wasn't sure whether May Anne was interested, but she seemed to be listening. When Lindy fell silent, May Anne stepped off the blanket so she could pull it up over the fresh sheets.

"That's the most ridiculous story I've ever heard," she said.

"It's why I need help so badly," Lindy said.

May Anne stared at her, one edge of the bedspread dangling from her hands. "I don't believe you, but I've heard sicker things, so here's the truth in case you can use it."

Lindy drew a long breath.

"Karl and Timmy thought Owen was everything. He was in the dark ages, but he could be fun, so you forgave him. And he had all these *stories*."

Lindy nodded.

"That's how all the guys got into moonshine. Owen would tell about possums crawling into the vat to sample and liking it enough to drown in it, and everything like that. He could spend *days* talking. I think he remembered every batch of moonshine he and his dad ever bootlegged."

"Was he making it up?" Lindy asked.

"That's what I thought, too, any woman would. But Karl said no, and Timmy never lets you say *any*thing about Owen that's less than perfect."

Lindy nodded.

"But Owen wouldn't tell them how to do it. Whenever they asked, well, then he had a million boring warnings."

"So it really was Vance who knew?" Lindy asked.

"Yeah, but Owen got them started asking, so I blame Owen."

"Where did Vance find out?"

"Some book." May Anne dragged the bedspread off the floor and spread it over the blanket before tucking it around the pillows.

Lindy's heart began to labor. "Do you know which book?" she asked.

"Gray paperback. Orange printing. No picture."

"Where did he get it?"

May Anne shrugged.

"Who has it now?"

"Who knows? They always acted like it was some big secret."

"Because moonshine's against the law?"

May Anne twitched her shoulders, looking more annoyed than a mere shrug could express.

Lindy watched her use a pillow case to swipe crumbs off the table. "May Anne, this is a terrible thing to ask, but could I tell my insurance you'd be willing to describe this book under oath, if we have to go to court about it? It might help me, and it *surely* would help what people believe about Owen.''

May Anne leaned on the table. ''My mother'd kill me. She thinks I'm a fool to stick with Karl, now he's a criminal, and especially where I almost walked in on Owen after he was dead. Thank God you got there first!'' she interrupted herself. ''I'm going down to the tech school for computers, and my folks are letting me live at home until I finish and get a job. I know you think I'm eighteen, but when you're still living at home, your folks don't think so.''

''I can see that.'' Lindy nodded several times to emphasize how true it was. ''It helps me to know, even if you can't risk swearing. So, thanks—a *lot*.''

May Anne bent to scoop up the rest of the soiled laundry.

She had to find the book, Lindy thought as she went back to her car. Maybe it wouldn't tell her anything, but she wanted to know. A paperback with nothing but orange printing on the cover. It didn't sound like a public publisher, and if it gave instructions on something illegal, like making moonshine, it might be an underground press. How was she going to trace it?

She went to the university library and spent the afternoon reading through the subject index to publishers' lists. She ran her search back for twenty years. She doublechecked through chemical and social science indexes. She used journalism indexes.

When she couldn't think of anything else to try, she bought a milk and muffin from the student union's takeout window and drove to Post Point Park. Since the upgrade had spoiled the park, no one else was there. She sat alone in the early twilight, looking across the dark bay. The point buoy groaned occasionally. A few lights showed on the Lummi shore. As she ate her impromptu meal, she tried to focus on the beauty—it was still a beautiful view—but her thoughts were everywhere.

The hard part about investigating, she decided, was that

details didn't help. This book was a good example. Apparently she wasn't going to be able to identify it. Did that matter? Knowing it existed proved Owen wasn't at fault, but she had already decided that. On the other hand, the police might not agree. Should she risk telling them? They might conclude any handbook must have come from the Sunstrike, along with the copper kettle. That explanation seemed perfectly possible, much as she didn't want it to be true. Was there any way to know? She could ask the boys, but if they weren't talking to anyone, they weren't likely to talk to her.

Very ready to be distracted from thoughts which circled to nowhere, she turned on her engine and left Fairhaven. Crossing Happy Valley through a slow rain, she headed for the Old Mall. She had to park on the outer rim of the lot because *Ours* was surrounded by an unusual number of cars. She sighed. Evidently the Thursday group had finally heard about her trouble.

She went into the bookstore and smiled at the owner as if it were any other night. When she joined the group, she forestalled avidity by asking for the same discussion she had brought to the Tuesday regulars. She listened for an hour, bemused to find that, for the first time ever, the two groups reacted in the same way.

22

SLEEPING ON IT DIDN'T HELP. LINDY DAWDLED OVER HER COF-
fee and toast, next morning, trying to balance everything
out. If she kept quiet about the moonshine book, that
wasn't fair to Owen's memory. If she reported to Brent, he
wouldn't use the information to attack the Sunstrike, but
he would discuss it with Richison, and she would end up
being questioned twice. If she called Richison, that would
be an act of trust toward a man who had sought out Nathan. They were all bad choices, so she might as well take
the most obvious.

She called the Bellingham police. "I'd like to talk to
you," she said when her call was transferred to Richison.

"Stop right there," he cut in. "I don't want to hear it on
the phone. You've got so many do-it-yourselfers out there,
it's not possible to know who's listening."

"Why would anyone listen?"

"I don't know which ones they are, so I can't ask."

Lindy sighed. "Let's just assume they're not."

"No. I'll come out. If it isn't urgent, I've got a few messes
to cap off, here, if I can. It may be close to noon."

"That's okay."

When he still hadn't arrived by one o'clock, Lindy decided to go ahead with lunch. She was standing at the stove,
dropping sage dumplings onto simmering sauerkraut when
he knocked and walked in. She didn't know whether to be
irritated or amused that he had decided to partly copy her
Sunstrikers.

"Go ahead and eat," he said, looking at the stove, "I didn't intend to be this late."

"Have you had lunch?" she asked.

"Yeah."

"This has to steam for twelve minutes, so we could talk while I wait."

"No, I wouldn't mind a break." He hung his parka in the microwave alcove and came to the stove to inspect the pot.

"Is that ethnic?" he asked.

"Not that I know of. My mother makes it, but I don't know where she got it. It was one of my favorite meals as a child."

"You keep in touch?"

Lindy nodded. "By phone. My parents live in Oklahoma." She put a lid on the pot and set the timer. "I hope you won't call them."

"Good idea, I hadn't thought of it."

When she glanced at him, he smiled. "Just a joke."

Lindy didn't smile. "I'm not sure it's a joke, because you talked to Nathan, which also seems unprovoked," she said as she led the way to the living room.

"No, that was provoked. I wanted to hear the worst that can be said about you," he said as they sat down in front of the fire.

"Why?"

He sighed. "I'm trying to figure out if I'm a fool for taking you as you seem."

"Why would that make you a fool?"

He looked at her steadily. "Any cop in his right mind would dismiss all the other suspects in a situation like this. You found Owen, which puts you in control of the scene and excuses prints and fibers. Solid-citizen witnesses identify you at his house at the right time for the killing. Your alibi is offered by someone who's in your debt. You're involved in the earlier crime that we have to connect."

Lindy could feel her face turn white in response to his efficient summary. She willed her heart to do its job, but it seemed to have its own opinion. Richison looked interested, which made self-control even harder to achieve.

"I don't see how that involves Nathan," she said in a rusty voice.

"Here's my problem," he said. "The sheriff's department doesn't think you're guilty—I set that aside because you're his prof. But *I* don't think it, either, so where am I? You mask your reactions, so acting innocent proves nothing. What else? I can't think of much. So I head for Adair, to hear the poison."

"What did you find out?"

"He says you're damned."

Lindy laughed.

"It doesn't bother you?"

Lindy shrugged. "Everything about Nathan bothers me, but that doesn't more than anything else."

"I'd like to hear your version."

Lindy hesitated.

"I assume it won't sound the same as when he tells it," he said.

"Well, once when he was furious at me," Lindy said slowly, "I told him about this time I was asking a lot of questions the Sunday School teacher wasn't used to hearing. She got tired of it, so she finally said, 'the way you act, a person would think you're damned and don't even care.' "

"Okay, that sounds more reasonable, talking to an eight-year-old, but why tell Adair when he's already enraged?"

"He had been trying to shut me up, I don't remember what about. I hoped to show him it wasn't going to happen. If you have to defend your ideas when you're eight, you've had a lot of practice by the time you're grown."

"It doesn't seem to work that way with most people."

"Because most kids are asked to defend their behavior," Lindy insisted. "Behavior's different—you either did whatever it was, or you didn't do it, so you either apologize or smart off. But with ideas—most people don't think children have them."

202

He sighed. "I've got an eight-year-old sister. Maybe I'd better take another look at how I treat her."

"What's she like?"

"Full of herself." He grinned.

It was appealing. Appealing enough, almost, to make her forgive him for Nathan.

The timer dinged and Lindy got up to go to the kitchen. "Would you like coffee?" she called.

"Not coffee, I drink too much. You wouldn't have any milk, would you?"

"Yes." She brought two glasses of milk to the small table between their chairs and went back to the kitchen for her plate.

"Did Nathan tell you anything else?" she asked as she sat back down.

He shook his head. "Nothing to matter. Let's not spoil your appetite."

She shot him a rueful glance which earned her a grin, and so she was able to eat.

"I could see why you divorced," he said, reaching for his milk, "but I always can see that. That's the strangest thing about the Northwest. Around here, you meet people who are still married to the first person they married, no matter when that was."

Lindy laughed.

He launched into a discussion of the couple he had been trying to help deal with a violent son. "They've been married sixty-two years," he summed up. "I can't grasp it."

When Lindy finished her lunch, Richison stood up. "Do you mind if we walk while you tell me whatever it was you called about?" he asked. "I've never seen a place like this. I'd like to look again."

When she nodded, he grabbed his parka. Lindy was wearing a silk turtleneck under her sweatshirt, and so she simply went outside.

"I talked to May Anne," she said as they started along the path toward the woods.

"Karl Patrick's girlfriend?"

Lindy nodded. "She said they learned about moonshine out of a book," she said as they approached Tim's pond.

When Richison paused to look, the small-mouth bass came forward like bright shadows under the surface of the water. Lindy smiled in response to their learning—when someone approached quietly, they expected oatmeal to descend onto the water since she so often brought them some.

She described her conversation with May Anne as they moved on to enter the woods. When she finished, they walked in silence for a little way. Richison stopped to admire a line of odd white growths which had sprung out like an extra layer on the bark of a downed tree trunk. Their surfaces were slick enough to look like the first heating of meringues.

"What is that?" Richison asked.

"I don't know the names of any of those things."

"You ought to get a handbook."

"I probably should," Lindy agreed, not intending to. Naming was owning, which wasn't her view of other lives.

"Why did May Anne talk to you?" he asked as he started walking again, veering east. "She's hostile in all directions, so far as I could see."

Lindy decided not to admit she didn't walk along the riverbank anymore. "She probably wanted to talk to somebody," she said, "but she doesn't know how to get started because she assumes adults are going to be on Karl's parents' side. His parents think Karl's making nothing of his life."

"Are they wrong?"

"I don't know." Lindy frowned. "The real problem probably is that teachers aren't very good parents. Teaching, you start where anybody is and coax growth if you can. If you can't—oh, well. But parenting seems to work better if you're mindless and absolute. Sit up straight. Chew with your mouth shut. Look at people when they speak to you. Wipe your feet before you come inside. All that kind of thing."

Richison laughed. "That insight comes from being a teacher's kid yourself?"

Lindy nodded tentatively.

"I'll look into May Anne's information," Richison said, circling back to their earlier topic in a way she was becoming accustomed to.

"Mr. Crayson told me he used to have a book, but he traded it in at one of those secondhand places."

"Okay, I'll have that checked out."

"If they used a book, it proves Owen wasn't their source."

"Right. But I didn't think he was to blame, anyway."

"Who *do* you blame?"

He frowned. "Good question. No one here on the Sunstrike is a communard in the moonshine sense. Fuller has talked to the tax-resistance types in the community around here, and all he gets is that everybody knows moonshine costs more to make than a bottle costs at the state liquor store. He says that isn't true, but they're standing pat. The subsistence types he questions seem to have known Owen, but almost everybody knew Owen, so linking that up isn't a help."

"Have you been pestering my residents?" Lindy asked, focusing on the important part of his account.

He stopped walking in order to offer a clear view of aggressively empty blue eyes. "We've solicited the cooperation of community members," he said formally. "We've told everyone we know this is private property, and we've reminded them they can shut their door in our face. Nobody did."

Lindy looked away, imagining it without wanting to. They would have been trying to protect her, even though some of them hadn't even met her, so far as she knew. She felt bad, realizing she needed their protection.

"This book might give us a new angle," Richison said, turning back to the trail and moving forward again. "Maybe one of the kids will talk, if we show we know this much. What I'd like would be to interview Al Crayson without his doctor, his lawyer, his counselor, and his parents all standing between us."

"I'm glad they want to help him," Lindy insisted.

"Don't you have any self-protective instincts?"

"Sure. Everybody does."

"Maybe. But I came out here thinking you were going to tell me something to contradict what I hear every morning at our case conference. What you give me instead *strengthens* your connection."

"I was afraid it would look that way to you."

"Not to me, necessarily, because of checking you out, but if I say you wouldn't have identified a book as the knowledge source if it came from the Sunstrike, everyone is going to inform me that campus types are too clever for their own good, which means you must have decided I'd hear about this book eventually, so you obviously decided to tell me right up front in order to give the impression you couldn't be guilty because if you were, you wouldn't mention it."

When Lindy stopped walking, he turned to look.

"Do police really talk like that?" she asked.

"I probably make it sound more polite than it is."

She bowed her head. "If the boys read a book wrong, then what happened was just an accident, just horrible luck."

"No, it works the other way, if somebody deliberately gave this book to them."

"Does that mean you aren't assuming it came from the Sunstrike?"

"I won't know where it came from until our investigation is complete," he said. "Could it have been lying around here somewhere for them to pick up casually?"

She inspected a tiny, lacy hemlock struggling for a place among the overshadowing cedars it had dropped among as a seed. "I don't know," she admitted. "I didn't inventory any of the storage areas when I moved in."

"Yeah, well, we'll be doing that for you. If there aren't any other how-to books, we can justify believing this moonshine text didn't come from here, either."

And if there *is* something else? she asked silently. A text on bulk cooking? A wiring guide? The Sunstrikers she had met seemed to operate from inner knowledge, not from texts, but that might not always have been the case.

She couldn't bear to discuss it. She was relieved when they moved on, walking single file where the trail narrowed to wander among the cedars lining the edge of the cliff. Small wild plants had begun to grow in the lookout spot Lindy no longer used, but Richison stopped there anyway. Lindy looked sadly down at the alder bottom, where the main attraction was the birding cabin, its police tape making it look distressingly hilarious, as if someone had TP'ed it with bright yellow tissue.

"I'd like to tear it down," she admitted, "it upsets me because of the tragedy for those boys. But you need as many permits to remove a structure in wetlands as it took to build it, and I can't seem to scare up the strength."

"Don't get on the run about this, Lindy. Compared to what I normally see, it isn't much."

She started to protest that crime looked different to cops, since they got to decide which laws applied and in what way. But just in time, she remembered his story about his brother.

"What you told Sunny about living on a commune," she said. "Is it true?"

"Yeah. I spend so much time encouraging people to embarrass themselves by forgetting what they told me, I try not to fall into the trap myself. Which means I pretty much stick to the truth."

Lindy smiled slightly.

"I made my brother's situation sound nicer than it was, though," he went on. "I figured Sunny probably prefers your pretty world."

"If this is pretty, I don't want to see ugly," she said.

"No. You don't."

"What really happened about your brother?" she asked after a moment.

"Oh, just the usual." He gazed at Mount Baker, its cap bright with new snow, its fumarole trailing an iridescent plume in the clear air. "It was lucky I spent time on the commune, because they wouldn't have called me if they hadn't known me. Or at least they thought they knew me."

He let his gaze follow the meandering valley as the river approached their spot. "My brother was a serious user. He collapsed and would have died. They'd have hauled him out into the desert and dropped him where he'd have never been found. But they called me instead and I got him into treatment."

He looked down, remembering. Since they were standing on the very edge of the high bank, down included an extra two hundred feet.

"He's on his third try at treatment. He swears he's going to make it work, this time. Maybe he will. It costs a fortune, but my stepdad is in the military, so that covers it, for now. Our mom—" He shrugged. "My brother really needs treatment, but my mom can't handle it."

"Drugs are horribly hard on parents," Lindy agreed.

"If my mom comes up to visit me, I'd like to bring her out here."

Lindy nodded, surprised by a request which sounded trusting. "I'd like that. If I'm still here," she added.

"Yeah, well, we're working on it."

He gazed down at the river, which had turned to a seething pale khaki because of the rains. Suddenly he frowned. "Did you see something move inside the cabin?" he asked.

"No. With those crime scene tapes everywhere, who would go inside?"

He cast her an ironic glance and stepped over the edge of the cliff onto the narrow trail which shone with recent rain.

"No, don't! That's clay! It's slick, now that it's wet!"

"Tell your insurance company you warned me," he said without a backward glance.

Lindy decided to follow him. He seemed to be a totally city person, and so, if he fell, he wouldn't know what to do about it. Even if he didn't fall, she might as well go to the cabin with him. She knew she would never go alone, with all the feelings the place had triggered, but going would give her a chance to decide whether she wanted to destroy it. She hoped letting time pass might seem like change enough.

"It's probably just a Sunstriker, exploring," she said. "Remember what Sunny said about everyone knowing when I won't see them? We're off my schedule."

"Whoever it is, they're not supposed to be there."

They worked their way slowly downward, clinging to the crumbling clay wall. Richison made his task harder by watching the cabin as well as the trail, determined to know if someone spotted their approach and tried to run. He lost his footing once, slithering over the side as he landed on his hip, but an elbow saved him and he hauled himself back up to the trail without commenting. Determined not to follow suit, Lindy pressed herself against the bank until her front was clay-covered and her fingernails were painfully full.

As they neared river level, the trail lost its slope. They had almost reached the beginning of the catwalk when they heard a groan. Richison leaped forward as if slick clay had to cooperate, in crisis situations. When he reached the elevated walkway which kept them from slopping through the alder bottom and endangering wetlands, he moved more confidently. Lindy tried to copy his silence, but the boards creaked under her lesser weight. She wondered what his secret was.

When they reached the cabin's wraparound porch and ducked under the yellow crime scene tape, they heard a wretchedly drawn out groan. Richison reached inside his parka to clean his hand on his sweater before pulling out a gun. Lindy reached forward to grab his elbow.

"Sergeant!" she whispered urgently. "Wait!"

He slammed her against the cabin wall with his empty hand. Shifting his grip to the top of her head, he pushed her down. It took her a moment to realize the attack was only sudden, not rough. By the time she had adjusted, she saw there was no point in struggling—he was startlingly strong, besides having a cop's physical confidence. As the easiest way out of the problem, she sat down.

When her back was against the wall and her heels against her hips, he released her. He ducked under the window and flattened himself against the door frame, listening with his entire body. Grunts began, at first irregularly, gradually gathering speed, as if someone were being beaten up and the attacker had decided it was fun.

Richison stepped inside the cabin door, making a silhouette of himself as briefly as possible. Lindy stood up and followed him in a normal way. He had moved quickly—he was already out of sight by the time she entered the house to follow the animal sounds toward a bend in the hallway.

Richison stepped into the bedroom doorway just as Lindy turned the hall corner and could watch. It made an arresting tableau, Richison with his gun pointed up but ready to drop and fire at the least provocation, Opaline with her back against the wall, her legs wrapped around Al's body to soften the impact of his lunging, one naked arm around his neck to steady herself while the other hand cushioned his forehead from the wall behind her and above her head, Al naked as well, his clenched olive buttocks and bare back contrasting with Opaline's very fair legs and arms, his splayed hands cupping her bum to support her at a level convenient for him, his straining thighs slamming them both against the wall with rhythmic total oblivion.

Opaline saw them, but of course Al did not. Her face froze. A red shadow under the skin began at her belly and crept upward across her breasts, her throat, finally reaching her face.

"Honey," she said breathlessly.

"You have fifteen seconds to organize yourselves," Richison said, putting his gun away as he headed back down the hall toward Lindy, his face expressionless.

Lindy went back to the porch. She tugged a sliver off one of the railing uprights and began clearing the clay out from under her fingernails. Richison leaned against the corner post to watch.

"You'd better call me Dan, with all the stuff we seem to face together," he said as she finished with one hand.

Lindy was relieved to laugh. Evidently that was his admission that he should have listened when she tried to stop him. She knew she ought to look at him, but she couldn't lift her gaze further than his mouth. He was obviously intensely annoyed, but her giggles seemed to help.

She perched one thigh on the railing and looked down into the swirling river. "I wonder if she minds it that he can't see how beautiful she is," she asked after her smile had faded.

"She looks good to you?"

"Not to me personally." Lindy glanced at his eyes. "But she's beautiful, isn't she?"

He shrugged. "Maybe I see too many naked bodies in elemental situations."

Thinking he might talk about it if she didn't ask, Lindy looked down at the muddy river. It hadn't been rain-swollen when Vance plunged in, but probably it had been even colder since it would have been mostly glacier melt. She gazed along the main channel, where the water seethed against the sheer clay face of her cliff, generating foam. She could almost see a blond head bobbing out of control in the midst of a splashing. But, no, Mr. Crayson had said Vance looked like him, so it would have been a dark head. She looked again.

"Sometimes I worry the people I deal with are going to turn me just clear off of sex," Richison said.

Lindy was glad to set her own reverie aside. "May Anne's waiting for you to ask for a date, if you feel like checking your reactions," she said, getting to work on her other hand.

He looked rueful. "I don't date suspects," he said.

"She can't be a suspect. She has an alibi," Lindy answered, glad of a chance to check on that.

"An alibi supplied by her mother." Richison sighed.

"I've never interviewed a mother who admitted she ever lost sight of her child."

"Even so," Lindy said.

He shook his head. "May Anne's strong enough to do Owen. And she has a better motive than most of the people on the list—she's the angriest of everyone involved."

"But her anger makes sense. Think of what's happened to her life. She's working really hard, to achieve her plans, and now this happens to Karl."

"Anger always makes sense to the person feeling it," he said.

"You can't suspect her," Lindy insisted. "She's just a kid."

"Which means her values aren't fully developed. Her grip on consequences isn't fully in place. And have you talked to her parents?"

Lindy shook her head.

"They're good people. Standing by her. Worrying about her. I wish every kid had a home like that. But the dark side of being loved by your peaceful, decent parents is that you get used to someone fixing whatever goes wrong. After I met them, I could see it makes sense to her to fix this situation for Karl."

The feeling in his voice told Lindy he was talking about a great deal more than simply May Anne's home life. She remembered that Maggie Anderson suspected he might be in distress.

He didn't seem to be. He stood idly, looking at the view.

"What are your rules about dating?" he asked after a pause. "Setting suspects aside," he added.

It appeared to be a theoretical question, and so Lindy groaned. "You surely know the answer to that. When Nathan and I were first divorced, I couldn't even sit through a movie where anybody kissed, never mind facing it live. I figured time would solve that, and it did, more or less, but before I got around to hating Nathan as an individual instead of blaming men generically, I had begun to notice what all these women keep saying in every one of my groups."

He inspected her face. "Which is?"

She gazed across the river toward the spindly alders, chlorotic from having their roots flooded too much of the year.

"They complain," she said finally.

"You're not different? I would have thought you were."

"Oh—" She rubbed at the clay drying on her shirt front. "When I was in grade school, they used to ask us a bunch of questions every year, including what we were going to be when we grew up. Now, I know it must have been just somebody working on a PhD dissertation project about personality development, but at the time, it was totally confusing. I finally got my courage together in the fourth grade and left it blank about my plans. The principal called me in and said I had to answer. So I put that I wanted to grow up to be an adult."

He grinned. "Did that work?"

She smiled. "They sent me to detention. But why I mentioned it—I *didn't* say I was going to grow up to be celibate. It's just that, now, compared to the alternative—"

His vivid eyes became less shadowed. "AIDS?" he asked.

She shrugged. "Sex leads to a lot of things besides AIDS. All AIDS does is kill you. In my experience, marriage is far worse than that."

He laughed at last.

23

RICHISON PUSHED OFF FROM THE RAILING. "I'M GOING BACK in there," he said. "They might be willing to say things now that they wouldn't before, and if Al doesn't yell for a lawyer, here's my chance to talk to him."

Lindy nodded.

"I'll send Opaline out so he doesn't worry about a witness. See what you can do with her? You're both teachers, maybe you can figure out what to say to each other."

Left alone, Lindy studied the sheer face of her cliff, trying to compose herself. When she heard uncertain steps behind her, she turned.

Opaline was wearing a two-piece knit dress in a bronze which brightened her flowing blonde hair. Her matching flat shoes made her look like a child, since she was small to begin with, and the fear in her greenish eyes increased her air of being young. But Lindy could see the signs of maturity under her eyes. Not lines exactly, just a lack of the slick featureless skin typical of the very young.

Opaline clamped her lips between her teeth, creating dimples above her mouth. "You don't have to stay," she said nervously. "I won't run away."

Lindy nodded. "But I've been wanting to talk with you, if you don't mind."

Opaline approached the railing. "I'm sorry about this," she said. "I guess you've about had it with trespassers."

"It's all right."

"I guess not," Opaline said. "Richison says if you cross a

214

crime scene tape, you're neck deep in sewage, regardless of anything else."

"It probably depends on how much you worry about cops," Lindy said. "Why did you risk it?"

"Where else can we go?"

"I don't know where people go," Lindy admitted, "I hadn't thought of it."

"Al's mother is just—" Opaline searched unsuccessfully for an adequate word. "I'd feel uncomfortable going to his room at his parents' house, anyway." She was silent for a while. "I've got an apartment, but the landlord has teenage sons, and he told me if Al comes over one more time— He's afraid his kids will be corrupted."

"This new puritanism, according to the magazines," Lindy said.

"*That's* for sure." Opaline glanced briefly at Lindy's sympathetic face. "I wanted to bring a mattress out here, but we were afraid the cops might notice because there's not really any furniture, and Al doesn't mind standing up. He *likes* it, I think—it's one of the ways you really notice an age difference."

"I've never— I mean, I don't know much about it," Lindy said. "My former husband was my age, and I haven't done a whole lot of serious dating."

Opaline looked her over. "How come? You're attractive."

Lindy made a show of gazing down at herself, her mud-covered sweatshirt and jeans contrasting ridiculously with Opaline's careful grooming. "Maybe if I got cleaned up, or something—"

They laughed less uncomfortably.

"I thought with the police tapes, we'd be private. I forgot it isn't fair to you."

"Don't worry about it, truly." Lindy held her gaze a moment. "And as far as being private, normally it would have been. We just happened to be out walking. Richison thought he spotted some movement down here."

"You're interested in him?"

"We were just talking about all this trouble," Lindy said. "He thinks you probably know more than you've told him."

"That isn't true."

"He's brand new from California, and he can't quite figure out about Northwesterners."

Opaline rubbed a love bite which her collar didn't quite hide. "I called in sick today because Al said he wanted to talk. He has trouble talking about the future, so I thought it was important."

"Did you get it figured out?"

"No. We were just getting started." When she heard what she had said, she flushed, but she didn't try to correct it.

"Do you know where the guys got their moonshine information?" Lindy asked.

Opaline shook her head. "They never talked to me about it." She rearranged her gold bracelets. "It's a mess. Most of the time Al treats me like a woman. Like his woman. But every once in a while there's this wall. All of a sudden I'm a teacher, and they all hate teachers. In a flash, they remember I'm older, I'm an adult, and they don't trust grownups."

"It must be hard."

"Love's always confusing, I guess."

Lindy nodded. "I was never interested in my students. I mean, a lot of them were attractive, but they were students, if you know what I mean."

"You're lucky."

"I don't *feel* lucky," Lindy said.

"I guess people never do."

They stood quietly side-by-side, looking out but seeing nothing. Lindy wondered if Opaline was worrying about what Richison might be doing to Al. Al's handicap was still so unfamiliar, it seemed unfair for him to have to be alone while facing a sighted man who was a cop besides.

"Could you marry Al?" she asked impulsively. "I know it's none of my business."

"Anything's your business, under the circumstances," Opaline said as she scraped at a thumbnail which looked already perfectly groomed. "I'd like to marry, we'd both like to marry, but there's this awful dilemma about money. I hope that doesn't disgust you—my putting a dollar price on it."

"No. I have the same problem with being sued. I can't fight it very well because I keep being afraid it looks like I'm more worried about money than I am about these kids."

Opaline nodded. "You never dream how insurance is going to control your life. If we don't marry, Al's included on his dad's health coverage, for rehabilitation, and Al needs that."

"Teachers have insurance, haven't they? Wouldn't yours cover him, if you marry?"

"Yes, but not preexisting conditions."

Lindy sighed.

"I'd gladly just pay, if I could, but Al needs more than I can afford. This residential program his mother found for him in Seattle sounds excellent. I've promised I'll move down there, go unemployed if I have to, whatever it takes so he's not alone, but he keeps saying he's not going to live like he's blind." Opaline rubbed her forehead to dispose of her worried frown. "Disbelief is natural, but I've talked to his doctor, and he *needs* that program. So I don't want to marry him yet. I want him to get his retraining and we'll go on from there. It's what I was hoping he would agree to today."

"You really do love him."

Opaline flushed. She nodded without looking up. "But his mother thinks I'm the Devil in clothes," she said.

"Are they Fundamentalists? I got an announcement of the services for Vance, but I didn't recognize the group."

"They're nondenominational. I'm not sure what they say about the Devil. But for her, it's personal—more like she's always thought the Devil was a woman, and now that she's met me, she takes it as proof."

"She's just grieving," Lindy said gently. "She's not a public person, and so she doesn't think how it sounds."

Opaline shrugged. "To tell you the truth, she's not even the worst—Barney is. I guess you'd expect that, but I didn't."

"Barney?" Lindy repeated.

"My former husband. He's a coach over at the other high school. I used to teach over there, but they let me transfer when we divorced. Barney's used to being this hunk, but he started in on steroids, so he's losing his looks early and takes it out on everybody. He's twelve years older than I am, and he hates it. The first time he hit me, I moved out, but that was just a symbol, really, because the constant quarreling bothered me more. It still does." She glanced at Lindy's eyes. "Barney keeps track of everything by gossiping, and then he calls and cackles and jeers."

"Has he been calling about this?" Lindy said.

"*Believe* it."

"Did you tell the police?"

"No," she said with an anxious glance over her shoulder. "I keep being afraid it might be better for Barney to talk. If he hassles me by phone, maybe it will be enough so he doesn't decide to do anything worse."

Lindy frowned.

"It's just noise," Opaline said quickly. "Any teacher in the public schools has to take a couple of courses, every three years, to keep their credentials current, and you should hear him gripe. He puts it off to the last minute, and this time he took incompletes because I'm not there to write his papers for him, the way I did when we were married. He has to finish these courses or they won't let him teach next year, and he says it's my responsibility. He claims he tries to study, but he thinks they're prejudiced against jocks."

"It might be true," Lindy admitted. "At least, I've heard rude remarks sometimes."

Opaline shook her head. "Whose side are you on?"

Lindy smiled faintly. "Sorry."

"Oh, well, like he says—what's the big deal? He swears he's got everything I need, you know—books, notes, syllabi. All I have to do is write the papers. I don't *want* to, but he talks you to death."

"I hang up on my ex," Lindy said.

Opaline looked at her. "I'd be afraid to make Barney *really* mad, like that."

It took Lindy a moment to follow the thought. "My former husband is artistic. Not physical. But I suppose a coach must be as bad as a cop."

"If you're filing an impact statement about cops, I'd prefer hearing it face-to-face," Richison said from the cabin door.

The women turned.

"Were you rough on Al?" Opaline asked.

Richison's face darkened beneath his tan. "I'm sure he's going to tell you I was, but from my point of view, I wrapped him in Styrofoam."

Opaline scowled.

"I want the truth out of you, Opaline," he went on. "I'm up to here with people talking my ears off but never quite getting around to telling me anything. Now. Al's waiting inside. The quicker you tell me the truth, the quicker you're going to be able to go in there and hear all about everything he thinks I did wrong."

The shadows in Richison's eyes didn't look like anger to Lindy. She decided to leave them alone. If sympathy was getting in Richison's way, he was more likely to give in to it if no one was watching.

"I'll head back," she said as she crossed the porch.

"I'll drive you, if you want to wait," Opaline said, reaching toward Lindy in a panicky way. "Our boat's tied up under the porch, here, and my car's on the other bank, around the bend."

"Thanks, but I'm used to walking."

"I don't want you scrambling up that trail alone," Richison said.

Lindy managed not to remind him that he was the one who had slipped, on their way down. "Going up's easier."

Opaline paled under her careful makeup.

Lindy stepped aside, so Richison couldn't see her. She assembled all the reassurance she could manage, and held Opaline's gaze while she nodded. And then she followed the catwalk toward the landing at the base of the cliff.

She worked her way up the slippery trail, grateful for the demanding exercise. She would have liked to question Al, but she could imagine how defensive he must be after dealing with Richison. And besides, what point could there possibly be? If he wouldn't talk to Opaline, he obviously wasn't going to talk to a stranger.

But she could talk about him, she decided as she reached the top of the bank. Opaline and Mrs. Crayson both wanted the same thing for him. Apparently they couldn't sit down together and talk it over, womanly, but she might be able to serve as a go-between. It was certainly worth a try.

By the time she reached her home clearing, she was thoroughly chilled. She stopped at the foot of the steps, where normally she would have stripped out of her clay-sodden clothing without a thought. But this time, she wondered. Richison was surely still occupied down at the cabin, but Sunny or in fact any of the Sunstrikers might be watching.

But it's my house, she thought as she peeled off her filthy shirt. And at least for the moment, she added as she slid out of her wet jeans, it's still my woods. If anybody's out there, they're on my property so they're obligated to shut their eyes.

She left her shoes outside to be hosed off and carried everything else directly to the laundry room. Dumping soap along with her messy clothing, she started the washing machine.

She went upstairs to stand in the shower, washing her hair, scrubbing at her nails and cuticles, scouring her hands until her skin was raw. She got out to dry and dress quickly, in a tunic over pants so she could seem like a shopper. Hurrying to Bellingham, she went to Nordstrom's. Not finding Mrs. Crayson, she toured the mall. Coming up empty, she went to Sunset Square, even though she was fairly sure Mrs. Crayson wouldn't enjoy an outdoor-style mall. When that didn't work, she tried the Old Mall, despite her doubts that Mrs. Crayson would be willing to dodge sky hooks and patches of broken pavement. Sure enough, Mrs. Crayson wasn't there.

I can't go to their house, Lindy thought, letting her engine idle as she tried to decide where else to look. Her husband's bound to be there, and everyone acts different when a family member's looking on. But what else was there? She stared through the windshield without seeing it.

Downtown, she realized. There were some nice boutique-type women's stores scattered around downtown.

She took the throughway along motel row and past the sprawl of services attached to the northern edge of the university. Coasting down the long hill toward the commercial city which had sprung up around a railroad spur which no longer existed, she parked on Railroad Street and started to walk.

Peering past the displays in windows fronting stores which were almost empty, she began to feel like a peeping tom.

"Oh, great! Dr. Adair? It's lucky seeing you here," a young woman said, rushing to her side with a big grin. "I was down here buying envelopes. I'm sending out grad school applications. I know it's early, but I've made up my mind. Would you do recommendations?"

Lindy returned the smile while she scrambled to remember. Light-brown hair tumbling down her back. Small blue eyes. Cheerful mouth softening a pointed chin. Round cheeks.

"Cathy Winterset?" the young woman asked.

"Sure, I remember," Lindy said, relieved to recognize the name. "You did a project on Osage beliefs, is that right?"

Cathy nodded, her grin widening. "I'm still interested in

221

that, you know, it wasn't just a project."

Lindy smiled as she dug her wallet out of her shoulder-bag. She pulled out a business card. "Here's my address to send the forms."

"Terrific," Cathy said before rushing down the street toward the office supply store.

Lindy lingered in front of a health food store. It made her nervous to be recognized while she was at so difficult a task. When she had convinced herself it didn't matter, or at least couldn't be helped, she set out again. At last she saw a familiar back in front of a triple mirror inside a tack shop.

Of course, she thought—Ellie had said Mrs. Crayson boarded a jumper at her stable. She went in awkwardly, never having shopped with riders. Mrs. Crayson had been admiring the way a pair of white riding breeches outlined her muscular thighs. Her athletic body showed no signs of middle age, Lindy noticed—no wonder she liked to look at herself. When she realized Mrs. Crayson was staring at her in the mirror, she smiled.

"You aren't shopping," Mrs. Crayson told her.

"No, I've never been in a tack shop," Lindy said, glancing around to be sure she didn't know what she was looking at.

"I suppose I ought to give up competition," Mrs. Crayson said.

"Why should you? Ellie says you're really good."

"There's a meet in a couple of weeks," Mrs. Crayson said. "I suppose people think I should be in mourning."

"I don't know what people think, but I don't see any reason why you should miss it."

"I wanted to have something that fits," she said. "I've lost weight."

"Those pants sure fit—you look good."

Mrs. Crayson studied Lindy's reflection. "What did you want?" she asked without turning around.

"I've been talking with Opaline," Lindy answered to match Mrs. Crayson's directness. "The two of you want the same thing for Al—this school. It's wonderful that the

222

most important women in his life can agree on it. I know you're having trouble talking with each other, but maybe I could serve as go-between."

Mrs. Crayson stared at her as fixedly as a child might do. "You don't have a son, do you," she said.

"No."

Mrs. Crayson reached for a riding jacket, which hung on a peg beside the mirror. "Then you don't know what you're talking about," she said as she slipped the jacket over her silk shirt.

"In terms of what you're feeling—no, I don't know. But I do know you and Opaline agree about the school."

Mrs. Crayson held up one manicured hand to interrupt. Her pale skin looked lovely against the wine of the jacket. Lindy looked down at her own hands, realizing that, after all, she hadn't scrubbed hard enough to get her nails free of the stains left by clay.

"If help is really what you meant by coming here, I should thank you, and I do. But I'll remind you what you're asking for. That woman wants me to supervise Al's medical care, his therapy, pay his bills while he keeps on seeing her. I know how they spend their time. No mother ought to pay her for that."

Lindy's mind filled with the scene she had walked in on at the birder cabin. What if Mrs. Crayson had been with her, then, instead of Richison? But maybe not actually seeing it, maybe only imagining it was worse, she thought, because there had been real tenderness in the way Opaline had been embracing Al. Would a mother see that, though? The torment in Mrs. Crayson's eyes suggested not.

"I hadn't really thought of it—not that way," she admitted.

Mrs. Crayson nodded. She turned back to the mirrors, clearly using her image as armor against her thoughts.

24

LINDY RETURNED TO HER CAR IN A QUANDARY. SHE couldn't see how to sympathize with everyone at once, since they were in such contradictory states. She needed to talk with someone sane. A campus type, she decided, since any of them would take a larger view. Not Maggie, who would want everything explained, even though it couldn't be. Greg. Greg was certainly sane. And he already knew.

Heading toward the south campus entrance, she passed through the Visitor Center to pick up a parking permit. She drove on slowly, in the midst of a cross-country team which filled the campus roadway, their glittering nylon suits providing a bright cluster against the gray day. Relaxing since she couldn't hurry them, she felt drawn into campus life. They smiled at her with the automatic friendliness she used to love, and she responded wholeheartedly.

She was almost at peace by the time the cross-country team peeled off toward the athletic building, thumping knuckles and flat hands on the hood of her car as they passed in front of her with bright grins. Lindy continued around the curve giving access to the tennis courts which had been built on top of a sump which had settled predictably, allowing water to accumulate often enough to make them useful only as parking lots.

Parking in a one-inch-deep lake, she splashed toward the science building. Climbing the stairs quickly, she walked through the Friday afternoon emptiness toward Greg's office.

"Well, *this* has been a while," Greg said, looking up

from his computer screen when she tapped on his open door.

Lindy smiled. She glanced around his office, which didn't seem to have changed since she left campus. Like most science offices, it was little more than a cement cubicle, holding a filing cabinet topped with spilling stacks of file folders, a desk entirely occupied with a computer and its peripherals, a conference chair piled full of student papers, crammed floor-to-ceiling bookshelves, a hemp carpet almost hidden by paperwork.

She straightened a stack of books to make them seat height and sat on the stack. "I want to ask you something that's going to sound awful, Greg."

"Won't be the first time." He grinned at her, his hazel eyes alight. "Remember when you wanted to know whether your husband's posing nude for life drawing classes was hurting your chances with the university tenure committee?"

She nodded, almost able to smile.

"I repeated the whole conversation where it did count against you," he went on, "and then the rest of the committee swore under oath that your husband's behavior wasn't the issue."

"Where I'm at now is even worse," Lindy said.

"Couldn't be."

She half-smiled. "I'm scared Mrs. Crayson is willing to wreck Al's life rather than let him be happy with Opaline."

Greg drew a breath deep enough to stress his shirt's buttonholes. "I'm afraid to comment for fear of sounding sexist."

Lindy tried to keep on smiling, but it didn't really work. "Your problems with your son's friend might help you understand Mrs. Crayson's attitude, I was hoping."

He rumpled his hair. "I'd like to insist my son isn't Al, and my son's girlfriend isn't Opaline, but everyone concerned might want to swear the difference doesn't matter."

She gestured with one hand to brush that thought aside. "I'm not the right person to ask about the feelings of wives," he said finally, rubbing one cheek with the back of his thumb. "Ellie and I are divorced."

Lindy nodded. "But not the way Nathan and I are."

"That's true. Ellie and I are friends, we always were. Our situation is just that friends stop sharing living quarters as soon as they graduate and can afford their own place."

Lindy wasn't sure it looked that way to Ellie, although the difference wasn't hers to comment on.

"Do you know the Craysons?" she asked.

"Not really." He frowned at his desk. "I've talked to him a little bit. I don't have the impression they talk to each other."

Lindy nodded.

Greg hammered the edge of his desk with a pen. "This isn't just a problem for Al."

"I know."

"I meant—" Greg threw the pen against the wall beyond his desk as if nothing else would make him stop fidgeting. "Mrs. Crayson keeps worrying Tim by swearing Owen killed himself. Tim feels lost, thinking his grandfather would bail out on him."

"Everybody knows the suicide was faked."

Greg shrugged. "I keep telling Tim, but Crayson knows better, apparently, and it's hard to answer her arguments when I don't have anything better to offer. What *did* happen, does your cop say?"

"No, they don't seem to know. Do you have any ideas?"

"I do hear the kids talk," he answered. "They blame themselves for the still. They grieve for Owen. When a swarm gathers, I hear a lot of crying, so I'm sure their friends are following the same line. I normally leave them their privacy, but I've listened to this, because it's hard to think of any reason to kill Owen unless you blamed him for the moonshine."

"I'm afraid the police would like to suspect May Anne, because they can prove she blamed Owen," Lindy said.

Greg frowned. "She isn't the only one, is she?"

"Mr. Crayson seems to blame him."

226

"Well, he's got to blame somebody," Greg said, fidgeting his fingertips along the placket of his shirt in an unconsciously eye-catching gesture. "I don't *like* them, especially not her, but I feel for them, you know? My kids are both alive, and they can see. Tim's even swearing his eyes are a blessing in disguise. He's deafening me demanding a voice-activation package to add to this computer he inherited from his grandfather—he wants to be able to talk to Owen's computer and have it obey." He turned his mouth down in an indulgent smile. "He's claiming he can't do close work for long times, but what's really true is, he loves machines, and these voice-responsive programs fascinate anyone."

Lindy smiled.

"Yeah, he's a nice kid," Greg said.

"May Anne feels like you aren't fair to Karl," Lindy said.

Greg sighed. "She's probably right." He reached for another pen so he could fidget. "Okay. I'll cool it. He's got enough on his plate without me, and if the cops are after her, she deserves to win something."

"Greg— If this won't work, I'm not really butting in," Lindy said after a moment, "I just wanted to suggest it."

He grinned at her.

"I guess Al really can't see, and his parents want him to go to this special school in Seattle. But he won't."

"Yeah, Mother Crayson blames that on Tim, too."

Lindy frowned. "She told me she blames Opaline."

"Well, yeah, she blames everything on Opaline, and maybe I would, too, in her situation. At least I know Ellie does. But she's right to blame my kids as well, because as long as he's here, Al's got these friends, ready-made. Tim looks up to him, and Karl's his buddy."

Lindy nodded. "Okay, and that's what I was wondering. I never really read our health coverage, when I worked here. Would your insurance pay for Karl to go to this school with Al? At least for a while, to get him started? Mightn't it help both of them?"

"*Good* idea, Lin." He thrust his wrist out of his sleeve in order to see his watch. "I wonder when that school stops answering its phone?"

Lindy stood up, catching the books she had been sitting on and restacking them so they wouldn't fall. She waved good-bye and walked down the empty hall, feeling grateful to Greg for sharing her attitude without a second thought. It *wasn't* just on the Sunstrike that people tried to help, she thought as she left the science building and returned to her car. Richison was wrong to call her vision pretty.

BY THE TIME she had finished changing her clothes, she heard feet on her deck. She glanced out the upstairs hall window while she buttoned a denim shirt over a red silk turtleneck. Her Subaru was the only car in the meadow, which meant her visitors were from the Sunstrike. She went downstairs without any dread. Nick had wandered into the kitchen, with Stash at his elbow. Neither of them smiled when she appeared.

"Stash has something he wants to say, Lindy," Nick announced as if he were the parent of a much younger child.

"Yeah," Stash said, lifting both hands to tuck his long brown hair behind his ears. "Because I know how many ways I ought to be saying thanks."

"Never mind that," Lindy said. "If we're working out for you, that's all I want to hear."

"It's working out," they both said.

"Good," Lindy answered. "Now. What can I get you?"

Nick went to the fridge to get himself a beer.

"Juice?" Stash said.

Nick pulled a pitcher out of the fridge and opened the nearest cupboard for a glass.

"For me, too, please," Lindy said.

Nick got a second glass, and they trooped into the living room to settle in a triangle of chairs.

"What you did helps," Stash said.

"Sergeant Richison is the one who figured out how to move you out here," Lindy said.

"Okay, you both helped," Stash insisted. "I want you to know I know it."

Lindy felt Nick's frowning gaze. It's a preamble, she realized belatedly. What he really wants to say comes next. She decided just to nod instead of modestly hushing him.

"All the guys agreed not to say anything, but Nick says in real life you don't choose between right and wrong, you choose between which is more important among several things where all of them are right," Stash went on.

"That's how it always looks to me," Lindy admitted.

Stash glanced at Nick as if the agreement had been important. "I can't tell you everything that happened because it's hard to remember," he said as he turned back to Lindy. "Like we were drunk to start with, and then when you get to the hospital, they get you drunker."

"Really?"

He nodded. "You're like a test tube," he explained, tapping his stomach while looking at hers. "So they add more alcohol to keep you from making some chemical inside yourself, I forget what."

"Formic acid," Nick said.

Stash nodded. "The doctor said it's like rubbing nettles on your nerves. Your eyes first, but what matters more is, second, you stop breathing."

"We should have done something!" Lindy said, trying to remember what Tim had told her that first morning. "But one of the guys thought it was better to just wait," she said, "or— I'm not sure I understand."

"No, that's okay," Stash said with an unnerving calm. "We got to the hospital in time. We called Tim a butt for wanting to go up to your house like he did, but he was right. And about warnings—I did ask the doctor, but he said most people don't need any."

"That isn't as cruel as it sounds," Nick explained, "because you have to drink more than you think, before you hurt yourself. Unless you build up to it, you're likely to vomit everything you've eaten for the past month, which

229

rescues you, or some people black out before they get enough."

Lindy sipped her juice to keep herself from commenting.

"We had this book of instructions which said you have to keep the temperature steady while you're distilling, but it didn't say why, and have you ever tried to keep a fireplace steady?" Stash said.

"I'd like to know everything you can tell me about that book," Lindy said.

"Nick thought you would." Stash breathed heavily. "I *can't* tell the sheriff, we all *swore*. But if you do, I can't stop you."

"I won't say how I found out," Lindy said.

Stash shook his head. "I'm not a butthead. Say whatever you want."

"Thanks."

"The book sends you through these safety checks," Stash went on. "Like if it comes out of the collection tube milky, you'd better age it. For seven years, if you can believe that."

"I suppose," Lindy said.

"Or else you can add some wood alcohol to strip out the bad part, if you can't let an oak barrel do it for you, taking all that time," Stash said.

"Was yours milky?" Lindy asked.

"No, but we wanted to be safe," Stash said, "and the book didn't say how much."

"So you added enough, for no matter what," Lindy said. Stash nodded.

"It didn't say how dangerous that might be?"

Stash turned his mouth into an inverted V. "The only warning it gave was about federal agents."

"What a wonderful help."

Stash nodded.

"Where did you get the book?" Lindy asked, trying not to sound as if it mattered.

Stash gazed at the floor for a long time, his struggle painfully visible. Welcome to the real world, Lindy thought sympathetically.

"Vance took it," he said at last.

"Vance really was the one who got the information, then," Lindy said.

Stash nodded. "Everybody thinks we must be just dumping on Vance because he can't tell his side, but how they could check that out would be to try lying to the sheriff. He asks you the same thing too many different ways, when you're messed up already. You catch yourself telling him things, and then you're stuck with the truth."

Lindy nodded. "You said Vance took the book," she repeated. "Where did he take it from?"

"He never said."

"Could it have come from the Sunstrike?" she asked.

"I don't think so, because—" He turned to look at Nick. Nick was watching him with no trace of anything beyond a purely intellectual interest, as if lives, futures, weren't at stake.

"Look—I was the one who took the kettle," Stash said, not looking at Lindy. "There weren't any books, and Vance didn't realize how much stuff lies around here, so even if there'd been a book, he wouldn't have found it."

"It's all right about the kettle," Lindy said. "I wish you hadn't used it for what you did, but everybody's welcome to borrow what they need."

"The sheriff keeps asking about it," Stash said. "I've been afraid to say, in case they wouldn't let me live here."

Lindy brushed her hair off her forehead. "I don't know if it would matter about your living here."

"Nick thinks it matters about blaming someone for the moonshine, so the next time the sheriff asks about it, I'm going to say."

Lindy didn't want to tell him how *much* it mattered to her. If both the instructions and the equipment came from the boys' own resourcefulness, she ought to be able to fight even a civil suit. But would anyone believe Stash? It would be so easy for a lawyer on the other side to claim he was just protecting the Sunstrike in exchange for permission to live there. But that wasn't Stash's problem, and so she shoved the thought aside.

"It's brave of you, Stash. I think it'll be all right. The sheriff and that city detective are the ones who arranged for you to move out here, so I think they'll want to let you stay."

"When I borrowed it, it was just a big cooking pot."

Lindy nodded. "And it still is just a pot."

Stash frowned at his glass of juice. "About the book—I only know two places Vance could have found it."

Confessing was a struggle for him. He sighed and watched Lindy's mouth a while, and then shifted his focus to her hands. She tried to sit comfortably, hoping to suggest nothing mattered very much, but his view of himself was clearly at stake.

"Owen always talked about the past," he said in a ragged voice, "so that puts him out of it, no matter what anybody says. Any of us knew only two people who ever talked about learning moonshine *now*."

"Vance's dad told me he studied it up," Lindy said.

Stash met her gaze, his eyes large with relief at being not the only person in possession of such knowledge. "Right. He learned from a book, and so did the coach."

"Your *coach*?"

Stash glanced at Nick. Nick smiled at him. The approval seemed to be enough to keep him going. Lindy was touched by Nick's patience, by his understanding Stash's need for a mentor he could rely on absolutely.

"Mr. Barnett's divorced, and he says divorce makes you broke, so he thought making his own stuff would save money—he really likes to drink, but not beer. He's always on and on to all of us about not marrying so we don't have to divorce."

"Maybe he's just talking tough about distilling for himself. But even if it's true, surely he wouldn't bring a book like that to school."

232

Stash brushed his hair behind his ears. "He likes people hanging around his house, since his wife moved out," he said. "I went over a couple of times, before he restricted me off field sports unless I cut my hair. He's a butt about haircuts."

"That sounds dumb, all right," Lindy said.

"Vance thought he was terrific. He was over at his house all the time."

"To show he was welcome where you weren't," Nick said.

"People who compete all the time—that's hard to deal with," Lindy agreed.

The low-keyed approval seemed to make talking easier for Stash. "I don't know if it matters, but the sheriff keeps asking how we learned."

"It might be important," Lindy agreed. "Do you know where the book is, so we could look at it?"

"It's in the river. Vance took it out on the deck where there was better light. We didn't realize he was getting mad, so we didn't stop him in time. He couldn't find anything in it about hangovers, so he just ripped it and threw it."

"It's probably in the bay, by now, but we could organize a work party to comb the banks," Nick said.

"Shouldn't the cops do that?" Lindy asked.

"No, I want to get there first," Nick said. "That publisher needs a reality check. At the *least*, they're going to revise their script. Anybody who's ever come within a mile of moonshine knows better than to run a still too hot, and it's their obligation to say so and say why."

Lindy looked at him.

He laughed. "Don't worry, I'm not firing up for the Sunstrike. I studied it because I keep putting people in these totally isolated situations, and they've got to have something to do besides work."

"Like where?" Stash asked.

Nick seemed to think the question was perfectly reasonable, and Lindy was glad for the conversation to move on.

The tension had been too much, she thought. They all deserved a break.

"I've been thinking about these planets they discovered around this star," Nick said. "All their home base gets is an electrical signal which some of them doubt is really planets. My crew goes out to check. Planets are there. So I land on one of them, but now what? My crew finds only one thing they're sure enough of, as a vegetable, to use for whiskey mash. It grows in clusters sort of like bean sprouts and makes helium as a by-product of photosynthesis because this sun is weird. The helium stores in these small pods where it keeps the clusters of these plants afloat in the air."

"Will the helium change the moonshine?" Stash asked raptly.

"My question exactly," Nick said, "now look—"

Lindy smiled. Promising herself she would give an encouraging report to Faith, she watched them dive into speculation about off-world chemistry.

25

WHEN STASH AND NICK WANDERED AWAY THROUGH THE woods, happily wrangling over helium, Lindy called the Bellingham police. The desk officer demanded her name before admitting Sergeant Richison was out of touch for the rest of the day. She called the sheriff's office, expecting the same result since it was Friday afternoon. To her surprise, Brent Fuller answered his phone.

"Brent, I have some information that might help."

"That's terrific, Dr. Adair, what is it?"

Lindy described Stash's information. "It means the book must have come from the coach," she explained, "because Mr. Crayson said he traded his book in."

"If he's telling the truth."

"I suppose that's true."

"Why would a coach leave a book like that lying around?"

"He probably wouldn't, normally," Lindy said, "but he's struggling with divorce, and that can really wreck your concentration. I also wondered if he's connected in another way, because Al's friend is divorced from a high school coach, and it seems like the same name—I'm not totally sure because I didn't make a point of remembering. But if it is the same man, then his ex-wife says he's an abuser."

"They always say that."

"Yes, I guess, but it might be true sometimes."

"So if he's involved, maybe he killed Owen?"

"I hadn't thought of that," Lindy said, "but I guess it might be easier for an abuser to kill someone."

"Whoever gave you this information—you felt like they were telling the truth?" Brent asked.

"Yes, I'm convinced of it. I really hate accusing anybody," Lindy said, "but I don't have any way to talk to this coach on my own."

"No, no, leave him to us. This call's an anonymous tip line type of deal, right?"

"However you want to handle it."

"I'm going to get right on this, Dr. Adair. There's no reason why you're involved, but stay where we can reach you."

"I'm sorry, Brent, I'm working for a retreat this weekend. I've been scheduled for months. I won't have a phone."

"That's a problem. We don't encourage people to leave town during active investigations."

"I'm not leaving town. The retreat's on campus."

"That's good," he said.

LINDY GOT UP THE NEXT MORNING determined to set her personal concerns aside in order to concentrate on the retreat. A marriage renewal weekend wasn't what she normally would choose, and she had reminded the organizers she was divorced, but they had assured her the participants had ruined their lives by engaging in too much blue sky about love. An exposure to reality was supposed to rescue them.

She packed an overnight bag and a sports bag and headed for the university. She wouldn't have wanted to go back if fall classes had begun, but the campus was still almost empty and would be for another week. The retreat was happening at one of the most beautiful of the dormitory clusters, in a part of the south campus she had never used as a teacher. Built inside a natural amphitheater, its low buildings ringed a bricked courtyard more like a ski resort than a school.

She parked outside the natural ridge and entered the gateway which had been blasted through the sandstone to give level access to the courtyard it helped enclose. She turned right and followed a group of breakfasters into the dorm. All the rooms were standing open, pointedly denying privacy. Retreat rules were posted on the doors and also on the beds, in case anyone had any doubts as to whether they were part of an organized group.

As Lindy started down the hall toward her room assignment, she was spotted by one of the organizers, a tall woman on the comfortable side of middle age, her confidence resting so firmly on tenure, a full professorship, and a developmental psychology PhD that she had long since forgotten what life was for other people.

"Hi, Lindy, we missed you at breakfast," she said.

Lindy smiled. "Hi, Barbara. It looks like people are getting into it."

"Absolutely." Barbara paused for Lindy to drop her bags in her room and then scooped her into her wake as she went on down the hall, checking rooms to be sure no one was escaping. "People assume marriage renewal is an orgy situation, but that's not it. We keep them busy and separated from who they've got doubts about. Single rooms. Mostly separate activities."

Lindy adjusted quickly, keeping herself mild for the sake of participants who might find Barbara's cordiality overwhelming. Participants had been assigned to conversation groups, gender-sorted to start with so fewer secrets would be kept. They were scattered through the open spaces in the dorm, and some were using the larger bedrooms.

Lindy spent the morning wandering, joining each group for half an hour, listening in, answering questions, affirming. She would have felt awkward, being paid for such activity, if she didn't notice how all the conversations energized when an expert listener was added.

Box lunches were distributed at noon, without interrupting the talk. Lindy stayed with one group for the meal. As soon as the packaging was collected again, everyone returned to their room to dress for sports. One group assembled to be escorted to the weight training room. Another set out toward the outdoor track. A third lined up to go to the pool.

"I'm going to try the horseback riding," Lindy said as Barbara looked into her room. "I borrowed these boots."

She held up one leg to show a western boot in scuffed black calf which didn't fit inside her jeans.

Barbara stared at the boot. "I don't know the least thing about riding."

"I don't either, but I thought I might as well see."

"Well, get running, the horses are here," Barbara answered.

Lindy tromped outside in her unfamiliar boots. She gazed at the dozen horses which filled the courtyard. Standing at ease, they seemed to be mostly round, well-muscled rumps, but whenever they moved, all Lindy could see was bright steel hooves. One jerked his reins loose in order to turn and look at her, lifting his surprisingly detached lip to expose long, curved, ridged, yellowed teeth.

"Beginners on this side! Advanced over here!" a familiar voice called from the middle of the pack, and Lindy was relieved to recognize Ellie.

"Where do you go if you're not a beginner yet?" Lindy asked.

Everyone laughed, and Ellie joined in cheerfully. "Everybody starts," she said.

When the experienced riders were mounted, Ellie instructed each of them to take a riderless horse by the reins and keep it still while a novice tried to mount. Lindy joined the rest of the beginners in fits of giggles which left them in no condition to climb when it was their turn.

Ellie obviously was used to it. "A horse is like a boat," she said to each of them as she stood them beside a horse and placed their hands on the leather. "You want to spend your time topside."

Each time she said it, everyone laughed obligingly, except for the person being told. When Lindy's turn came, she was amazed at how big the horse was, a bay she might have admired, if she weren't involved. She couldn't believe

238

she was expected to put her foot in a stirrup which was level with her waist.

"Bend your other knee and don't drag yourself up," Ellie said, "give a little spring."

Lindy laughed. "Spring? Maybe I—"

"Forget it!" Ellie interrupted, "you're going up."

She stepped behind Lindy, prepared to boost. Ellie was bigger than Lindy, and well-muscled. She clearly would be able to lift her. But being helped hurt Lindy's pride, and so she managed to spring. When she was seated, and Ellie had adjusted her legs, the horse sighed.

"I've never been patronized by a horse before," Lindy protested.

Ellie laughed. "He knows he's going to have to do everything for you," she said, "he's letting you know he's resigned."

When everyone was ready, Ellie mounted and came to ride beside Lindy. They led the way out of the courtyard onto the trail toward the top of Sehome Hill. The rest of the group followed in pairs. At first, all the talk was helpful suggestions from the experienced riders, and complaints from the beginners, but the horses knew the rules, and so real conversations stragglingly began.

"I'm glad you chose riding," Ellie said, when she felt the trail ride had settled down. "I saw you on the program and hoped you would."

Lindy smiled. "I saw your name, too. I thought maybe we could talk." She looked ruefully at her horse. "I didn't visualize how it absorbs your attention, feeling insecure up here."

Ellie glanced at her lower body. "Grip with your thighs, if you want to, but don't squeeze, or he'll think you want him to trot."

Lindy looked at Ellie for comparison. It was obvious that she was hanging on with her legs, but her clasp was so light that her mount evidently didn't feel it as a command. It was automatic for Ellie, but it also looked like nothing a beginner should attempt.

"If he's going to have problems interpreting, I'll stick with feeling like I'm going to fall off," she said, letting her legs hang.

Ellie nodded. "Probably easier."

They rode silently for a few strides.

"I've been over there going through Dad's things," Ellie said. "Dad owned the house free and clear. Karl wants to move in with his girlfriend, instead of us selling it and splitting the money."

"That's a good solution, isn't it?" Lindy asked.

Ellie sighed. "Greg's having a cow. Young men were supposed to stop being young when he stopped being one of them."

Lindy smiled. "Could you remind him of a situation or two?"

"I have been. He's started saying 'shut up' before I open my mouth."

Lindy laughed.

"Dad's neighbors say they saw you hanging around, the day he died," Ellie said.

Lindy's smile vanished. "I asked him about the moonshine."

"They say you visited Dad three times that day."

Lindy's mount shifted his lead. She grabbed for his shoulders.

"Sergeant Richison mentioned that, too," she said when she had a good grip on a handful of mane. "I visited around noon, and also in the evening, but someone else must have been there in the afternoon. Did the neighbors describe the other person?"

"Yeah, let's see," Ellie said, turning to look at her straggling crew. She rolled her eyes when she turned back to Lindy. "Average height, medium build, dress-up conservative clothes."

"That could be anybody."

"Yeah. One of them thought you changed your dress, for the afternoon visit, but two others said no, you just put on a jacket and floppy hat."

"I don't have a hat."

Ellie shrugged.

"I wish it *had* been me," Lindy said, "because whoever it was might have seen something that would help."

Before she had finished her sentence, Lindy suddenly realized who the afternoon visitor had to be. A woman in a dress. About her size.

It couldn't have been Ellie, because the neighbors would surely recognize Owen's relatives. Faith's schedule was so demanding that when she wanted to visit, people had to come to her. May Anne might borrow a dress, but it was hard to imagine her in a hat. Opaline was so tiny no one would mistake her for Lindy. That left Mrs. Crayson. Lindy had noticed a tension which her grief for her sons more than explained, but something else might be involved, as well. If it was Mrs. Crayson, then she must have seen something, discovered something at Owen's house—something so frightening she couldn't tell the police.

"I try not to think about any part of all this," Ellie said, making Lindy realize how long she had been silent, oblivious even of the motion of her mount. "Dad's still dead, whatever the cops do."

"I wish that weren't true," Lindy said.

26

DAN KNOCKED AT THE FRONT DOOR OF A SMALL HOUSE ON the north side of Sehome Hill. A Saint Bernard put his head through a diamond-shaped cutout in the wood fence next door, checking out the noise.

The two of them had been doing the same routine since Friday night, when Brent Fuller had located Dan with Lindy's new information. Nostalgic for city life, Dan had driven to Seattle at the end of his shift. He had mentioned his plans when he left work—unfortunately, he thought, when a Seattle uniform picked him up on the waterfront and told him to call in.

When he complied, he discovered Fuller had continued working Lindy's information while Seattle cops searched for him. Fuller had a current address for the coach Vance had liked. He had researched the name—the coach had legally changed to the nickname version of his last name, Barney Barnett. He had verified that Barnett was Opaline's exhusband.

Fuller's promptness made it obvious that Dan should forget about time off. In case Lindy was right in identifying a man who didn't appear on their suspect list as even so much as a bystander, he wanted to be sure the interview went correctly. And even if this wasn't a new lead, he wanted to be sure the questions didn't overlook any possible direction.

And so he had driven back to Bellingham and started knocking at an empty house. When Barnett hadn't answered his door by three o'clock Sunday morning, and his car hadn't been spotted anywhere else, it was apparent he was on a two-day all-nighter on unknown private property where he could park out of sight. Dan had gone home for some sleep.

But now, here he was again on Sunday morning, he and the Saint Bernard. This time, however, there was a battered black Mustang in the driveway. Dan stepped out into the grass to inspect the house. It looked as vacant as before. There wasn't any walk, so he tramped through the sopping, unmowed grass toward the back. Under the Saint Bernard's watchful stare, he glanced around the empty alley before pounding on the back door.

"*Stop that racket,*" a rough voice bellowed. The command was followed by a fit of coughing which promised to dislodge lung lining at the least.

Dan tried the door. It was locked. He hammered with the side of his fist in a rhythm intended to suggest he wouldn't stop. The door flew open at last, exposing a furiously frowning man wearing nothing but old-fashioned blue pajama bottoms which were coming untied.

"Barnett?" Dan asked, holding up his shield and identifying himself.

"What do you want?"

"Talk to you."

Barney stared at him for a while. "I don't think so."

"Come down to the station if you want."

They eyed each other. Barnett was heavily muscled, although his condition was less than peak. Suggesting why, his hangover was almost comical in its intensity. He was the taller by maybe two inches, but it wouldn't be a problem, Dan knew.

Barney evidently agreed. "Come in," he said at last, returning to the kitchen table with a rocking gait which suggested he had trouble balancing. He dropped into a kitchen chair and propped his elbows on a table in need of wiping. Using both hands, he lifted a white cafeteria mug to drink noisily. A jar of instant coffee stood open beside his mug.

"Is this why she left you?" Dan asked.

Barney looked around as if he wasn't sure where he was. "No, no. She always kept the place clean."

"The bottle?"

Barney glanced toward the cupboard over the stove. "No. I never used to do this. But I'm too old to date, for God sake. I always think liquor'll help."

"It doesn't."

"*Tell* me."

"You know why I'm here," Dan said.

Barney started to nod but stopped abruptly and closed his eyes. He sat utterly motionless for a moment and then leaped to his feet and stumbled toward the hallway.

Dan listened to him retch. It went on for a while. While he waited, he gazed around the foul kitchen, which seemed almost crowded because of all the pots holding the twisted and blackened remains of long-dead plants.

A toilet flushed. Water splashed. Barney came back slowly, his face dripping. He spooned coffee crystals into his mug and filled it at the hot water tap. He sat down again, his head hanging.

"This is about that god-forsaken book, isn't it?"

"Start with that," Dan agreed.

"I shouldn't have talked. I'm a *coach*, for God sake, a health freak."

"Yeah, it looks like it," Dan said.

Barney gazed around the room again in an even more disoriented way. "There are lots of books around here. The boys wouldn't have noticed any particular one, if I hadn't been running my mouth."

Cookbooks were propped in a sloppy row on one window ledge. Dan silently agreed that no one would notice them.

"I was just going to thumb through it again," Barney went on. "I don't *make* liquor—I was just going to read it. That's when I discovered it was gone."

"How would you know?" Dan said, gazing at the chaos. "Maybe it's still here."

"No, it's gone all right." Barney looked around as if

wanting to be contradicted. "I should have told you right away—come forward right away—but I thought you'd jump to conclusions. Which you obviously are doing."

"What conclusions?"

Barney let his head fall back until the base of his skull rested on his spine. He sighed explosively. "About Opaline. About getting back at her."

"How does that work?"

Barney straightened up and reached for his coffee. "I know all these boys. From school."

Dan didn't comment.

"Al's just a punk. I don't know what she sees in him. He's a fair defensive center, but that's nothing to her."

"Some women turn on to athletes."

Barney shut his eyes. "She never changed to my name when we married, so he didn't know who she is."

"Was," Dan reminded him.

"*Is*," Barney bellowed, provoking another explosion of coughs. "It's freaky how fast anything turns into ancient history around a school," he went on when he found his voice again. "She transferred out because of the divorce, and you'd think she'd never lived."

"If she works at the other high school, how did she meet Al?"

"No, no, she only transferred over there starting last school year. He was in her history class, while she was still here in my school, is what I heard." He swigged his tepid coffee. "That's when it seemed like the total end—when she left school. You're still working together all day, you're not really divorced."

Dan nodded. "So what about the rest of it."

"I was in the bookstore, looking for pictures about frontier life—I teach history, too, you know, we had it in common."

Dan nodded.

"They had this how-to on moonshine. It caught your eye. I thought, well, why not? It turns out to be too much trouble. I never even tried it."

Dan took a moment to remember high school, wanting to visualize this man's world. "What did you tell the boys when you gave them the book?"

"I didn't *give* it to them."

Dan frowned. "Contradicting isn't good enough. You'll have to tell me a different story, something that makes sense."

Hangover sweat slicked Barney's gray face. He wiped at his forehead and closed his eyes. "Okay, I talked about it, sure. Maybe you don't know what it's like, having teenage boys hanging around all the time. Anything reasonable, they claim it bores them. All they want to hear is stuff they can't discuss with their dads. That doesn't mean they were supposed to rip me off."

"Criminals always blame their victims," Dan said.

"Have they been blaming me? Those *thieves*!"

"You've got it backwards," Dan said coldly. "You're the criminal I notice doing the blaming. Supplying minors with information about abusable substances is a crime. Probably doubly so if the supplier is in a trust relationship, which a teacher supposedly is—I'll have to research that."

"Forget that kind of remark, if you want this conversation to continue."

"Keep talking."

Barney debated it only briefly. "I was sitting right here one day when Vance and a couple of new kids walked in. It hit me you might take wine and distill it to raise its proof, which would be a lot easier than starting from scratch, and I was looking that up, but there wasn't anything."

"You discussed it with these kids?"

Barney's total attention disappeared into his coffee mug.

"I need the names of the other boys," Dan said.

Barney kicked the table leg. Dan thought about it as part of a sequence. Fuller had reported that this man was an abuser, in the opinion of his former wife. Pounding on objects might be the beginning of an abuse sequence. It didn't look good.

246

"The names," he repeated.

Barney tightened his right hand into a fist, leaving it lying on the table where they both could see it. Finally he croaked out a short list.

"When the kids left and the book was gone at the same time, I thought about reaming Vance for stealing, but he was pretty unhappy at home, and I didn't want him to start thinking he wasn't welcome here, and at that point—before we knew what was happening at the birder cabin—any of those boys could have taken this book, although it wouldn't very likely have been the new kids because they're always on good behavior for a few visits. Besides, the book hadn't turned out to be any real use. And anyway, I didn't realize—" He rubbed his face, his hand grating against his two-day growth of beard. "Did you know that stuff was dangerous?"

"Yeah. Everybody knows."

"Not me." Barney gestured with one hand. "Well, now. But not then."

"What about the old man?"

Barney straightened in order to meet Dan's gaze. "I absolutely and eternally had nothing to do with that."

Dan watched his eyes. Barney slumped again, but his gaze didn't waver. It could prove honesty, or it could prove lying was easy, a habit.

"I got to feeling bad. Reading in the newspapers. Listening to school gossip. I was working up toward coming in, talking about this." He shook his head even though he had to squint to bear the motion. "But then the grandfather died, and it wasn't just a dumb mistake anymore."

Pity lost the battle with anger inside Dan. "Dumb?" he asked. "Aren't you being a little easy on yourself?"

"Dumb, dumb, dumb," Barney said as he might have done with one of his teenage athletes.

"I don't believe you about the grandfather," Dan said.

Barney looked at him with eyes so bloodshot they seemed ready to bleed. "Yeah, you do," he said despairingly.

247

It was true, but Dan had no reason to relent. "Start at the top."

Barney made himself another mug of tap-water coffee and started in.

27

AFTER DRIVING BARNEY TO THE STATION AND INSTRUCTING A team of questioners, Dan went to the university. The Visitor Center helped him locate Lindy's meeting and gave him a parking permit. He left his Cherokee outside the natural berm and followed his campus map to the small auditorium where the last event of the retreat was scheduled. At the top of the stairs, he picked up a program which told him Lindy's Sunday address would give everyone touchstones to keep them going through the rest of the year. He saw her hand in the description—her wrap-up speech wasn't going to be full of absolutes.

He walked down the hall quietly and paused before he reached the closer of the auditorium exits. At first it seemed nothing was happening inside, but finally he heard a woman's voice, confiding. Standing just outside the open door, he focused intently. Lindy's slightly slow lilt became evident as he adjusted an internal volume control.

He grinned as he realized what she was doing. She was telling them about the nine kinds of marriage in what sounded like the same faith she had described at Owen's services. His eyes gradually sobered as he took in what she was saying. It wasn't the faith itself she was speaking about, Sunday morning or not. She was pleading against being one-way.

A different voice spoke up, a woman, asking a question Dan couldn't make out. In answer, Lindy distinguished between faith and law, and then moved on to discuss conflict resolution in this faith which offered so many kinds of marriage and the lives to go along with all that variety. Her reasonable, confident explanation made him think about her ex-husband's complaints. Marriage hadn't worked for her, and maybe she thought that proved the need for all these other options, which weren't available outside Owen's faith.

And what about the rest of her theory? he wondered. Would it work in the real world? She seemed to be wiping away the whole structure of enforcement—his job, in other words. What if offenders had to sit down with the people they hurt and work it out, conflict-resolution style—as she was describing? Could they?

He grinned at the vision, but he also remembered that she had wanted to shunt lawyers aside and talk to the families in this case. Was that just her personality? Or was she acting on this faith she seemed always ready to describe?

Wanting to judge, he crossed the hall and moved just far enough past the opposite door frame so he could watch her. The shadows ought to keep her from spotting him.

She was standing beside a lectern, focusing on her audience, alert for any least movement which might indicate a question. She was wearing a light-colored tunic over a skirt which barely reached her knees. Her gestures were spare, not distracting. She came across so convincingly she seemed to be speaking totally individually to every person in the room. And out here in the hall, he added ironically.

He knew exactly when she noticed him. She didn't look toward the back of the auditorium, but he already knew she had an unusually wide range of peripheral vision. She didn't hesitate in her confiding speech, but she stepped behind the lectern.

He sighed. If she was so persistently on her guard against him, there might be a reason for it. He would have to check. It was tiring always to entertain the worst possibility, even about people he wanted to like, but it was a job he had chosen.

He left the building and crossed the brick courtyard toward her dorm. One of the organizers was standing in the middle of the resident advisor's office, frowning at a handful of paper.

He showed his shield. "I'd like to wait for Professor Adair in her room. She knew I would probably have to meet her here, and she didn't want the retreat participants to be aware of it."

"Thank . . . you . . . Lindy!" the booming-voiced woman answered with a glance of appeal toward the ceiling. "She certainly gets into the scrapes, doesn't she?" she added as she strode down the hall.

Richison didn't answer. When the organizer pointed, he stepped inside Lindy's room and closed the door. The horse smell came from her boots, he realized after puzzling a moment. He went over to stare down at them. They looked well worn, but that didn't make sense. If she were a rider, she wouldn't have made only walking trails through her woods.

He wandered to the desk. It held nothing but an open program with her responsibilities hi-litered. A totally low-impact life, he thought, noticing that she had already packed.

Hearing footsteps, he moved to the blank wall, in order to have nothing to inspect so she wouldn't feel invaded. She turned the doorknob while someone was talking to her. She lingered to answer questions, the door barely open. Finally the good-byes and thanks began. At last she stepped inside.

She stopped at once, but it took her a moment to turn toward him. "It's like being able to walk through walls, isn't it?" she asked.

He half-smiled. "I thought I'd catch you here so you'd be able to relax, once you got home."

She pulled out the desk chair and sat down. He sat on the edge of the rumpled bed.

"You seemed so calm in there, but I know how you're really feeling," he said. "I've often wondered about public speakers. Do you use valium for that?"

She shook her head. "When I was getting fired and divorced at the same time, I was in a state, so my doctor gave me a prescription. I took half of one pill and slept for two days."

They both laughed.

"Do you still have them?" he asked.

"No, I threw them out." She suddenly looked intent. "Are you— Did you want to borrow some?"

He was surprised by the question, which played into his hands perfectly. Hoping she would misinterpret, he sighed.

"Look, Dan, it's none of my business if you don't want it to be, but that stuff isn't really very good for you. What would help more—there are some top notch vocational counselors here at the university. I've got some friends. They could arrange you an appointment off the books, as a courtesy among government employees. You'd like them. It would be just like talking to anyone, except that they know what they're doing." She smiled. "Whereas I obviously don't."

"You obviously do."

She rubbed her eyes. "Seriously, I know counseling isn't fashionable at the moment, but they can help if you treat them like people."

"I like my job," he said.

"Okay, but Brent says you overreact to anything involving kids, so this case is bound to work you up."

He refused to let his irritation show. "You and Fuller did discuss me then. That's what I surmised since both of you went around acting like 'what private conversation,' after Owen's services."

He watched her face heat, but embarrassment didn't pry a confession out of her. Not that he would have expected it to.

"So what about a vocational counseling session," she persisted. "It takes one phone call, Sunday regardless."

He shook his head. "Not needed."

"It *is* needed. At the least you'd learn not to ask for valium. That's *old*. I forget what's fashionable now, but all the students who live on the Sunstrike have something else.

252

Well, except for the ones who've gone green and use nothing but chamomile."

"I'll go with the chamomile."

She laughed. When she rubbed her forehead, he could sense how tired she was. He decided to get it over with.

"You're right about campus types. They really are willing to go out of their way to help another government employee," he said. "It takes forever to get official tissue analysis back on autopsies, so I asked your friend, Professor Patrick, to set something up for me. Just unofficially, so I know what the official lab will find, whenever it gets around to it, but in the meantime I can work on this investigation."

He watched the color leave her face in slow increments.

"Valium?" she whispered.

He nodded.

"Then it *was* suicide. Oh, I have to be glad."

"No."

She looked at him doubtfully.

"There's no valium in his house, and his doctor says he didn't have a prescription for it or any other tranq. But he was chock full of it. Not enough to kill him. You have to take a surprising amount to die, which is one reason it's such a durable prescription—doctors feel safe because they figure you'll get bored with all that swallowing and change your mind, if what you want is to OD. But Owen took more than enough to keep him out cold no matter who was busy doing what to him."

Lindy pressed her fist against her mouth, rubbing her wrist with her other hand.

"Right. He couldn't have done himself, the way his wrists were cut, and the autopsy bears that out. So we're looking for somebody under medication for stress."

"Everyone's stressed."

"Right. But it has to be long-term stress, as you just proved with your discussion of valium as the past."

She bowed her head. He studied the sloppy part in her dark hair which proved she combed her hair with her

253

hands, even for public performances. The discovery was oddly touching.

"I did have access to valium," she said in a painful voice. "Are you accusing me?"

"No." He waited for her to look at him, but she continued to study the floor, and so he went on. "Valium's amazingly easy to get hold of, so this tissue analysis isn't as much help as you'd wish. But now that we know the method, I've been putting it together from the other end. I've got a witness who swears Karl wasn't at Owen's house, but that doesn't clear May Anne. I know her mother says they didn't go, but Ellie says they did."

She looked at his mouth but didn't meet his gaze. "You think Karl refused to hassle his grandad, so she went on her own?"

"The timing could be close enough."

"It can't be true."

Her answer was so automatic he almost laughed. "Is there anyone you *are* willing to suspect?"

"Did— Did Brent— I mean—" she stopped.

He nodded. "Yeah, your tip was good. We've got Barnett going through a variety of questioners, even though we probably ought to wait. He's in no shape to say with confidence whether it's his foot he's looking at if it isn't in his shoe."

"His foot?"

"He'd been drinking," Dan said.

"Oh."

"His story is, he bought the book on an impulse and made the mistake of talking about it one day in front of some of his young athletes and when Vance left the house, the book was gone."

She cleared her throat. "Do you believe him?"

"I'm inclined to. He seems understanding of kids."

"Then the tip line was wrong. What happened was just a dreadful string of accidents."

"Maybe. But the tip line was probably about something else. Where did you hear it?"

"I— Uh—"

"Come on," he said, letting his irritation show, "if this investigation is springing leaks, I need to know."

"One of my women's groups includes the friend of a friend of a friend who heard something from an official source who talked in confidence," she murmured.

"Okay. If we're talking about the same thing—a caller who swore everything was planned—that probably was Mrs. Crayson. They tape those calls, and we've got a voice specialist who thinks he can identify her speech patterns."

"That would make sense," Lindy agreed. "Grieving is easier if you have somewhere to focus blame."

"Maybe. But why would she claim there's malice, which stacks up charges against Barnett? They're on the same side, wanting to fight this relationship between Al and Opaline."

"Maybe she didn't know who was involved."

"She sounds like she knows—I've listened to the tape until I hear it in my sleep."

Lindy rubbed her eyes. "I found out something yesterday, talking to Ellie. This makes sense of it—she probably did know."

"Let's hear it."

"Owen's afternoon visitor has to be Mrs. Crayson, if it's someone involved with these families."

He waited, watching her face, which told him nothing beyond how tired she was. "Ellie told you this?" he asked.

"No, but she described the visitor, and it's obvious once you focus on clothes. Faith dresses out of the Good Will, as a matter of policy, except for shoes—she likes shoes. Opaline dresses young, because she's dating a kid. May Anne's still wearing high school clothes, saving up for a place of her own. Ellie never wears anything except boots and jeans because being in business for herself means she works around the clock. But Mrs. Crayson cares about her wardrobe. She could have put on an outfit she'd feel anonymous in from dressing down and it would look like what I choose for nice. Which is what I wore at noon, a dress, to show respect."

"What would Crayson be doing there?" he asked.

"She must have wanted to tell Owen what she thought of him. Calling the tip line couldn't have helped very much because you don't see the results. She must believe her life won't get better until everyone says how bad they feel."

"What good would that do?"

"She keeps talking about what people think she should do, or what she shouldn't do. If you always pay too much attention to what other people think, wouldn't you want them to get in line about something as terrible as this?"

"Maybe."

"Greg says she's been making Tim feel guilty," she went on, "so wouldn't it make sense that she tried with Owen, too, that afternoon before we found him?"

"We?"

She breathed deeply. "That night— I called you as soon as I knew what was wrong," she murmured. "I've been saying 'we' to myself. I— It helps a little bit."

"Okay." He waited a moment. "No one was with you? One of your communards you're protecting, someone like that?"

She shook her head, not looking at him, not even knowing she ought to.

"I've been planning to talk with her about it as soon as this workshop is over, because she must have seen or heard something scary. I hadn't connected her with the tip line, but if she called, then maybe she knows quite a bit. Her husband admitted he started out to study moonshine. She could be protecting him. She might have asked Owen about moonshine because she's afraid Mr. Crayson is involved."

"Okay, he's so busy being folksy, none of us got anything out of him, but I could try again. If he thinks his wife's running around asking questions, he might worry enough to try to cover up."

"I'll do it," Lindy said as if she hadn't noticed she was talking to a cop. "I'll be there anyway, discussing this new stuff with her."

He shook his head. "If she knows something she hasn't said, then getting it out of her is police work."

She straightened up. The symbolic refusal to yield interested him since she was so rarely physical.

"Okay, let's compromise it," he said. "You can come along, when I interview her."

"I can *come along*?"

He nodded.

"No."

He waited, not wanting to resort to his authority, knowing it would be better if she talked herself around. She sat looking at him with nothing in her eyes except intelligence. Apparently finishing an internal discussion she wasn't going to confide, she stood up and reached for her overnight bag.

Dan picked up her sports bag and boots. She didn't grab her property away from him, but her face told him there were nonphysical ways of scuffling.

"We're both leaving," he reminded her.

She hesitated. After a moment, she glanced around as if she were alone, scraped up her program and left the room. He felt her tension as they walked down the hallway and left the building. They crossed the courtyard silently. In the parking lot, he put her sports equipment in the back of her Subaru.

"I want to talk to them alone, Dan," she said as she slammed the hatchback. "If you're not there, she might tell me things, and even he might let something slip when I explain that we've located the source of Vance's book and so we know it didn't come from him."

He decided not to argue. She didn't seem to realize what her insistence implied. Could a cop never be considerate, in her opinion? Well, maybe not, he admitted, maybe she was right.

Retrieving his Cherokee, he left campus at pedestrian speeds but when he reached the street, he drove like a cop, amused to see how easily she stuck with him. As they approached the home which looked the embodiment of peace, he spotted Mr. Crayson in the side yard, working an empty border with a trowel.

Dan parked and got out of his car, loitering until Lindy joined him, looking ready for combat.

"You go on inside," he said quietly, before she could launch a debate. "I'll tackle him. If neither of us gets anything, we can trade places and try again."

28

FOLLOWING MR. CRAYSON'S DIRECTIONS, LINDY WENT TO the miniature barn, where the top half of a split door stood open. She looked into a room furnished with sling chairs of saddle leather around a fire pit under a smoke hood. The day was bright enough to make her presence obvious, not as a real shadow, but as a sudden loss of light.

Mrs. Crayson turned reluctantly. "Oh, it's you."

"Your husband said this is a trophy room," Lindy answered. "I've never seen one."

When Mrs. Crayson gestured vaguely, Lindy opened the half door. Inside, the impact of the decor made her feel awkward in a dress. The floorboards were the right width to be in a stable, although they were finished to a high gloss no horse would walk across. Flakes of hay tumbled loose in one corner, pleasantly scenting the room. Rugs woven in saddle-blanket designs were scattered artistically. One wall was taken up by a wet bar, but two others featured a counter displaying ribbons and cups at a level to be inspected and admired. The walls above the trophies were covered in a gold satin which offered a glamor background for framed photographs.

Dressed for riding, in breeches and a soft shirt, Mrs. Crayson had been standing facing the wall. Lindy went across to join her. It took her a moment to understand.

"The photographs match the trophies?" she asked.

"Yes," Mrs. Crayson said, pointing toward the photograph she had been looking at. "This was my last competition, the weekend before all this started about the boys."

The counter held a small statue of a horse and rider. Above it on the gold wall was a photo of Mrs. Crayson in an elegant riding habit, seated side-saddle on a powerful horse so large he made her seem small.

"We costumed," Mrs. Crayson said. "It's surprising what a difference it makes—all those flapping skirts. But my horse didn't spook."

Lindy smiled. "I barely managed on a beginner's trail ride yesterday. I can't imagine getting good enough to compete."

"It takes concentration."

It clearly does, Lindy thought as she stepped back in order to see the entire display. The pair of walls was a kind of diary, she realized, the photos moving into the past in a way which wasn't immediately obvious since styles for formal riding clothes didn't change much over time. But the woman inside the clothing changed. In the full bloom of confident middle-age, Mrs. Crayson looked athletic, well turned out, dominant. But as the photos stretched away along the wall, she became more slender, more flexible, her smile more spontaneous and radiant. Turning the corner and starting along the second wall, the photographs recorded a very young woman who seemed hopeful, rather than triumphant, who slipped gradually back into girlhood, growing smaller, finally ending as a child young enough to have teeth missing, sitting perkily on a fat pony.

Lindy smiled. "It's like a biography, isn't it?" she said.

"I was on my way over to the stables," Mrs. Crayson said as if she didn't want to talk about her life.

"Could we talk a minute, first, though?" Lindy asked.

Mrs. Crayson looked her over, but she didn't move.

"It turns out we were both over there to visit Owen, that last afternoon," Lindy said, "and I thought maybe we could brainstorm, figure out some way to know what happened."

"I leave that to cops."

The answer didn't deny that Mrs. Crayson had visited Owen. Lindy was relieved to have her guess proved right.

"Have you talked to the police?" she asked.

"They talk."

Lindy nodded. "I was hoping you would talk to me."

Mrs. Crayson turned toward the wet bar.

"Owen must have been expecting someone else to visit pretty soon after you. I think he must have told you so. You wouldn't have known what it meant, at the time. But now, looking back, you have this dreadful knowledge. I've tried to imagine how it feels, in your shoes. Since you haven't come forward with your story, I have to figure what you know is even worse than not knowing."

"Saying someone's guilty—what good would it do?"

"We all need to know, so we can get on with our lives, move on to the next thing."

"The next thing." Mrs. Crayson stared at her most recent trophy.

"Holding a secret as important as that," Lindy said, "it preoccupies *your* life, too."

"My life?" She scanned the walls which recorded a competitive, successful past. "I don't understand what's happened to my life," she said.

"I guess all of us feel that way."

Mrs. Crayson frowned. "But that's different, for me, because I've always done what you're supposed to."

"I guess I haven't. But I doubt it matters, as to what happens."

"Of course it matters," Mrs. Crayson snapped. "Doing what you're supposed to is what it takes to win. If it weren't, then why are you supposed to do it?"

"I'm not sure why. But what people tell you—that can't be just so you'll win, because life isn't a competition."

"Indeed it is." Mrs. Crayson paused to study her trophy walls. "The reason you don't think so is that you always lose."

Lindy was surprised. "Does my life look like that to you?" ·

"They say you got fired. They say your husband left you. They say you're losing your home."

Lindy waited for her heart to stop hammering. When it simply kept on, as if it would pound forever, she sighed.

"Those are just problems," she said, hoping to convince herself, "just stuff for me to deal with. They aren't a question of winning or losing."

"An attitude like that is exactly why you don't have a trophy room."

Lindy gazed along the pictures again, taking a new look at what they implied—pride in a glamorous skill. As a teacher, she had always been interested in the athletes in her classes. It had seemed to her that they knew what they could do and would endure any pain to accomplish it. They didn't aspire to what was impossible. That self-acceptance had made their personalities seem open, centered. She had liked them.

But those were the successful ones, she realized now. The ones she had identified as athletes were in school on scholarships and sometimes asked for extra help to maintain the grade they had to have, or they were pictured in the paper after some event, or they asked for leaves of absence from class while their team was traveling. She had never before realized there must be others, who had tried as hard but didn't make it.

As if they shared the thought, Mrs. Crayson said, "I don't know what people do, when they don't win."

Lindy smiled and swept a hand toward the wall. "It looks like you don't have to know."

Mrs. Crayson began tightening one hand over and over, as if she were working a grip-strengthening spring. "You think if you marry a tax accountant, that's going to be real power, because everyone's afraid about their taxes. You never dream he'll use it as an excuse to work only half the year."

Lindy tried to see it from Mrs. Crayson's view. She hated paying her taxes, but she wasn't afraid of her accountant, a kindly woman who gave her useful advice. Which of them was wrong about accountants?

"You have your two sons, the way you're supposed to,"

Mrs. Crayson added. "They're handsome, just the way they should be."

Lindy smiled. "Al sure is attractive."

Mrs. Crayson didn't seem to hear. "Their teachers comment a little, but who wants an intellectual? When you remind them of that, it shuts them up."

Lindy thought about her classes. Not all of her students had been intellectuals, but some of them were, and she had liked them all.

"I'll admit it was disappointing when neither of them would even glance at equestrian sports. Horses are for girls, was all they'd ever say."

"In the part of the country where I come from, men ride. A lot. They take pride in it," Lindy said.

Mrs. Crayson sighed. "They went in for other sports."

Lindy frowned, realizing there weren't any photos of the boys. Was there another trophy room for them?

"Not that they ever lettered," Mrs. Crayson said. "Which was stupid. That stupid high school. I wanted to transfer them, but they kept talking about friends. As if friends matter."

"I can see that, though," Lindy said softly. "Friends still matter to me, at my age, and for teenagers, there's just nothing else of any importance, is there?"

"The people I know talk about their kids all the time," Mrs. Crayson said as if Lindy hadn't interrupted. "Brag about them. I come in first. The woman who comes in second stands there for the lineup and instead of talking about our competition, she tells me all about her son, his science contest, his scholarship. You'd think she didn't even notice she was only second."

"I guess it's a stage—glorying in your kids."

"Winning just isn't enough. Your kids also have to win, or it doesn't seem to count."

"It must be so hard," Lindy murmured, realizing she hadn't understood how complicated it truly was. Faith's attitude had seemed normal to her, because she worried over a young man she loved and granted independence to. Ellie's blend of demanding rules and cautious freedom, Greg's exasperated friendship and frustrated protection—she easily grasped their feelings. But Mrs. Crayson's attitude wasn't the simple lament she had assumed.

"Vance dead. Al handicapped," Mrs. Crayson said harshly. "People call—people I've been competing against for years—" She frowned at the trophy walls. "You should *hear* them. Their *voices*. *Dripping* pity—I despise pity."

"I guess we all do," Lindy said.

"They think, if my sons did it to themselves— They think, since their children aren't in trouble— It always ends up hanging there—not quite said—that I must have brought my sons up wrong, for this to happen. They *triumph*."

"Oh, no, please—surely not."

"They're wrong."

"They can't mean that."

"I've always done what you're supposed to," Mrs. Crayson said again in the circular thinking which locked her into her despair. "They're not going to deny my whole life."

"They surely don't mean it that way," Lindy insisted.

"So I tell them the boys didn't do it. They were *victims*. Sacrifices. They change their tune. I'm *not* going to lose this."

Lindy felt overwhelmed by the grief which filled the room. "Maybe it would help at least a little if you could think about it a different way," she said. "Life isn't winning and losing. Truly. I think it's just what happens and what we do."

"You think that because you lose."

"No," Lindy said, half smiling to take the sting out of contradicting. "I think it because winning costs too much. But if you really feel you need to win this, then help me figure out what happened to Owen, would you please? That would be the only kind of winning there is left, for this."

"You think so?"

Lindy nodded. "I'm sure of it."

"You're investigating?"

Lindy nodded again in an abashed way, not wanting to seem self-important. "I try to help the police a little. The sheriff's deputy is one of my former students, and I liked him, so it's natural to get involved, I guess."

Mrs. Crayson faced her with the bold stare which had worried her when they first met—the stare which didn't actually seem to see. After a few moments, she shrugged and turned away.

"I'll have a drink," she said. "You can tell me what you know."

"I really would like to brainstorm," Lindy agreed, wondering if she should learn to drink. Everyone seemed to find such comfort in it. Would this be a good time to start? Mrs. Crayson had wanted to share clothes with her in Nordstrom's. Maybe she would share drinks, talk about drinking as a way to lead up to whatever it was she couldn't face. To show she was willing to participate, Lindy followed Mrs. Crayson to the bar.

Mrs. Crayson dug a lighter out of a drawer. She started a Bunsen burner–style heater and adjusted the flame. She rummaged in a cupboard and pulled out a large shallow stir-fry bowl. Settling the bowl on the rack above the flame, she watched it heat a few moments.

"I don't know much about drinking," Lindy said. "Is that how you make a toddy?"

"Some drinks are better mulled," Mrs. Crayson explained. "We have parties here, sometimes," she added.

"It's a charming room."

"I suppose you think I shouldn't remember what a party is."

"No, I don't think that. I can't imagine anyone who would."

"What happened at Owen's house was simple," Mrs. Crayson said without looking at her. "That's what you're here for isn't it—to hear that."

"Yes."

"All right." She drew a very long breath. She reached for

265

a bottle of clear liquor and poured it slowly into the bowl.

Lindy watched the heatwaves rise.

"I found out Owen was a fool for courtesy, just like I thought," Mrs. Crayson said as she opened a cupboard door and dropped the empty bottle into the trash. "I took a tub of homemade ice cream with me when I dropped over. I told him I'm allergic to dairy products, so I'd need plain tea." She paused to think. "After what he did to me and mine, he shouldn't have eaten that ice cream. But he was busy *sharing*. I hate that word," she interrupted herself. "So he ate a big dish. I make good ice cream," she added.

"I'm sure you do," Lindy said.

"For that batch—if I had listed ingredients, I'd have put pulverized valium at the top of the list." She smiled bitterly at her own joke. "I waited, to give him time. He ruined my life, luring my sons into danger, and I would have enjoyed explaining how he was going to pay for it, but—"

She paused, and Lindy was grateful, because she felt she needed to catch up somehow.

"What?" she whispered, leaning closer in order to be sure she heard. "What about valium?"

"I didn't want a scuffle, and he was going to lose, so what difference would it make if I told him? His knowing wouldn't have lasted but a few minutes anyway, and why should he see my butchering knife? I've never liked all those kitchen knives."

Lindy's mind seemed to stall, but her body understood. Small fires seemed to break out on the inside of her skin, her heart labored, her vision tunneled. She was so sure Mrs. Crayson couldn't have mentioned a knife that she struggled to figure out what word she had misunderstood, what other word could sound like "butchering knife." She couldn't think of any, but she absolutely knew there must be one—there must be several, if she could just think of them.

She drew a quick breath, but before she could ask, Mrs. Crayson picked up the lighter and flicked it over the stir-fry bowl. A lovely blue and white flame danced at the edge before spreading with a burst across the entire surface of the liquid in the bowl, leaping surprisingly high. As the flame established itself, it brightened to yellow.

Mrs. Crayson pulled a pair of hot mitts out of a drawer and bent them over the lip of the metal bowl in order to pick it up.

"Wait," Lindy said, concerned about the awkwardness of the arrangement, because the pan looked too big to pour anything that wasn't chunky, like stir fry.

Mrs. Crayson didn't wait. She lifted the flaming bowl and turned, holding it in both hands. Everything else happened too fast for either of them to know for sure. Did Mrs. Crayson deliberately fling the contents to spill over Lindy? Or did she drop one side of the bowl because the hot mitt caught fire and burned her fingers? The residue flamed upward strongly, catching her shirtsleeve, climbing rapidly in the dainty cloth. Frantic to escape the fire, she threw the bowl. It clanged across the counter, coming to rest against the wall where its heat encouraged the flames dancing above the spilled liquid which had puddled against the wall. Fire sprang up the satin-covered wall, strengthening as it caught in materials more substantial than the liquor where it began. Reaching the ceiling, it ran with amazing speed around the room.

But Lindy wasn't watching. Her tunic was fire-proofed and so it blackened without actually bursting into flame, but her skirt was a completely natural fiber, and so she was on fire around her knees. She looked up desperately for something to use to put it out, but the whole room seemed to burn.

29

DAN TURNED SHARPLY AT THE SOUND OF SCREAMS. A woman was running toward them, her hair in flames, her arms flailing fire. He grabbed his pocket cellular and dialed 911 as he ran toward her. He dropped the phone as soon as he gave the address. Diving in a football tackle, he knocked the burning woman down and rolled with her in the rain-wet grass as if they both were afire—as in fact they were, before he had her flames extinguished. When he rose to his knees to check her over, she continued to scream and reach for her face.

"Come here, Crayson, deal with this," he said roughly as he stood up. He stripped out of his scorched jacket and dropped it while he ran toward the trophy room, where rapidly blackening smoke poured from every opening. Pausing to free the tail of his shirt and sop it in the grass, he pulled it up to cover his mouth and nose before opening the half door and entering the room at a crouch. He tripped at once and went sprawling. For a moment the world was full of arms and legs, but eventually he made out a soft body which yielded under him.

"Lindy?" he said.

Choking coughs were the only answer. The smoke stung his eyes too painfully to let him see, but he kept hold of the clearly feminine body as he fumbled back toward the door, crouching to stay below the smoke.

"Come on," he said before joining in the coughing.

"Roll just in case," he said, when they were outside.

"I was crawling to keep below the smoke," Lindy said,

268

lying on her stomach, her cheek against the grass as if she would never rise from the wet ground. "It never occurred to me I'd trip anyone, doing that."

He croaked a laugh. "Are you okay?" he asked, inspecting her blackened clothes and reddening hands.

"Yes, I rolled in one of the rugs," she said, gagging and clearing her throat between words.

"Good. I don't know why people run when they're on fire. It fans the flames, but they all seem to do it, except not you, thank God."

"They do it because you can't believe how much you want to get away," she said fervently. "I tried to stop Mrs. Crayson, but she's really athletic."

"It's okay. We got her down in time."

"No, it isn't okay, Dan," she said, her voice breaking. "She killed Owen—she's truly not okay."

He wondered if she was in shock, but she seemed to know what she was saying. "She told you that?"

She nodded.

"This fire wasn't an accident, then? She was shutting you up?"

"I'm not sure." She stopped to cough. "She had this bowl of something clear. Gin or something. She might have just dropped it, I think."

"What's that got to do with this?" he asked as sirens became evident in the distance.

"She lighted it."

"What for?"

Tears cleaned wavering streaks down her cheeks. Tasting salt, she wiped at her mouth. "She said it was going to be a drink," she said. "I don't know anything about drinking. My parents don't drink, and by the time I would have tried it on my own, I knew an alcoholic, so I didn't start."

"That doesn't stop most people."

"I just meant, that's why I'm not sure what happened."

"Okay."

"I'm afraid she meant to throw it, because why else would she pick it up? It was too big to pour into a cup. If

269

she was making a drink, she needed a ladle, like a punch bowl—she said they have parties in there sometimes."

"She threw it on you?"

"I must be wrong," she contradicted. "It spilled. Some of it went on me and some splashed back on her. I don't believe it. I saw it, I mean, but—" her voice dwindled.

"What were you talking about, before the fire?"

"I—" She tried to press her hand against her mouth, but her burns obviously hurt, and so she let it go. "She asked if I was investigating—"

"She thought you hadn't talked to us yet?"

"I guess so."

"So she was protecting herself, trying to, at least."

"I guess. But Dan?" she whispered, "she knew about the valium."

The sirens were deafening before they cut off. Dan stood up to signal for the medics, staying clear of the firemen dragging hoses across the lawn. When the medics ran toward him pulling a gurney, he turned back to Lindy.

"Go with these guys," he told her.

"I'm all right."

"Go with them. I want an official record of your condition."

She looked up at him with tormented eyes.

"It's got to be faced, Lindy," he said as he turned away.

He beckoned to the cops as he crossed the lawn toward Mrs. Crayson, who was sitting half dazed in the way usual with burn victims. Her shirt had crumbled into black across one shoulder and down one arm. A charred scarf knotted around her throat explained her crimson face. She had no eyebrows, and her head was covered with blackened threads which made her look painfully like a burned-over field where there hadn't yet been enough wind to crumble the ruined grass into ash.

"Read her her rights," he said to the closest uniform, "and then stay with her in the hospital."

"Look here, now—" Mr. Crayson began.

"Come inside," Dan said, leading the way toward the house, "I need to talk to you."

LINDY CROUCHED BY her firepit on Wednesday morning, struggling with her first slash fire of the season. A gunmetal Cherokee drove slowly into the clearing. Lindy straightened up as Dan got out and crossed the wet meadow toward her, staring at a giant maple on the lip of the river bank.

"Is that really a bald eagle?" he asked.

Lindy turned to look. A huge dark oval balanced on one of the lower branches, its top covered with a snowy cape. "Yes. He likes to sit there and watch the river, when there's no commotion. I have to be careful which way the breeze is coming from because he hates smoke."

Dan looked at the firepit, where twigs were neatly stacked above crumpled paper which had charred without the smallest trace of flame. "I don't think he has to worry," he said.

Lindy laughed. "I decided fire is like horses," she said, "if you get bucked off, mount up again right away. If you get burned, light up again under better circumstances."

"Good plan." He began looking around in his usual way. His worn leather flight jacket looked comfortable. It topped jeans and a new-seeming sweatshirt which matched his eyes. It meant he was off duty. She hoped.

"My insurance says, with the boys telling how they got their copper pot, not involving me, and with the how-to book coming from the coach, even if not maliciously, and with Mrs. Crayson being in no shape to accuse anyone of anything, and with Mr. Crayson wanting only criminal charges, even to begin with, and not even wanting that, now that Mrs. Crayson is in such trouble so he sees it from a different side, I'm going to be okay," Lindy told him. "They might raise my rates," she added.

"No doubt."

"Thanks for letting Stash stay here," she said.

"Your residents are doing a good job with him."

"Yes, they're glad he's here."

He gazed at the cedars, which had begun their autumn molt, russet fans of dying needles soaking up enough rain to lose their hold on living twigs in the light drift of air. She watched soberly, trying to understand how close she had come to losing everything.

"I can't make sense out of what happened," she said.

"Crayson does, though. She says violence is everywhere." He shrugged. "She's right."

"But what she told me is that she wanted to win," she contradicted tentatively.

"No, not 'wanted to,' *had* to." He adjusted her dead fire stack with one toe. "Her real life was competing. The rest of it was just what she was supposed to do, to get the life she wanted. She loved the show ring, and she was willing to pay her dues to get that, but she never bargained for a husband and sons who expected to live their own lives. The older the boys got, the more they spoke up about it. It just seemed like chaos to her."

"Did she talk to you, it sounds like?"

"Yeah." He was silent a while. "I managed to convince her I wanted to understand. Which was true," he added, looking at Lindy's eyes as if he knew how dubious his claim must sound, "I always hope I'll understand."

Lindy nodded.

"In her mind, the beginning was first grade, where she learned about competition. Schools ought to quit using that to motivate."

"I'll mention it to my mom."

"Except for the trophies, things already weren't going well, and then Vance died and Al hurt himself, and it was just too much. The only emotion she ever feels is triumph, and everything else is just frustration. She explained that when I tried to talk about family affection, loyalty."

"That's just defensive. It can't be true."

"It sounded true." He shrugged. "The boys took pride in being underachievers, which a lot of kids do. Their

272

moonshine was pure defiance of her, is how she saw it—an endless supply of free booze so they could be drunk all the time. Owen made it seem charming, which was a relief to her, I think, because she didn't want to blame the boys. Blaming Owen let her take control of the situation by cutting him up. You made it easy for them to ruin their lives, so she was going to win that by throwing you onto the street so you'd experience what it means to have a ruined life—bad as hers had become, yours would be worse. This property offered the boys a place to get out of hand, so she was going to punish it by turning it into bare apartment lots."

"Did she *say* all this?"

"I'm giving you just the essentials—she explains it better," he said. "She admits setting you on fire was taking a risk, but you were out of control with your questions, so she had to act fast. And give her credit—if you hadn't lived through it, we really might have believed it was an accident."

"I thought it was, so you might as well," Lindy agreed.

"Your student didn't, though. When he heard about it, he came storming. There were limits on what he could do, being a deputy, so he threw that curse, that malediction in her face. She took it the other way, as proof that she was fighting God, which is a battle you don't expect to win. It left her her pride. Fuller meant it to be crushing. His face was a study when he realized he'd helped her, instead." Dan grinned.

"You make it sound so *reasonable*."

"Yeah, to her it is. I realize people want murderers to be crazy, but most of them aren't. It's why you get so many hung juries and innocent verdicts in spite of the evidence— people can't believe this coherent, well-dressed accused person could be complex enough to get into killing on a part-time basis. The truth horrifies them, so they convince themselves murderers can't be ordinary, even though most of them are."

"Surely that isn't how it works."

He looked at her intently, as if her body could tell him more than her words. "Are you hiding your head? If you are, just say so. But a cop has to understand. In Crayson's case, you're talking about a person who led a really physical life and believed absolutely in rules. That also describes any cop."

"But you don't do murder."

"Right, because the law backs us up. Crayson wasn't into killing, either, until she felt like society wasn't behind her anymore."

Lindy remembered what Maggie Anderson had said about him—that he might be having trouble with stress. Was he? she wondered. Empathy was one of his important traits. That might make murder especially dreadful to him, but it also might help him to understand, in which case he might be right about this. Could that be? She looked him over, trying to decide.

"Your hands are burned," she told him.

He spread his hands to look at them. The painful red extended into his sleeves. "They'll heal." He sighed. "I was glad I got her fire out, even after I found out she caused it."

"Is she all right?"

He was silent a little while. "Deep burns leave heavy scars," he said at last. "Skin grafts hurt like hell. It's harder to go on, I think, if you used to be attractive."

"She was. Attractive."

"Yeah."

As if seeking distraction, Dan crouched and flicked a lighter under the twigs. Lindy knew the heat must hurt his burned hand, but he held the flame steady. The rain-wet twigs maintained themselves. She smiled as she watched his sober, intent look, as if the fire mattered equally with everything else he encountered.

"I think you're going to lose this one," he said as he snapped his lighter shut and stood up.

Lindy laughed. Remembering how Mrs. Crayson had tried to badger her with that word—lose—she felt intensely free, grateful to be amused instead of hurt.

274

"I can't believe she admitted what she'd done," she said.

"Yeah, I'm always surprised when they confess," Dan said as if confessing, himself. "But I guess when you've caught them, most people want to talk."

"It's like she was standing there waiting for us."

He shook his head. "I know the social services say they want to be caught, but they don't. What they want is to be *admired*. They think everybody's dumb, and who wouldn't, as much floundering around as we do. They took control of their situation, and they want you to know it. When you figure it out at last, they see you don't truly understand, as who could, so they want to show you the fine points."

Lindy looked at him doubtfully. "Surely not," she said.

He shrugged. "A couple of weeks ago I was looking into this supposedly simple accident. This gravel truck following this passenger car. The gravel driver got distracted by a wasp inside the cab and veered into the oncoming lane. He plowed head-on into a logging truck with a full load. The impact broke the logs loose and spilled them down onto the passenger car and killed the driver. Perfectly straightforward."

Lindy watched him study the tops of the cedars.

"I was interviewing the drivers," he went on after a while. "My report was going to be so routine I didn't separate them to ask my questions. Telling it together, they got to giggling and topping each other and ended up spilling the whole thing. The driver of the car was the logger's wife, and he was sick of her. He got his buddy to crash into him after he didn't properly secure his load. From genuine accidents, they knew the trucks could withstand the impact, but the logs would break loose and solve his marital problems. They'd gone to a lot of trouble figuring speed and distance and so on, and they just had to tell somebody who could appreciate how clever their plan was."

"You don't think of truck drivers as giggling," Lindy said faintly.

"You don't, do you?" He turned back to the eagle.

"There's a bit more to it, with Crayson," he said.

She studied the feathering of coffee-colored hair across his nape, wondering if police work was as hard for him as it seemed to be.

"She chose her life—a respectable life," he explained. "Worked hard at it. Succeeded. But nobody cooperated—not the boys, not her husband, not me, not you. She deserved better, she feels like."

"Will she find some kind of closure?"

He shook his head over and over, as if talking to himself. "Barnett knows what he did—how careless he was with his moonshine book. We've got him in detox, which he isn't facing very well, so he feels like he's paying his price. But Crayson's situation is harder. She feels like life owes her."

Lindy studied her failed fire. "I shouldn't have been in her face. If I hadn't been trying to ask, or— If I'd just have left her alone, she wouldn't have gone after me."

"Don't start down that road," he said sharply. "Owen wasn't in her face."

"That's certainly true."

"She used tequila on you," he said. "I was glad it wasn't white whiskey. I hope I never see another batch of that."

"How come everyone knows so much about alcohol?" Lindy protested. "I didn't know it would burn."

"Depends on how social you are, I guess. I've been served these flambé meals, sometimes. People don't realize what a cop thinks about when he sees fire."

Lindy tried to read his eyes, but he seemed to be thinking about the women who had set flames in front of him, rather than about domesticated fire.

"She says she learned about it from her husband," Richison said after a while. "He was in the service. They used to drink their tequila that way—light the shot and toss it down, flames and all. Singed his beard, once, is why he remembers it enough to tell."

"I didn't know he had a beard."

"While he was in uniform, apparently." Richison gazed toward Tim's pond. "He's having to rethink his adult life.

His dreams have exploded in his face, too. She forgets that."

"It must be awful for him."

Richison inspected her face. "He'd probably appreciate it if you dropped in."

"I might."

"With the fire, and the arrest, Al consented to that boarding school in Seattle. His mother's innocent until proved guilty, in the school's opinion, confession or not, so they're refusing messages to her son, on her orders," Richison added. "But I talked to Opaline. She's a teacher, she ought to be able to get a love-letter-type tape smuggled to him, to keep him going. A professional courtesy from those teachers down there."

A love letter, Lindy thought, remembering his reactions at the cabin. She smiled. It took him a moment to grin.

"I was about ready to stop this and go have lunch," she said. "Are you on duty?"

"No. I'm not. Thanks."

"I usually eat my main meal in the middle of the day," she said as they strolled across the soaked meadow together. "It's one of the luxuries of not teaching anymore."

"Supposed to be healthier," he agreed.

In the kitchen, they both washed up, using cool water for the sake of their burns. Richison rummaged in cupboards for tableware while Lindy pulled a baking dish out of the oven.

"Smells good, what is it?" Richison asked as he poured two glasses of milk.

"Stuffed cabbage heart. It's vegetarian, a French peasant recipe, but I add julienne beef."

He laughed.

"I usually cook a triple batch, so I can freeze some."

"Makes it handy for us drop-ins," he said.

She carried a basket of homebaked rolls to the table, and they sat down together. He picked up her plate and served it before picking up his own.

"This is good!" he said.

"Surprise," Lindy said.

He smiled.

As they began to eat, the silence was tense with whatever it was he wasn't saying. Lindy decided to let it go. She'd been through enough, talking to doctors and lawyers and sheriffs and insurance adjustors and family members and friends, and refusing to talk to journalists. She wasn't curious.

When he finished his helping, he reached for the serving dish. "Split this with you?" he asked.

"No, you go ahead."

"I want to propose something," he said as he served himself. "Or, I mean, create an arrangement."

"I'm probably not interested, Dan."

"Okay, but let me try it."

She sighed.

"Bellingham cops don't have partners," he explained. "This time, I partnered with your student because the county was involved, too, but mostly, we're on our own."

Lindy didn't comment. He drank half his milk.

"The closest we get to a partner, normally, is these compassionate ride-alongs," he went on. "I'm not asking you to sign up for the regular rotation because I can't swear for some of my fellow officers, as to after dark, which is when compassionate calls usually hit."

"I'm not a cop groupie."

"Okay, but you saw how well it's been working with the two of us. Every one of these people was willing to talk to you. The same with that mess on Sunday. I never suspected Mrs. Crayson of anything more than being a witness. But I should have. You noticed her ice-cream bowl sweated on his counter. You also identified that afternoon visitor. We're trained to ask for bodily details, but you saw we should have focused on clothes. If we'd known we were working together, one of us might have realized what everything meant, maybe soon enough to have spared you your hospital trip."

"Everything seems easy when you look back," Lindy said.

"If we were working together, it might get easier to see while it's still happening."

"I'd hate to think people trap themselves by talking to me."

"I hate to think of people killing each other and getting away with it," he said.

"That's true."

Dan set his fork down on his empty plate and held her gaze. "I've talked to the chief. He understands you're available only upon special request from me. Can I count on you?"

"Okay. Yes, sure. You saved this property. I owe you."

"No. Not because of that."

She gazed at him while she thought about his attitude. "Well— Then— For just the usual reasons."

He grinned.